THE SECRETS THAT THEY KEEP

T. M. LORE

This story is for the broken and battered.
The twisted and abused.
You are not alone.
I am in your corner, rooting for you.
You are strong. You are loved. You are a warrior.

CONTENTS

Introduction　　　　　　　　　　　　vii

CHAPTER ONE - MONDAY

Client One: Jennson　　　　　　　3
Lunch　　　　　　　　　　　　15
Client Two: Davis　　　　　　　21
Client Three: Thwaite　　　　　27
Manor　　　　　　　　　　　　45

CHAPTER TWO - TUESDAY

Midnight　　　　　　　　　　55
Return　　　　　　　　　　　67
Preparations　　　　　　　　77
Sempers　　　　　　　　　　85

CHAPTER THREE - WEDNESDAY

Day Off　　　　　　　　　　　97
Later　　　　　　　　　　　105
Lunchtime　　　　　　　　　119
Visitors　　　　　　　　　　133
Run Before Dinner　　　　　143
Dinner...and a Show　　　　159

CHAPTER FOUR - THURSDAY

Knights　　　　　　　　　　175
Boxes　　　　　　　　　　　193
Rearranged Schedule　　　　203
Shower　　　　　　　　　　215
Shopping　　　　　　　　　225

Trouble   237
Bracelets   251

CHAPTER FIVE - THE ISLAND
The Island   263
The King's Tour   273
Queen   283
The King's Feast   293
Vixens and Dollies   311
New Friends   327
A King's Bed   341
Sunday Brunch   349
Finding Ruby   355
Compromised   373

Epilogue   383

Acknowledgments   399
About the Author   401

INTRODUCTION

A note to you the reader,

This novel touches on sensitive subjects that could bother some readers. To make sure that everyone is informed before they dive into this book, I want you to know that the subjects include drug use, grooming, sex, kidnapping, sex trafficking, and one scene of forced sex.

I want to tell everyone that, when there are victims involved, it is never ever, ever, ever the victim's fault. If you've been a victim, please know that it was nothing you did, or didn't do. The fault lies with the perpetrator of this crime. It doesn't matter who they are, it is their fault for being a monster, not yours.

If you need to talk to anyone, please contact the National Human Trafficking Hotline 1-888-373-7888 or visit www.rainn.org to chat with someone online.

They offer services for any victims of sexual assault, no matter your gender.

It is 100% okay to seek counseling, or group therapy. You are not alone. I'm right there with you, too. We are strong. We are survivors. We are warriors.

There are many additional resources at rainn.org that include...

National Domestic Violence Hotline 1-800-799-SAFE (7233).

National Center for Victims of Crime 1-855-4-VICTIM (84-2846)

National Sexual Assault Hotline at 1-800-656-HOPE (4673)

And many more. Please do not hesitate to reach out if you need help.

THE SECRETS THAT
THEY KEEP

CHAPTER ONE - MONDAY

CLIENT ONE: JENNSON

I'm up by 4:30a.m. to start my week, dabbing concealer under my tired brown eyes.

It takes me hours to apply my makeup, but when I'm finished, I'm flawless. I slip into my black mini dress—the front is open down to my navel. My Louboutin Alta pumps will make today's outfit pop. I'm out the door by 6:25a.m. New York traffic is less busy at this time of day, and my driver—Sasha— knows her way around so we'll arrive early.

"Mean girls suck." Sasha laughs as she opens the car door for me. She greets me this way every morning.

"And nice girls swallow." I give my usual quip and slide into the backseat.

"Good thing you're not nice, Alyx." She closes my door.

I'm thankful for the warm tea that's waiting for me.

Sasha must've gotten up early to get me this drink. I didn't know she'd left the apartment while I got ready.

Sasha and I live together. It's a requirement from my handler—Estelle. Sasha is my driver, slash body-guard, slash babysitter. She reports everything I do to Estelle. I must behave, so those reports glow like damn LED headlights. If not, I'll get demoted with a giant pay cut—no thank you.

Sasha stops at Mr. Jennson's office building at 7:25a.m.; she hurries and opens my door. I'll have enough time to prepare everything. I wink at her then walk toward the alley beside the tall building.

"Go get'em tiger," Sasha yells as I walk away.

I throw a thumbs-up into the air without turning. Sasha cackles and the car door closes. I can imagine her short brunette hair bouncing as she laughs.

I've worked with Jennson for the last six months—what I do for him pays my brother's medical bills so that's why I continue. If my parents hadn't... I stop myself; I need to focus, not spiral and ruin my makeup. Mr. Jennson requires me in his office when he walks in precisely at 7:52a.m. I have to be there before everyone else, and I have to be ready.

That's how it is; if you want to get paid, you do what you're told.

There is a rear entrance—a secret door with a magnetic lock—that's only for me. I wave the keycard and the door pops open. My entrance has a small gray foyer with a mirror and a black cabinet filled with supplies. The most important thing it holds however is money. I check the cabinet for the thick brown envelope.

Payment is required before, not after. I count it.

The agreed Monday morning price is six thousand dollars. My handler gets seventy-five percent; the rest is mine. I'm one of the lucky girls. Most get five percent —usually less. But I've been doing this for years, and my handler trusts me to do what I'm told. I think she's preparing me to take over her position one day— another benefit of behaving.

After confirming the price has been paid, I shove the envelope into my bag. Next month's rent and prescriptions for my brother are now paid for. Grabbing the required supplies from the cabinet, I head into the office.

Jennson has a closet about ten feet from his desk. It's where I set up shop every Monday. I open the door and roll out the clear plastic self-adhesive film. I start up by the closet rod and roll it down the wall, covering the flooring, too. The plastic catches anything that may drop—hair, clothing fibers, skin cells, and such.

Rule number one: leave no evidence behind.

After the plastic is in place, I set various condoms on the top shelf, then put everything away. I check over the supplies to make sure I don't need to leave a list for Jennson. Hefty trash bags—check. One roll of thirty-six inch by two-hundred-feet self-adhesive film—I used the last of it today, so that'll go on the list. Jennson's preferred brands of condoms—Caya and Magnum— there's an entire shelf of those so we're good there. I toss a Caya in my bag for my next appointment.

I walk over to his desk and grab a post-it-note— leaving a message on his monitor about the adhesive film. I have two other appointments today, but Jennson comes first because, let's face it, he pays to get what he wants—and what he wants… is me.

After everything is put away, I undress, leaving my clothes and my bag in the tiny foyer of my secret entrance. I look myself over in the mirror. My mother always called me her little Snow White. It's because— no matter how much sun I get—I'm pale. My hair is jet black, like my mother's was, and even without makeup, I look as though I'm wearing bright red lipstick. I see myself naked more often than I see myself clothed, but I look great naked, so it's no bother to me.

Rule two: never tell them how old you are.

This rule is easy to keep and ninety percent of the reason I'm still employed. I've learned all the secrets on how to appear young, so I look about seventeen. However, if a *John* asks, 'how old are you now, fifteen, sixteen?' The answer should always be the lowest number they'd offered, with a fraction added at the end. 'I'm fifteen and three-quarters.' The honest answer doesn't matter because the *Johns* I work with like young girls, and I like getting paid. Money is important when, like Snow White, I don't have any parents to take care of me.

Stop. Focus.

I check my phone before I put it in my bag—it's 7:48. I turn it to silent, leave the room, push the secret door behind the tapestry into place, and get into the closet—closing the door behind me. The closet is dark now, but I've been doing this long enough that I don't need the light.

Rule number three: stay in position until told otherwise.

Jennson will be here in about two minutes, and I *have* to be in place before he comes in. I sit on the floor, cross-legged, back straight as an arrow, chin up, with my palms flat against my thighs—like every other Monday.

The door to the office opens and the fluorescent lights hum to life. A stream of bright white light flows under the door and into the small space. It's Mr. Jennson and his assistant, Christina; they're talking about his morning. Christina pretends to be aloof, but she has to know what's going on—because she always locks the door behind her on Monday's. Though she doesn't say a word—I get it—why should she lose her job because her employer isn't faithful to his wife?

She tells him about his morning schedule. He thanks her, and she leaves, bolting the door behind her.

His steps sound against the floor as he goes over to his desk. A cork pops from a bottle and liquid pours into a glass. A drawer slides open. "Ah," he smacks his lips together as he closes the drawer and his glass clinks onto his desk. He must've taken a pill. Sometimes he has to; so he can stay hard for as long as he desires.

I sometimes have to take things, too. Though the things I take aren't prescribed—they're provided by Sasha on days when my schedule is a bit more *difficult*.

My Thursday roster comes to mind.

Jennson opens the closet to put his jacket away. I try my best not to react to the onslaught of light as he watches me. He must've dyed his hair because there is no longer any gray in it, it's dark brunette. Jennson always wears high end clothes. His Dolce & Gabbana suit is dark blue today; it makes his pale white skin look sick though. Blue is not his color. I remain still.

The jacket slides from his shoulders and I'm there, right where I should be. He doesn't look down or greet me, but he never does. He places the coat on a hanger. I do not move.

Mr. Jennson unzips his zipper and grabs my hair. He lets me know where my mouth should be. I perform the day's first blow job, but before he can *finish*, he pulls away, and closes the door.

He likes the anticipation.

He also likes what the air conditioning does to my nipples while I wait on him.

Jennson makes his first phone call. I know when he's talking business because his voice is loud. I'm sure even Christina—who is at least twenty feet from his door—can hear him, too. It's when he lowers his voice that I don't know what he's saying.

Rule four: don't listen too close.

The first call is a loud one. I stay in my place, not moving. If he hears the plastic crinkle while I'm in the closet, he has another game he likes to play. It's not one of my favorites as it involves *my* backdoor—and he gets a little rough when that happens.

The call ends, and the closet door opens back up.

He leans down and looks into my eyes. "Good morning." A bright smile pulls at his lips. He gives himself over to it, and I see his perfect white teeth. "You've done well this morning. That pleases me." He takes my hands and pulls me into a standing position.

I don't speak—he hasn't asked me to yet—but I smile, ignoring his coffee breath.

"You know, Alyx," he grabs the belt from the shelf above the closet rod, "I almost called you back here on

Friday. Would you have been able to make that happen?"

He has asked a direct question, so now I can answer. "The fee for an off-schedule visit is double, you know." My handler always charges double for callbacks. "My schedule is booked solid right now, but," —I tease him by licking my lips slow and deliberate— "the next time I have a cancellation, I'll text you." I wink.

"That would please me." *B*rother smiles as he wraps the belt around my left wrist. All the *J*ohns have names like this. *U*ncle, *C*ousin, *F*ather, *G*randpa, and so many more. It's a hierarchy of who gets first dibs and so on. He pushes his body closer to mine and sniffs my hair.

He nibbles and kisses my collarbone—working his way from left to right. I'll have to wipe his coffee breath off of me later. As he approaches my right ear, he comes up for air. He wraps the strap once around the closet rod, then around my right wrist. When I am bound, he pulls the belt tight, and locks it in place.

Nothing is off-limits. Jennson pays handsomely to do what he wants with my body. He trails his hand between my breasts and down my belly until he finds the treasure he seeks. He always starts with his thumb. I don't know why, but that's his go-to move. I bite my lip the way he likes and lean my head to the side—it's not like I can roll my eyes or anything. He growls with delight. He works his thumb in and out a few times before switching to his fingers. Stroking me until my body has reached *his* desired level of moisture.

He sucks my nipples, undoes his zipper, and then rips a condom open with his teeth.

Rule five: always use protection.

He puts it on and then penetrates me. I'm not allowed to make a noise—this time is about *him*, not me. I grab the closet rod with my hands and steady myself against his thrusts. He's taking what he wants while I think about what's for lunch today. Maybe waffles at The Sugar Factory.

The phone rings and disrupts him. He likes it, though. He smiles, pulls his pants up—as much as he can—and closes the door. I hang there, holding on to the bar. My feet can touch the floor, but I can't lower my arms. I'm lucky that my lifestyle requires me to work out. Otherwise, there's no way I'd be able to hold onto this rod for so long. Jennson answers the phone.

Ooh, Baja fish tacos at Playa Betty's. My stomach rumbles.

His voice is low this time. I try not to listen, but I can't do anything else. "They'll make the move next Tuesday. No, I'm leaving Friday. I'll return next Wednesday." I hear him open a desk drawer. "Tuesday morning works better for everyone." He pauses and waits for a response. "Because school is starting back up and no one will pay attention to a busload of kids."

Jennson huffs. "You will if you know what's good for you."

The phone hangs up.

The closet door opens, and we continue on with our morning. I'm his morning treat. He does with me as he pleases, and I'm not allowed to leave until lunchtime. He pays a lot for that honor.

Jennson entertains himself with my breasts—as I try to decide what sounds tasty. Eggs Benedict at ASSET would be so scrummy right now.

MY ARMS TREMBLE when he undoes the belt. He arches a brow but doesn't ask me if I'm okay. There's a rap on the door. Jennson puts a finger up to shush me —even though I haven't spoken this entire time—and closes me in the closet. The locks on the door click.

"Mr. Jennson, it's lunch. I'll hold the remainder of your calls." Christina doesn't come inside the room.

"Thank you, Christina." The office door closes, and the closet opens.

The smile on his face tells me enough. The morning of sex has caused his oxytocin and endorphins to increase. The hormones pumping through his brain have done their job. He is both relaxed and happy that he pays what he does.

He'll report good things to Estelle.

It's just sex, and I get paid—so, I'm happy, too. I have to keep the cash coming in if I want to pay the bills. Besides, a good start to my Monday schedule means a good day.

As the blood returns to my fingers, my hands tingle. I turn away from him, remove the plastic from the wall —rolling up the many used condoms with it as I go— and carry the sticky liner toward my private foyer, feeling his eyes on me the whole way.

I slip behind the curtain, put the plastic in a trash bag, and get dressed. I slide back into my dress, looking myself over in the mirror. It's part of my job to look fantastic between clients; so that I'll attract a few more. My hand trails down to my navel. Everything is in place.

I'm out of the building before Christina can come back into his office. I toss the trash into the dumpster and walk down the alley to the front of the building. This job isn't as glamorous as others, sure, but it pays better—and I have to take care of myself and my autistic twin brother. Living in New York is expensive, and his medicine is even more so.

When we were kids, I spent so much time in waiting rooms while Trent was observed, tested, poked and prodded. I was an outsider, until it all fell to me— then I became a caretaker. I love my brother. I'll do anything for him.

Anything.

It's not like we have health insurance, my parents literally…no… I have other things to do today. My brother has an appointment with his therapist soon, and needs new clothes, and a haircut. The money from Jennson won't cover everything—the next appointment might though.

Sasha is waiting for me—I hand her the envelope of cash; she'll count out my portion later. She nods, takes my bag from me, and opens my door. My next appointment is further uptown.

But first, lunch, and I know where I want to go.

"Sasha, let's go to Bubby's."

LUNCH

It's a hungry kind of day. Sasha and I are seated at our regular Bubby's table. She eats every meal with me on workdays. Even though I know that she spies on me for my handler, we're great friends. I don't have to pretend; Sasha is cool. She doesn't know I know about her spying, though. As it stands, Sasha is my driver, my roommate, and my sole companion.

The waitress comes over. She must be new because I haven't seen her before. She takes one look at my Balenciaga bag and smiles flashing her teeth. She doesn't know it's a hand-me-down. "Hi, I'm Tammy. I'll be your server today. Can I get y'all some drinks or take your order?" Her thick southern accent lets me know she's a fresh arrival in the city. She hasn't learned to blend. Even though she's at least five years older than I am. I'm happy that she hasn't *had* to learn such things.

"Let's get right to it, Tammy. I'll have the Pancake Flight and a mimosa," I say.

"She'll have the avocado toast and an orange juice," Sasha butts in. "I'll have the same." She grabs my menu and hands both to Tammy.

The waitress—bless her—looks back at me. She thinks I have options here. I nod and laugh like my order had been a joke. It wasn't, I'm starving. When I age out of this business, I swear I'm going to eat whatever I want, whenever I want, and get super chunky.

"Hookers don't eat like that," Sasha whispers to me as Tammy walks away. "Estelle would be pissed." Sasha's knee bounces up and down under the table.

Great, so she'll be texting Estelle an update after she drops me off. "For starters, don't call me a hooker. I prefer the term high-end call girl." I've been doing this since I was fourteen. It's a young age to start, but not as young as some girls are when they're forced into it. No, I'm not some poor white trash without better options. It's how my life played out. The truth of it though—it's all I know.

It's also how my twin brother and I have survived since our parents died.

"Why do you do that? There's nothing wrong with being a hooker. If I hadn't been in that accident, I'd still be in the game. It pays better than being a driver." Sasha quirks her brow at me.

"But somehow, being the driver, you still get less wear and tear on your *vehicle*."

"Nothing wrong with a little wear and tear." Sasha smiles and sips from the glass of water on the table. Her leg relaxes, too. Sasha had been at one of the annual summer parties two years ago and got attacked by a *John*. She now has scars all down her left leg, so Estelle took her out of the game because Sasha has a lot of pain there now.

"Too much wear and tear is tough on the back." I stretch my arms above my head, and my back pops.

Sasha laughs at my joke. To the other patrons, we look like a pair of young gal pals off on a shopping day.

At least someone thinks I have a life.

How and why, I do this are questions I get from time to time. When a *John* asks me those questions, I say things like, 'so I can meet sexy men like you,' and then I give them a little wink. My brother has never asked me how or why because he thinks I'm a personal shopper. I'm glad he doesn't ask—I hate lying to him. It wouldn't matter anyway—it's the best way for us to survive.

My chair bounces toward the table, and I look back. The family at the table next to ours is getting up to leave. The kid who bumped my chair doesn't even look back to apologize. The mother is setting money on the table while the dad is strapping one of their toddlers into a stroller.

Lucky kids.

My parents died right before I finished high school. I wasn't sure what would happen. My brother, Trent, and I were seventeen at the time. It was a late night in December when the accident happened. The police said Dad was drunk. Witnesses had seen the car swerving and driving erratically, so that's the assumption the police made. If they'd been alone on the road, they would have disappeared. We had a hard time with all of it because *our father never drank*. But we couldn't argue with the evidence left behind.

They'd never made any arrangements to determine what would happen to us. I suppose they never thought they'd die.

They were wrong.

After all was said and done, I begged my *U*ncle to step in and help, but he refused unless I agreed to certain *arrangements*. He wasn't my real uncle; he was my handler—before I was passed to *A*untie—Estelle—but there was a system in place, and I had to adhere to it. So, for all intents and purposes, he was my *U*ncle. My childhood friend, Ana, was the reason I got into this business. The money *U*ncle gives me is the reason I'm not out. I have to have resources to care for myself and my brother. I have no high school diploma, but this job allows me to make enough money without one.

As the happy family exits the restaurant our orders arrive at the table. "Let me know if y'all need anything else," Tammy says.

Sasha ignores her, but I give her a bright smile. "Thank you, Tammy."

The waitress seems appeased and leaves us to eat. I toss everything from my head and break the yolk on my egg, letting it run. I take a big bite. Which is not 'lady like' at all. I can feel Sasha's gaze on me. Let her tell Estelle about that. We've found several *Johns* by eating in high-end restaurants, but Estelle hates it when we eat like we 'came from a farm.' Whenever we act human, we're quickly compared to farm animals.

The rest of our meal goes by, and before I can give in and order a slice of cherry pie, we're back in the car, headed to my three o'clock appointment. I sit in the backseat imagining the warm tart cherries in my mouth. I'd text my brother and tell him to send me a cherry pie, but I don't want to piss Estelle off and have her cut my pay. Estelle reads all her girls' text messages, too. She doesn't know that my brother lives close, either —and I want to keep it that way.

My high-functioning-autistic-brother, Trenton, lives right here in New York. Not in the apartment that Estelle makes me pay for, but one in the adjacent building. If I'm ever in a pinch, I can get into his place by going through a set of fire doors. Luckily the alarm is never set because so many use it as a cut-through, which makes it easy for me to see him whenever I can.

Trent and I both had to learn how to be alone after our parents died. I trained him how to deal with his anxiety in public; and he trained me how to not care what others think. Though, the first few times he went out alone I followed him. Once he could handle himself, I was less stressed watching him go out unaccompanied. Though, now he has most things delivered —and I'm thankful he does because I still worry.

I'll always worry.

CLIENT TWO: DAVIS

Sasha drops me off at West 61st Street and Central Park West. This afternoon's client prefers hotels over offices. Which is nice because I'll have time to shower before they arrive. I sometimes wonder if they plan it that way.

I don't mind either way.

I go inside the hotel and ask for the key to the Lachlan suite. It's a false name, but no one says boo. There's too much cash being paid for the room for anyone to push for answers. I'm sure half of the money goes into the manager's pocket. Especially considering it's only used for a few hours at a time.

It's definitely off the books of *this* hotel.

There aren't as many rules with this client, but they too pay for unlimited access to my body. I'll find an envelope of cash in the bathroom.

I ride up the elevator, enter the suite, and go

straight to the bathroom. The Italian marble is heated, so I take my heels off as soon as I'm inside. The envelope is peeking out from an open drawer. I count it out. Six thousand—it's all there. I turn on the tub, slip out of my dress, put the required condom in, and slide into the warm water. This client hates wearing condoms, so it falls to me.

I'm not sure when Mrs. Lennox Davis will arrive, but we have a three-hour window—and I have to be *ready* to fuck.

I must've fallen asleep in the tub because I'm awoken by fingers tracing the inside of my thighs. The acrylic nails leave an electric hum behind as they trail up and down my leg. Mrs. Davis's blonde hair falls into her face as she leans in and bites her bottom lip. I've told her that this drives me crazy, so I play along like it does. I kiss her and pull her into the tub. She's clothed, but I know she's got another dress with her. She always has extras hanging around. Water splashes out of the tub, and she squeals with delight.

"Alyx," she says out of breath. "Can you stay longer today? I've got the rest of the day off. I told everyone I had to take the kids school shopping. I left out that the nanny was taking care of that task." She laughs.

"Used the whole mom angle, did you?" I kiss along

her jawline. "You know, I'm sure that's considered a Bad Mom move in some circles."

Lennox trills. "I don't care. I pay well enough for their nanny and the children love her. Besides, I need time off to be a good mom, too." She tucks my hair behind my ear and her blue eyes stare at me. "Besides, seeing you keeps me young."

"Thanks," I whisper as I rub her breasts through her soaking wet top. "Everyone needs a little 'me time.' Why don't you let me help you make the most of yours?" I lean down and nibble over her shirt above her nipple.

Lennox moans her response. I unbutton her blouse as her hand trails along my thigh. Pulling her wet top off, I undo her front latching bra with my teeth. Making quick work with my tongue, tracing circles around her nipples. I pull up her skirt so she can straddle me, then slide her panties to the side with my thumb. I tease her clitoris with my index finger while I suck on her nipple, biting hard enough to make her reach ecstasy for the first time.

Lennox climaxes easier than most. She'll see six before she leaves the hotel today. It's part of the agreement—if she gets six, I get a bonus. A bonus will cover getting Trent groceries, and a new pair of sneakers— there may even be enough to tuck some away.

I put my hands against her chest, move her off of

me while squeezing her breasts, and get on my knees in the tub. It's almost time for number two. She removes her skirt and sinks back down into the warmth of the water. It's my turn to be on top. I trace every inch of her with my tongue while my fingers seek out warmer pastures. One… two… three fingers inside today.

Her whole body shudders. Her breath is hot against my skin. I bite along her neck while my free hand cups her breast. I take her nipple in my mouth and suck hard. I can feel the tension leave her body as her warmth explodes into the water of the tub.

I pull the plug and let the water empty. I take Lennox's hand and pull her to the shower. I turn it on, so we don't get cold. She kisses me nipping at my lips with her teeth. I push her up against the shower wall, and her hands trail the curves of my hips. "I think it's time," I say.

She bites her lip. "Okay," rushes out in a hot breath.

I walk over to my bag and pull out the vibrating strapless strap on. Pressing the button, the phallic comes to life in my hands. Lennox moans and bites her lip *again*. She takes it from me and fucks me with it, using the smaller piece as a handhold until I cry out a moan, letting her know she's done a good job. She pulls it from me then inserts the handhold inside me.

I turn her around and push her breasts against the shower wall. I smack her ass as hard as I can and plunge the vibrating joy inside her. After several good thrusts, her body trembles, and I know she's reached elation again. "Alyx," Lennox moans my name, then reaches down and pulls the vibrator from between my legs.

I pull her from the shower and lead her to the bedroom. She lays me down on the edge of the bed and returns the favor I'd given her in the shower. Standing by the edge of the bed, thrusting into me over and over, she climaxes for the fourth time—as I do for the first.

Warm wet flows down my body, and Lennox can't help herself. She pulls the condom out of me, and her tongue laps up the wetness. Tasting me, sucking, and flicking her tongue. As gentle and forceful as I can manage, I grab her hair and pull her onto the bed. If she's going to go down, I'm going to return. I'll get paid extra for this.

I straddle her sixty-nine style and use my teeth to remove the vibrator. Lennox roars with excitement. Her tongue moves quick, and I find myself moaning, which makes her want more. I use two fingers inside her while I lick and suck her sweet spot. Warmth floods my mouth as number five passes us by.

I roll off of her and grab the vibrator once more. Setting it to the highest setting, her eyes go wide. It's time for the finale. It doesn't take long for number six to arrive, but when it does, she lets out a scream that would wake the neighborhood if these walls weren't soundproof.

I'm glad her body makes my job easier. Other women aren't so easy to please. Lennox thinks I'm the reason she gets six every Monday, and that's okay because I'll walk out of here with ten grand today. I won't bother telling her that *her* comfort is why she can climax so often. I mean, she's old enough to know that all on her own—if she wanted to know it.

Besides, I could use some new clothes, too. Summer will be over soon and winter in New York is cold—and coats are expensive.

CLIENT THREE: THWAITE

I got another shower after Mrs. Davis left the hotel. Her nanny found out she left work. Lennox left because she lied and said she'd stopped to get the kids a treat on her way home. I called down to the front desk and had them put a box together so it wouldn't be a complete lie. No need for those kids to suffer because their mother is a liar.

I'm out of the hotel by six o'clock. Sasha is right there. I hand her the envelope filled with cash. "I see you got a bonus." She weighs the envelope, feigning that it's heavy. "Went down on her today, did you?"

I laugh. "Yes. But she also got her six, so she gave me an extra four."

"Fantastic, Estelle will be pleased." Sasha puts the envelope in her back pocket and opens the rear passenger door. She looks down the road for a minute and nods. I follow her gaze but see nothing out of the ordinary. There are people waiting for the lights to change. Crowds pushing past one another to find their way to the subway. A man in a black hat walking toward the curb, and people hailing cabs. Maybe Sasha had given someone a business card and was letting them know I'd be on the other end of that card. I do a quick spin just in case.

"Are you ready for dinner?" she asks, looking back at me. This is her telling me I'm not finished with work yet. I slide into the backseat.

"Of course." I already know dinner will be either Bar Boulud or Lincoln Ristorante. I didn't *know* where my next client would be tonight, but those were his two favorite places.

I use the term client loosely, because he doesn't pay for my company, only my dinner. At least dinner wouldn't come out of my cut of the money—not tonight anyway. Estelle doesn't pay for the animals to eat; we pay our own way.

Most dinner dates for escorts don't happen before nine o'clock. Early dinner dates aren't always easy, but Monday dinners are another story. This guy doesn't know I hold the title—escort. All he wants is a *date* for *dinner*. No sex is required, which is nice, but I still have to play a role.

It's not like I can tell him how I spend my time.

Corwin William Thwaite is a handsome fifty-five-year-old widower who lost his wife a year ago to cancer. Soon after, he lost his daughter in some freak accident in a lab at college. I don't remind him of her, but I fill a void. He liked to introduce the pale white girl as his late wife's granddaughter anytime we ran into someone he knew. He got a kick out of it because he was a tall, fit, African American man. He'd laugh, and then we'd be seated—no one asking any further questions—because no one gives a damn anyway. I think it makes *him* more comfortable saying we were sort-of-related.

Mr. Thwaite is different from my other clients. Estelle knows him from her college days. When Corwin expressed being lonesome for his wife and daughter, she'd told him... 'Why not have my *n*iece come to dinner with you. It might fill the void.' Corwin had said, 'Oh, no. I'm not worth the bother.' Estelle then insisted. She'd told him that it would help her *n*iece. 'She needs to practice her networking skills. You'd be doing *her* a favor my love.'

Estelle told me the entire story before I met with him for the first time—four months ago. She also said that Corwin was loaded and could perhaps be converted or coerced into spending money.

Estelle hasn't pushed anything further with Corwin, though. Not because she doesn't want to. No, it's because my client list has grown since I started meeting

Corwin for meals. Most of the new *Johns* noticed me while Mr. Thwaite and I were at dinner. They'd seen how easy the meetings had gone. They'd liked how I *behaved*. They'd follow us to the car. Not in a creepy stalker way, but in an 'I'm intrigued,' way. After Corwin left, Sasha would give them a business card.

Sasha pulls up to Lincoln Ristorante, and Mr. Thwaite is right there. Sasha walks over and opens my door. Corwin takes my hand as I exit.

"Good evening, Ms. Alyx." He offers a sweet smile.

"Mr. Thwaite." I stand on my tiptoes and kiss his cheek. "How are you?"

Sasha gets back in the car and drives away without saying goodbye. I glance toward the car as she merges into traffic. It's odd for her not to say goodbye or tell me when she'll be back.

I turn back toward Corwin and smile.

"I'm well." We chit-chat while walking toward the restaurant. He has a reservation, so we're seated right away. "How is school?"

The waiter hands each of us a menu.

"It keeps me busy."

"A Pink Vespa for the lady, and a Fig Old Fashioned for me," he says to the waiter before looking back at me. Corwin and I have dinners together so often that he knows what I like. I smile, the waiter nods and leaves. "Will you get a summer break?"

I didn't know. It's not like I've ever had a chance to go to college—maybe one day. "You know, I've been so busy with homework that I haven't paid enough attention to anything else," I lie while scrutinizing the menu. Jesus, everything on this menu is mouthwatering. I decide the Chicken Milanese is the safest choice since Sasha will be waiting to take me home, and she *will* ask.

"It's good that you work so hard." He smiles at me.

I return the smile. "How about you? How was your week?"

"I sold the apartment," Corwin answers as he looks over his menu.

"Wonderful." He's been trying to sell for a while. He can't hang on to those memories anymore; he's too hurt by all of it. I ache for his losses. "Have you gotten it all packed up yet?"

"I hired a crew, but they can't come back and finish until next week. Which brings me to my next question." Corwin sets his menu to the side.

I follow suit and lay mine down. "Shoot." I give him my full attention.

"We've been having dinners for a while now," here it comes. Estelle had been right. She knew he'd ask me for a hook-up sooner or later. "I know you are aware of my situation."

"Of course," I reach my hand out and put it over his. "We've become close. I enjoy our time together." It isn't even a lie. I do enjoy my time with Corwin. Though a sexual relationship will change the dynamic a bit.

"As do I." He smiles and I pull my hand away. "My lovely wife and daughter." His gaze turns downcast for a moment. "Beautiful women that they were." He looks back up at me. "Had a taste for clothes. I can see from the outfits that you always wear to dinner that you do as well."

"I like a good dress with the right set of pumps." I offer a sweet smile.

Corwin nods. "I wonder. Would it be odd for me to ask if you would assist me in going through their things? I can't bear to think of all of their nice dresses, shoes, and other things going to waste. I have no idea what items are worth saving, or what should be donated or to whom." He leans back in his chair. "If I'm being honest, it's very overwhelming."

"Of course, I'd be happy to help." I must accept any offer to go to his place. Estelle wouldn't have it any other way—it could be an opportunity—but I also like Corwin. He's a genuine man. He's always been kind to me.

"I can't see hiring someone to come do this either. I need to know I can trust the person." His brow tightens.

This causes Corwin stress. "Mr. Thwaite." I look down at my hands.

"Corwin, please," he corrects me.

"Corwin," I smile and meet his gaze. "I would be honored to help you go through their things."

"It would be of a great help to me."

The waiter brings our drinks over. He sets them down and hurries off seeing we're in the middle of something.

"This dinner should be a celebration," I lift my glass, "to their life and their memories."

"To life and memories." Corwin clinks my glass with his and we each drink. "My Rita wouldn't want me dragging my feet around that house depressed as I worried about what to do with everything. She'd want me to get it done and move on with my life. She told me as much before she passed."

"She sounds like a wonderful woman," I say.

"It's settled then, you'll assist me." Corwin takes another sip of his drink.

I do the same.

"When do you think you could come?"

"I'll have to double check my schedule. Is there a particular time you'd like me to come?"

"Perhaps one evening, before next week? I'd like to have it out of the way before the movers return."

"I'd be happy to." Corwin's offer is genuine. It's a

nice change of pace. "I'm off on Wednesday's, perhaps that evening would work?" I offer.

"Sounds perfect." He smiles at me. "Also, the things I don't keep, if you'd like to have any of the items, they're yours."

"That's so thoughtful. Thank you, Corwin." I've seen pictures of his wife and daughter—his late wife's skin tone was pale like mine. Her tastes are closer to mine than Estelle's are, too. It will be nice to get a few new-to-me dresses. Most of the things in my closet are things given to me from other girls. Or things Estelle requires me to buy—like the dress I have on right now, but the remainder of my money goes to making sure my brother is taken care of.

The waiter sees his opportunity. "What can I interest you in this evening?" he asks with a smile.

Corwin looks at me. "Chicken Milanese." I pass my menu over.

"I'll have the Black Angus Filet Mignon," Corwin hands the menus to the waiter, who nods and leaves the table.

We carry on, bantering back and forth for two hours. I make up what I can and change the details on the rest. I tell him that I went to lunch with my friend Sasha today, but I don't say where I'd spent any other time. I make up lies about college and classes to appease his curiosity. I even say that I'm excited to see my brother over the summer but don't mention that I'll see him tonight when I get home. Corwin—like most everyone else—believes my brother is in Florida with my grandparents. He doesn't know that I have no grandparents.

Without asking me, Corwin orders me a dessert—Lingotto. He orders a Castagno Torta for himself but gives me first taste when it arrives. My mouth waters. I'm more excited than I should be. One day, I am going to be so fat! I *love* food.

After all is said and done, Corwin leaves five hundred dollars on the table, and we go.

"Thank you for another wonderful evening, Alyx." We pass by the maître d' who holds the door for us as we exit the restaurant. Corwin kisses the back of my hand.

"Of course, Gramps." I wink. "Anytime." He walks me to the bench. Sasha isn't here, which is odd because typically, she is waiting by the car with the door open.

"Shall I wait with you?" he offers.

"Not necessary." I touch his arm. "I'm sure she'll be along any minute."

"Alright then." He pats my hand. "I shall see you Wednesday. Let me know if anything comes up."

"I look forward to it."

"You have a fine evening, little lady. Don't stay out too late. I'm sure you've got homework to get to."

"I promise." I smile, showing my pearly whites, and drop my hand.

Corwin nods and walks away.

Mondays don't end awful, at least. Come to think of it, today wasn't a bad day at all. I managed to get six from Jennson, and ten from Lennox. Sixteen thousand is pretty good for a Monday. Which means four thousand will be in my pocket when I get home tonight. More if Sasha's late because of a new caller.

At least my brother's rent will be paid, and I'll be able to get him some new clothes. Hell, I'll be able to fill his freezer, too.

"Who the fuck cares where she is," I say after twenty minutes of waiting on Sasha. I have trackers in my earrings; she can find me when she's finished. I'm sure she's at the office counting out my portion of today's take and is running behind. Maybe Collin came in and wanted a taste of the retired Sasha. She was always giving Estelle's bodyguard some side action.

I am a few blocks from my apartment. Straight up West 65th Street toward West End Ave. If I hadn't waited on Sasha, I'd be home already.

The sun is setting, and the air is warm as I walk. I love walking in the city. The lights and sounds—action is always somewhere. Walking calms me, too. I slide out of my Louboutin Alta pumps and slip my finger through the loops. I want to go home and get prepared for tomorrow, but I'll need a quick nap before the workday is over.

My schedule for tomorrow starts at 2:00 AM with Mr. Ito. I won't get home until around six, but then I can sleep for a few hours before my 1:00 PM with Mr. O'Gorman. O'Gorman likes me to dress in the classic school girl outfits. Tomorrow I'll wear my red one since I wore my yellow one last week.

Right after that, Sasha will drive up 5th until we get to 56th—while I change clothes in the back seat— then I'll get out and hop into Mr. Mishra's limo. He likes his 5:15 PM blow job on his way home. I'll get out at 104th, walk over to Park Ave, where Sasha will pick me up, and I'll go to a late dinner with Mr. Kishimoto.

It'll be a long day, but for now, at least I can people-watch on my way home.

It's one of my favorite things to do while I walk. It's also the thing I miss most about being in Florida. My childhood friend, Ana, and I used to sit on the pier and fabricate stories of who people were and what they were doing. Where they were from was a fun one, too. Ana and I are still friends, but we've grown apart since our schedules no longer match up. Now that *U*ncle Fitzroy is no longer my handler, Ana's with him, and I'm with Estelle.

As I walk along the street, I see couples and wonder

what that's like. Most of my clients are married, yet they still come to me. What must it be like to trust someone so much and have them break it?

What is normal anyway?

I've never had a boyfriend, a girlfriend, or a partner of any kind—only clients. I'm not sure that I could trust someone enough to ever have any typical kind of relationship. They're all going to cheat one day anyway.

As I cross 66th street, a black SUV speeds by and stops right in front of me. "I'm walking here. Asshole!" My hands fly into the air; causing me to almost drop my pumps.

The back door opens up—it's Estelle. "Get the fuck in the car!" she roars.

Without hesitation, I jump in. The car speeds off. "What's going on?" I ask as I look around.

Estelle has her phone in her hands, texting like a madwoman. Sunglasses cover her eyes, maybe Uncle gave her another black eye. "Where the fuck is Sasha?" Estelle turns toward me.

Felix, who's sitting in the back row of the SUV, reaches forward and grabs ahold of my shoulders. It's like Rachel all over again. When my last driver went missing, they held me for three days until I could prove I had nothing to do with it. God damn it, Sasha! "I have no idea," I shake my head. I don't fight Felix. For one, it's no use. For two, it will make me look guilty.

"She dropped me off for dinner with Corwin and left." His grip loosens.

"Can you prove that?" Estelle sneers at me. A wisp of her brunette hair falls down from the scarf she wears over her head.

"You can ask Mr. Thwaite. I got out of the car. We went to dinner, and she wasn't there when we came out."

Estelle nods to Felix. He lets go of me as soon as she does. "You'd better not be lying." She grinds her teeth and grabs my purse. "Felix, take this." She hands him the bag.

"Estelle, I had nothing to do with it. Just like I had nothing to do with Rachel."

"Fucking drivers. Why won't they do as they're told?" Estelle dials Corwin's number.

I sit in silence while the line rings. On the fourth ring, he picks up.

"Corwin, love," Estelle says in her happiest tone. "How was your dinner this evening?"

"Mrs. Estelle, it was beautiful. Your niece Alyx is quite the young woman. Getting into college at seventeen is a wonder. Already in her third year, too. I hope you're proud of her."

It was nice to know that the lies I told him about college had been believed, but guilt hangs over me for it. Hearing Corwin tell Estelle to be proud of me, puts little knots in my stomach.

"Of course, I am." Estelle's voice goes high. "I wanted to double-check that Sasha picked her up on time and didn't give you any trouble about anything."

"There was no trouble." Corwin laughs. "But after dinner, her driver wasn't there. I offered to wait with Alyx, but she told me she was sure her driver would be along. So, I left."

"There were no other issues?"

"None."

"Would you like to set up for next week? You know how much your meetings help Alyx."

"I've got some things to work out for next Monday. Can we push it to Thursday?"

"Of course, Alyx will arrive with bells on," she chimes.

"Thank you, Mrs. Estelle," Corwin says.

Estelle hangs up the phone. I know Estelle will be excited for my Wednesday evening plans with Corwin, but I also know that right now isn't the time to bring it up. I'll tell her later.

Estelle stares out her window. "We found Sasha's car down by the river. Sasha, however, is nowhere to be found."

"Have you checked the apartment?" I ask though I know they already have. I have to show that I'm not going to run off, too. I can't run off—this job is all that stands between myself and my brother being homeless.

My head flings to the side. My cheek is on fire—Estelle has backhanded me. "Of course, we checked the apartment," she screams. "You stupid cunts are all the same," she growls. "You all think you're smarter than I am." She huffs and looks out her window.

I'd said too much. There was a slight ringing in my ears. I hadn't meant to question her. *Fuck*. What is wrong with me? I know better. My cheek throbs.

After a few minutes of silence, Estelle grabs my arm and pulls me towards her. "Damn it, dear." She cups my face in her hands. "I'm sorry, you can't ask me trivial questions when I'm this upset. Does it hurt?" She strokes my cheek.

I give her a sweet smile, "No, I'm okay," I lie. I'll be lucky if I don't have to cover up a bruise tomorrow.

"Collin," she addresses the driver. "Pull over so Felix can run and get some ice." Estelle had taken over my mother's role when my parents died. She may have been hard on us, but she tried her best to care for the girls she handled. As much as she scolded us for being stupid, she protected us from harm.

Collin does as he is bid, and Felix jumps out of the car without being told anything. He is back in a couple of minutes with a small cup filled with ice and a cloth napkin. He hands it to Estelle.

"Here, dear." She wraps the ice up in the cloth and places it on my face.

The coolness is nice against the ache on my cheek. I should have known better than to say anything when Estelle is upset. I take over holding the ice to my face. "I didn't mean to imply that you didn't know what you were doing." I run a finger under the cloth. There is a sizable welt on my cheek. Estelle's rings must have made contact when she smacked me.

"It's fine, dear." Estelle waves a hand, dismissing me. "I'll find her. Did she say anything today?"

I think over the day's events and recount the day. "No. She picked me up at 6:30a.m., dropped me off for Jennson. We went to lunch at Bubby's before Mrs. Davis. Sasha waited until I left the hotel, then she took me to Mr. Thwaite. She didn't seem *off* or anything." Though, Sasha's leg had been uneasy at lunch. Not a good idea to mention that, though.

Collin's phone rings. "Answer that!" Estelle yells. "It could be Fitzroy."

Collin answers. "Talk," he says in his deep voice. His dark hair is slick with product. The lights outside the car make his skin look green and sick. Collin has been Estelle's bodyguard for as long as I can remember. He has his share of kinky quirks. Each of Estelle's girls has had at least one bounce around the bed with Collin. I've had more than I'd like to say, but it's part of the job. If I want Estelle to be happy, on occasion it is my job to make sure Collin is happy, too.

Felix, on the other hand, is different. I glance over my shoulder into the back seat. His blonde hair is a little long for my liking, but he has beautiful green eyes. He is thin, but his muscles still stand out. As far as I know, he's never been with any of the girls. He's with Estelle sometimes. The rest of the time, he's with *Uncle*, or Fitzroy, as Estelle calls him.

"Misty found Sasha," Collins says over his shoulder. "She's taking her back to your manor now." Collin stops talking for a second and listens. "But there's one problem."

"What?" Estelle says with fire in her eyes.

Collin ends the call. "Sasha didn't have any money on her when Misty found her."

I put the napkin and ice back into the cup. I am careful as I set it in the cup holder. Don't want to upset Estell further. I buckle my seat belt, it's a two-hour drive to the manor, but it is far enough out of the city to be secluded. Which, in this business, is sometimes necessary.

"That little bitch is going to pay for stealing from me!" Estelle screams then she turns towards me. Her lip twitches. "Anyone who participated will also pay."

Fuck.

MANOR

Felix is the first one out of the car. He holds open Estelle's door and then takes my hand to help me. I'm five-foot-three-inches-tall, and my dress is tight, so it helps. "Thank you," I say as I get out.

Felix nods. He still has my bag under his arm.

"Take Alyx to the pool house for now," Estelle says to Felix. "Stay with her. I don't want anyone out of my sight yet."

Felix grabs my upper arm and follows behind Estelle and Collin. Misty is inside the front door, and standing next to her is Fitzroy. A shiver runs down my spine—I haven't seen him in at least a year. His hair is still dark, his face still brooding. He is handsome, wealthy, and untouchable. He gave me to Estelle after Sasha got hurt. The client who'd hurt Sasha had had his sights set on me, too. Fitzroy moved me straightaway, and I'm still not sure how to take that. Was he protecting his *investment*; because it seemed like he wanted to protect *me*.

Fitzroy ignores Felix and I. Misty looks me up and down before rolling her eyes. Her green curls bounce as she turns her head away from us. "Estelle, I don't know where she could have put it," Misty says as Felix pulls me past everyone.

Felix drags me toward the kitchen. I look around as we walk, but I don't see Sasha anywhere. Estelle yells, "that little bitch," as Felix and I go out the back door. At least they found Sasha. If she'd gotten away, I'd be the one to pay.

When my last driver—Rachel—tried to leave, Estelle punched her so hard she knocked some of her teeth out. I later found out that they took her back to Idaho where she'd come from. Collin told me that they dropped her off in her hometown—without a penny— and left.

Sasha won't be happy going back home, nor will she like being left *there* with no money.

Felix deposits me into a chair, then locks the dead-bolt on the door. He goes around the room, double-checking that all the windows and doors are secure.

"I'm not going to try and leave," I say. Felix turns his head to look at me for a moment but then goes right back to staring out the window. "Conversation would make this wait go a little easier, you know."

He ignores me but takes a deep breath in through his nose.

"Fine." I grab the television remote. I flip through the channels, not watching anything. Keeping the volume low, to hear if anyone leaves the main house. "Can I at least have my phone? I'd like to text my brother and let him know I won't be available tonight."

Felix doesn't look over at me, but he tosses my purse. He's lucky it lands on the couch. Even Estelle might fire him for throwing a Balenciaga around like that. "Do you have to be so stuck up?" I pick up the bag.

"Why don't you get your shit and sit down. We don't have to make nice." Felix turns and stares back out the window.

"Whatever," I say. "I'm going to the bathroom." I grab my bag and walk away. Felix leaves his post and follows me down the hall. "Are you serious right now?"

"Estelle told me to stay with you."

I stop at the bathroom door. "She didn't say you had to follow me into the restroom."

Felix reaches around me, opens the door, and flips on the lights. He takes a quick look around the room. "No windows. I'll be right outside."

I make sure to say, "Uptight, Blonde, Mother Fucker!" as loud as I can when I slam the bathroom door. What an asshole. I mean fuck! I know he's doing his job, but I'm not the one who ran off.

I splash some water on my face. My cheek is still red. The welt isn't as prominent as it was in the car. I'll have to use an inordinate amount of cover-up tomorrow morning though. I dry my face, then grab my cell phone from my bag. I send a quick text to my brother.

"Working late, don't worry. Talk tomorrow. Love ya!"

Trent texts back right away. *"No problem, sis, stay safe. I'm staying in tonight. Fortnite event!"* Several emoji that make no sense pop up. He is always doing that. He thinks it's funny. It makes me smile.

Well, that is that. Trent will be in front of his computer until further notice. My brother is on the spectrum, but the doctors told my parents that he is 'mildly autistic.' There is no reason he can't have a normal life. That, however, doesn't stop the severe depression and the severe anxiety that creeps in on him and puts him down. It doesn't stop the nervous rocking, that you can do nothing about—other than offer comfort and if possible, remove whatever triggered it in the first place. After mom and dad died, it took me three months to get him to leave the house.

Neither of us graduated high school. Go fucking figure.

I was lucky that I'd already been working for *U*ncle Fitzroy for three years. If not, the mortgage company would have taken the house a lot sooner than they did, and my brother and I would have been left to foster care. We were so close to eighteen, though, that *somehow*, we got missed by the system. Thank God! I can't imagine anyone trying to take my brother away from me. That would not have ended well at all.

I know it will be a while before Estelle comes to get me. She likes making us girls wait—especially when she's mad. Everyone else would freak out, worrying to no end until she came. I know better. Instead of worrying, I'll make good use of the Jacuzzi tub.

I fill the tub with bubble bath and some essential oils. The bottles aren't labeled, but one smells of lavender and rose. I undress and sink into the bubbles.

There's a knock at the door. "How long will you be?" Felix asks.

I grumble. I'm not about to answer him. I've been soaking for about thirty minutes. He can stand in the hall with his thumb up his ass for all I care.

"Alyx," it's the first time he's *ever* said my name. "Estelle will be here in three minutes. If I were you, I'd hurry it up."

Damn it. There goes my relaxing bath. "Can you find me a towel?"

Felix huffs, and his footsteps retreat. I pull the plug on the tub to let the water drain. The door opens, and a hand appears, holding a towel. "Umm, hello," I say. "I'm way over here. I can't reach that."

Felix comes into the bathroom holding the towel stretched out in front of him. I stand up and put my hand out. Bubbles run down my body; Felix averts his gaze. I realize—I've never been in a room naked with Felix before.

I take the towel from him. He turns his back toward me but doesn't leave as I tuck the towel around my body.

"Felix!" Someone yells from the other room. Loud steps echo on the tile floor, headed our way.

Collin comes into the bathroom. "Oh," he looks me up and down and smiles at Felix. "Hate to interrupt, but Estelle wants Alyx now."

Felix turns toward me and grabs my arm. "Let's go," he orders.

Felix drags me from the bathroom; Collin follows right behind us. He grabs my towel and tugs it a little. I look back and he licks his lips. A shiver sweeps over me as Felix pulls me out the door.

Estelle stands outside the pool house smoking a cigarette and talking with Fitzroy. Her white dress has a few wrinkles in it that weren't there when we got to the manor. Like she'd pulled her skirt up... oh... maybe her and Fitzroy had a quickie in the kitchen.

Fitzroy's gaze rolls over my form beneath the towel. "Good evening, Alyx," he says acknowledging me.

"Hello, *U*ncle." I go to his side and kiss his cheek. I'm not allowed to refer to him by his name.

"So." He puts his hand under my chin. "What do you know about this whole mess?"

I shake my head. "Nothing."

"Are you sure, my sweet Alyx?" He trails a finger down my neck.

"I swear." I bite the inside of my bottom lip.

"Well, I guess we'll see then, won't we." Fitzroy yanks the towel from my grasp and throws it to Collin. "Bring her," he yells over his shoulder.

It's warm outside, but the breeze is cool against my bare skin. I know I can't ask for the towel back but I'm unsure why he took it from me in the first place.

Two men that I've never seen before come from the manor dragging someone between them. I can't see who because their head is hanging down. When they drop the person at Fitzroy's feet, I notice scars down their leg.

It is Sasha.

There are a few places on her body that aren't black and blue. She is also as naked as I am. I take a step back. Felix catches my arm and shakes his head no.

"You see, Ms. Alyx," *U*ncle says, "Sasha told me that you helped her. That you gave her the money, all on your own."

All the hairs on my neck stand to attention. I swallow hard.

This. Is. Bad.

CHAPTER TWO - TUESDAY

MIDNIGHT

Water runs up my nose and down my throat as Collin holds me under the water. He pulls me up before pushing me under again and again. "That's enough!" A muffled voice says from the surface.

I cough and choke as Estelle swats my back, forcing the chlorinated water out of my lungs—which burn like I've inhaled fire instead of water. I gasp while air finds its way back into my chest.

"I swear. I did what I always do." I cough again. "I gave her the money, so she could count out my cut and then give the rest to Estelle. I had no idea Sasha planned anything." What else can I say? I'm naked ... paralyzed ... and barely breathing.

"I know," Fitzroy says. "But we have to set an example." He waves a hand to the upstairs windows.

I look up, and there are girls in all the windows. Chills run over my entire body. Some girls are younger than me, some older. I recognize a few of the faces, but Ana's face stands out among the crowd. Her blonde hair had been dyed purple to appease a new client, but I haven't seen her in months. She stares at me, shaking her head. Ana knows me better than anyone. How could she think I'd have anything to do with this?

"Felix, take this." Fitzroy points to me.

Felix comes over and grabs my arm, helping me stand.

"Get her up." Fitzroy points to Sasha.

Collin and one of the unnamed goons pull Sasha to a standing position. Her legs don't hold her up; the goons do. "Sasha," Fitzroy squeezes her face in his hand. "You've been a nasty girl. A bad investment," he sneers. "You know what we do with bad investments."

"Yeah, you fuck them and then give them to your cannibal clients." Sasha spits in Fitzroy's face.

The air leaves my lungs again. Felix's hand grips my arm tighter. I didn't even realize I'd taken a step back.

"Bryant," Estelle says. "Take care of it."

It's never good when Estelle refers to one of us as *it*. The other unnamed goon, who is apparently named Bryant, walks forward. He pulls a gun from underneath his jacket. He points it at my head. I inhale and close my eyes.

"Not that one," Fitzroy shouts.

I open my eyes, and Bryant turns the pistol toward Sasha, who is standing somewhat in front of me. He pulls the trigger. My ears ring from the boom. Before I can move, think, comprehend, there is blood all over me, and Sasha slumps to the ground. Her head rolls back, and there is a hole where her eye should be.

Sasha lays there, on the patio with nothing...

She's dead.

The rusty scent of blood hits my nose, and the gunshot echoes in my ears. I scream as blood pools by her head.

Felix picks me up and throws me over his shoulder. What is he going to do with me? I wail, and cry, and try to get out of his grasp as he carries me toward the manor. I don't want to die, too.

FELIX SETS me down in one of the many bedrooms. He pulls me into the bathroom, grabs a towel, and wipes the blood from my face. I stare into the mirror as the streaks of red begin to disappear. I cry, and Felix cleans. I can't think. Before I know it, I'm in the shower, warm water running over me. Felix washes the blood from my hair. He gathers Q-tips and cleans the blood from my ears. He washes every part of me, careful not to touch my bare skin with his.

Sasha is an ass for stealing and claiming I had anything to do with it, but she is also my friend. *Was* my friend. Maybe she needed to lie and say I was part of it. As the water pools and runs down the drain, all I can see is Sasha's blood pooling by her head.

Felix turns the shower off, wraps me in a towel, and carries me to the bed. He sets me down, but as he tries pulling his arm from under me, I hold onto him. "Don't leave me. Please," I whisper.

Felix nods and crawls onto the bed. He wraps his arms around me. He's the big spoon; I'm the little one.

THE SMELL of coffee wakes me. I don't know when I fell asleep, but Felix is still beside me. Though, he's no longer holding me, just sitting on the bed, drinking coffee. I'm under the covers, the towel still around my body.

"You, okay?" he asks.

I sit up, pulling the blanket with me. My entire body aches. My cheek feels swollen, and it seems as though there's still some water in my lungs. I cough. "I don't know," I answer honestly.

"You slept like the dead," he says.

Sasha flashes in my head. I need her to stop doing that. "You stayed all night?"

Felix nods. "Couldn't leave, required to stay." He gets up from the bed.

"Oh." I don't know why, but that feels like a lie. Maybe it's the way he looked away from me when he answered. It doesn't matter. Sasha is gone. Everything is wrong. "Why... Why did they kill her?" Why didn't they send her away like Rachel?

"You don't steal from Fitzroy and get away with it, Alyx." Felix turns toward me, and I notice the bloodstains on his shirt. When he tossed me over his shoulder the fluid must've gotten on him, too.

I grimace. "I didn't... I didn't take anything."

"They know that. That's why you're still alive." He hands me the coffee. "But you're going to have to help them now." He raises his arms high above his head and stretches. Pulling at one arm, then the other.

The mug is warm in my hands. Steam rising from the milky brown liquid. I take a sip. "Help them with what?" The coffee heats up my insides in a way that makes me realize I'm cold. I squeeze it tighter and take another sip.

"You spent most of your time with Sasha. She hid the money she stole. You have to help them find it."

"Sasha never told me anything. We talked about movies, food, work, and clients. About whether we should take fifth avenue or the subway. I had no idea she planned anything at all." I take another drink of coffee. The warm liquid feels nice in my empty stomach.

"Doesn't matter. Sasha lived with you. She was with *you*, more than anyone. You've got to know something." Felix sits down in the chair by the window and puts on his shoes.

"But I don't." My fingers tap against the mug.

"Figure it out and get dressed. Collin texted; they want you downstairs in ten minutes."

I look over at the clock. It's 6:30. "Thank you for last night." I hand the mug back to Felix. "I couldn't have…."

"I know," he says. "Don't worry about it." He smiles at me. It's a half-smile. Given the events of last night, I don't expect more. "You need to get dressed," he points to the closet. "I'll be outside."

I nod. He grabs his jacket from the back of the chair and leaves the room. I've never paid much attention to Felix. He's always around being a bodyguard for Fitzroy or Estelle, whoever needs him. Though, before last night, he'd never even touched me.

I find clothes in the wardrobe. Fitzroy had the closets stocked. A black pair of sweatpants and a pink halter top with the little fg emblem below the left strap. The fg stands for Fitzroy's Girls. Once you've reached a higher position with him, the lowercase turns to upper-case—FG. I have one of those tops at my apartment in a box. I haven't needed it since I was given to Estelle. Back when I started out, it's what all of *his* girls wore. That's how we knew one another when we crossed each other out and about. It was the uniform he preferred. Mainly because the tops were almost see-through and thin enough that our nipples made their presence known.

FELIX LEADS me into the kitchen. His hand grips my upper arm, but he's not hurting me. It's more for show. He places me on a stool next to *U*ncle Fitzroy and leaves the room.

"Good morning, sweet Alyx." *U*ncle leans over and kisses my sore cheek. I make sure not to wince. He puts a hand on my lower back. "Have you thought about your actions?" His finger plays at the elastic waist of my pants.

"I didn't help Sasha. I swear." My leg bounces up and down.

"But her boyfriend did. Did you know him?" He adjusts his colorful tie. I'd been with Estelle when she bought him that tie at Neiman Marcus. The Zegna. I'd picked it out.

"No. I didn't know she had one. She never brought anyone to the apartment. At least not that I was aware of. I can't know what she does all day because I have appointments."

Fitzroy's hand grips my waist. Pinching my side but holding me in place. "What was that?"

Shit, I just made an excuse. "Sorry, I meant to say that I'm not always with her." I look away from Fitzroy's gaze.

"Be careful how you speak to me, Alyx," he says but he lets go.

I nod my head. "Yes, sir."

"Have you learned your lesson?" Fitzroy's fists clench and unclench.

"Stop teasing her." Estelle comes into the kitchen wearing a bright yellow summer dress. She looks like she's hopped out of a 1950's sitcom. "Alyx will do what's best for us. Like she always has." She eyes me. "Won't you, dear?"

"Of course. I swear I didn't know," I say. "I would have told you if I'd known *anything* at all." I press a hand to my stomach. At least Estelle knows me well.

Fitzroy puts his arm around my shoulder and squeezes me close. "I know. We found her boyfriend last night. He didn't have the money on him, but he knew about it. So," he clicks his tongue, "you're in the clear."

I'm not sure if *U*ncle is lying to see where I stand or if it's the truth. "But where," I start to ask where the boyfriend is, where the money is, but Collin sneers a crooked smile. I close my mouth.

"People drown in rivers every day." Collin laughs. "Especially foolish ones who steal."

Estelle giggles and wraps one arm around Collin's neck. "He's a good boy, isn't he, Fitzroy?"

"Yes, Estelle, your bodyguard did well last night. Would have been better had he found the money, though." Uncle Fitzroy gets up from his seat and grabs a plate.

"It isn't Collin's fault that that Pig took what was ours." Estelle rubs Collin's arm in a motherly way as she bashes the now dead Sasha.

She flashes in my head. I need to stop thinking about Sash... *her*.

Fitzroy peruses the table. It has a breakfast buffet set up. He fills the dish with food. Eggs, sausage, bacon, toast, hash browns, gravy, and biscuits. He sets the plate down in front of me. "Eat something."

I look to my handler, Estelle, for permission. She nods her head, so I grab a fork from the counter next to the plates and begin eating. Careful to take small bites and not chew too fast. I'm on display right now. One wrong move and I'll have more bruises than I already do. Fitzroy sets a glass of grapefruit juice down next to my plate. I smile and take a sip. It's bitter.

"No, it isn't his fault, but he could have brought the boyfriend to me first." Fitzroy stares at Collin.

"Next time, I will." Collin rolls his shoulders. Had Fitzroy taught Collin a little lesson last night, too?

"Are you wanting there to be a next time?" Fitzroy stares at Collin.

"No sir." Collin takes a step back.

I don't clean my plate. If it were up to me, I'd eat the entire meal and go back for seconds, but I know better. I don't need to be compared to a cow *today*. Estelle's already referring to Sasha as a *P*ig. Which is her derogatory term toward any girls who don't fall in line. Fuck. Stop it, Alyx. Stop thinking about… *her*.

"Darling," Estelle looks at Fitzroy, "Alyx has a full schedule today. Is it alright that we get her back to the city? Or should I cancel her day and leave her here with you?"

"Send her back into the city. I'll see her this weekend." Fitzroy rolls his shoulders.

I'm not sure what he's referring to, but I know I don't have an option either way.

"Bring in her new driver." Fitzroy winks at me. "It's an old friend. You should be happy."

Collin leaves the room to retrieve whoever it is. He's gone a moment before he comes back in the room with Ana at his side. She, too, is wearing black sweats and a FG pink halter top. The purple in her hair is fading, and it looks more blue than purple. Dye washes out fast when you shower as much as we do.

"Ana," Fitzroy says. "I know you know Alyx. But I want you to take extra special care of her today, alright?" He runs the back of his finger down my cheek. "She's had a rough night."

"No problem," Ana says.

"Are you excited about your new position, *Driver*?" Estelle sneers as she looks Ana up and down.

"Which car will I be taking?" Ana smiles and inclines her head toward Estelle.

"Take the SUV," Estelle says.

Ana nods, and Collin hands her the keys.

"Come on, bitch." Ana winks at me and smiles. "Let's ride!"

I know she is joking for show. I smile back. The thought of leaving Sasha behind makes me sick to my stomach—dead or otherwise. What had they done with her? I drink the rest of the grapefruit juice and follow Ana. Not daring to look outside at the back patio.

RETURN

I don't know who put my bag in the car, but it's in the passenger seat when I get in. As is my dress from last night. My shoes are neatly placed on top of everything. I set everything in the back. I'll never be able to wear that dress again because it will remind me of last night.

I grab my phone from my bag and text my brother that I'm on my way back to the city. He doesn't reply. More than likely, he's asleep. After all, he'd played Fortnite all evening while I...

I don't want to think about it. I notice an unread message from Estelle.

It's my schedule for the day. Apparently, I have a meeting at noon with Sempers and a 4:30 with Blake. Estelle must have switched Tuesday with Thursday because those two are my Thursday regulars. I wasn't in the city to start my Tuesday at two a.m., so she must have changed everything around.

Thursdays were hard days with Sempers who likes violence, and Blake, who is a different kind of kinky. But it looks like my difficult Thursday is about to be my even more difficult Tuesday. Not only because of last night, but the bruises on my body will make Sempers worse than usual.

I sit in the passenger seat and mess with the air conditioning controls. Ana has it set too cold. "Aren't you freezing?" I ask as she drives away from the manor.

"If you had two percent more fat on your body, you'd be warm, too." She reaches over and turns the dial back to the coldest setting.

I shake my head and look through my bag. I find a t-shirt. Taking my seat belt off so I can put the shirt on as Ana gets on the expressway.

"You of all people should know better than to take your seat belt off while a car is moving," Ana snaps.

"It was just for a second. Geez," I say while clicking my seat belt back on. "Why me of all people?" I close the air conditioner vents on my side.

"Duh, your parents." Her lip quirks up.

"You don't have to be a bitch. Jesus. Every single time I'm with you, you bring up my parents' death. What the fuck for? How does it help anyone, Ana?"

Ana and I hadn't seen each other in a while. Why did she have to start off so bitchy?

"What, are you gonna cry about it?" She pouts her lip mocking me.

"What is your problem? I don't see you for twelve weeks, and you turn into a massive bitch. Fuck off." I look through my bag for a pair of headphones. I don't have to take her shit. I have to get home so I can get on with my day. I have bills to pay.

"Yeah, my problem." She scoffs. "The only problem I have is girls like you."

"Jesus, fuck! Seriously Ana, what is going on? Did you miss your period again? Is that why you're on driving duty? How is any of it my fault?"

"No, I didn't miss my period. I won't have periods anymore." She presses the gas pedal, and the car speeds a little faster.

"Don't kill us because you won't have periods anymore. Wait, why won't you have periods anymore? You're only a few months older than I am." Damn, the headphones aren't in my bag.

Ana shakes her head.

"Fine if you don't want to talk about it, but there's no fucking need for you to be rude to me because *you're* having issues." I give up looking and put my bag in the back seat.

"You're not serious?" Ana scoffs.

"Yes, I am. I don't deserve to be treated like this." I lean back in my seat and cross my arms.

"Fuck you, Alyx! You're the reason Estelle insisted that I have the damn surgery."

"What fucking surgery? I didn't ask Estelle to do anything to you. Is *surgery* why you're a driver?" I motion a hand toward her.

"Because you and Sasha fucked everything up! If not for you two, none of us would have been dragged to the manor months ago."

"I had nothing to do with that!" The image of Sasha lying on the ground with blood pooling beside her fills my vision. "I swear," my voice is soft. I shove the vision out of my head. "I had no idea. I don't even know why she did it."

"Well, it's your fucking problem now because *U*ncle deemed Sasha too hormonal, and that's why she did it. Estelle had fourteen of our uterus' taken because of you and fucking Sasha!"

"Damn it, Ana. How many times do I have to say it? I had nothing to do with it! I was with a fucking client when she vanished!" I fold my arms across my chest. "It's not like I took your damn uterus," I huff. Tension builds behind my eyes. I'll need my sunglasses if I'm going to make it through the day without getting a headache.

"They knew she was up to something." Ana seems

to be talking to herself. "They knew she'd be dead soon. They made sure to do the surgery before her plan went through so that I could be reassigned as *your* driver until the doctor releases me to active duty."

Fucking shit. "Is that why you were at the manor for all those weeks? Surgery?" Ana had been gone, but she was gone a lot. *Uncle is always taking her on vacations and to The Island. When she's with him, I never give it a second thought.*

"I hate you. I wish I'd never fucking met you."

"My God, what the hell? I did nothing to you, Ana. I'm not in charge of who works where. I have no say in any god damned thing! If you've got a problem with Estelle or *Uncle*, I suggest you keep it to yourself."

"If it weren't for you, I'd never have been in this shit in the first fucking place. Now I'll never have any more kids."

That throws me. "Any *more* kids? When the hell did you have a kid? What do you mean if it weren't for me? I'd like to point out that I'm in this business because of *you!*"

Ana shakes her head again. "I can't even believe what I'm hearing right now. You are so full of shit. 'I didn't help Sasha. I know nothing,'" her voice is shrill. "You are so full of it!"

"You know what, pull the fuck over. I'll get a cab back to the city." I grab the handle to open the door.

"Get a grip, Alyx. I'm not letting you out. I have to do what I'm *told*, and right now, that's to make sure you get back to the fucking city."

"Jesus you're being a bitch! I'm not stupid. I know when I'm not wanted. Let me out." Fucking hell Ana is in a mood.

"I know you're not stupid. I'm not stupid either. Why else would you help Sasha? You're lucky I didn't tell Fitzroy that you know."

"That I know what?" How will I be able to concentrate on work today when I can't even follow what Sasha…nope… *Ana* is saying?

"About your fucking parents."

"My parents are dead, Ana. You just said so yourself." My day is going to be hard enough with Sempers and Blake. Why does Sa… *Ana* have to add to it? I need to get… the other girl… out of my head.

"I know you *know* they were ordered to run your parents off the road."

"What did you say?" I'm floored. "Who was ordered to run *who* off the road?"

"You're such a bitch. Making me say it. Your parents. The *accident*." She makes air quotes when she says the word. "The reason they're dead."

"I thought you were accusing me of helping Sasha, and now we're talking about my parents," I huff. "Okay,

I'm game." Fine. If she wants to play, I'll play. "Who's the reason my parents are dead?"

"It was Fitzroy and Collin; who else?"

That's straight out of left field. "What on earth would make you say that?" My mind races. Sasha's image pops in my head, and my breathing hitches. Flashes of Collin forcing my head under the water in the pool last night intermingles with all the girls watching me. Their faces all flash in front of me. Fitzroy's hand pinching my side. The images won't stop coming. I force my eyes closed.

I'm losing my grip.

"Stop acting aloof," Ana punches my shoulder. "It's fucking annoying."

"Ouch!" I rub my arm and throw a glare her way.

"I can't believe you told your dad what you did for Fitzroy."

"Ana, you've lost me here. I never told my dad anything. Why the fuck would I tell either of my parents what I did for extra cash?" I hadn't either. I'd never said a word to either of them. I'd always told them the new things I came home with were from friends getting rid of stuff.

"Bullshit. Your dad's friend Peter told me all about it when the police found your parents' car."

"Peter?" Peter had been my dad's best friend for my entire life. Fuck, my father and Peter had grown up together. He'd been my uncle, not by blood, but an uncle all the same. "When and *why* were you with Peter?"

"You're not that stupid, are you?" Ana roars.

I look at Ana, baffled. My head spins as my mind races to keep up with her accusations.

"Peter introduced me to Fitzroy, Alyx."

"No, you already knew Fitzroy. You introduced *me*."

"Alyx! Fuck! Keep up. Peter is why." She punches my arm again. I rub my arm reflexively—I can't *feel* anything. "I met him at your thirteenth birthday party. Do you remember? Eighth grade, the end of the year. Your parents had that huge party for you and your brother at the country club? Peter was there?"

"Peter was at all our birthdays." I tear apart my memories, looking for it. What on earth is Ana talking about? It hits me then. Peter whispering to Ana by the pool. She was several months older than I was; her boobs had arrived in the sixth grade. By the end of eighth grade, she looked like she was sixteen. He tucked a stray hair behind her ear. He took her over and introduced her to another man. Holy shit. The other man was… "Collin," I whisper.

"Yeah," Ana scoffs. "I thought you were already in the business when I joined. It was later when I found out you weren't. When Fitzroy picked me up from school and spotted you. He told me there'd be hell to pay if I didn't get you over to his house. I didn't grow up with money, Alyx. I was already in too deep to go against him."

"I've never gone against him though, why would he…." I trail off. What reason would Fitzroy have to kill my parents? Mom and dad died when I was seventeen. I started work for him at fourteen. "They died *after* I began working for Fitzroy, not before."

"Did you do what was asked of you, though? Did you do all that *U*ncle required of you?" Ana shrieks. "I thought I had done all that was required of me. Until I fucking got pregnant. Do you remember senior year, after your parents died and I went into home-hospital?"

"Ana, I've forgotten senior year because my *parents* died! It's all a damn blur." That year was a haze, too. What I did remember involved my brother and I having almost no food. We'd had to do all kinds of things to survive. Things like thinning spaghetti sauce with water to make it last for several meals. There were weeks that we lived on microwaved potatoes. No butter, with some salt. After a few months, I agreed to work with *U*ncle more, and those days of no food drifted by. The more I worked, the more money I had to take care of my brother.

"Well, that's the year I had my daughter. Fitzroy has her on The Island. He's her fucking father."

The world spins around me. "You have a daughter?"

PREPARATIONS

Ana pulls up to my building. "Get the fuck out and go get ready. It's almost time for your first appointment."

I get out of the car without hesitation. I slam the door as Ana peels off. "Fuck." My purse is in the back of the SUV. How can I get ready without my keys? I see the doorman to the building, so I cross the street. "Excuse me, Marcus," I say.

"Ms. Beck, how are you today?" He opens the door for me.

"Umm, I forgot my purse in the car, and my driver left. Can you let me in my apartment?"

"Certainly," he says.

He asks me questions about my weekend plans while we ride up the elevator, but my responses are vacant and detached. My mind reels with everything Ana told me. Could it be true? Could Fitzroy be responsible for my parents' death? Could he be the father of Ana's *child*? Did Ana have a child on the island?

I try to find the memories in my head.

Ana.

Senior year.

Home hospital.

I don't remember any of it. To be fair, though, once my parents died, I was high most of the time. I'd go to school. I'd go to *U*ncle's house. I'd make money—but never enough to pay all the bills. I helped my brother the best I could, but that's all I remember.

Maybe Ana wasn't present in those memories because she wasn't there. She *was* at The Island, having a baby. However, Estelle always told me that any pregnancies would be terminated. Why would Fitzroy do it any different?

Marcus unlocks my door. "Thank you."

"Anytime, Ms. Beck." He nods to me and turns back for the elevators.

I go into my apartment. The first thing I notice is a pair of Sasha's shoes. I fall to the ground, pick them up, and start crying. Why am I crying over shoes? I lived with Sasha for a year. I've known her for... shit, Sasha started the same year I did. She'd lived two towns over. Misty had brought her in. Fuck, she was Misty's cousin.

Misty is the one who found her by the river and brought her back to the manor.

"I'm sorry," I whisper to the shoes. I take the shoes into Sasha's bedroom and lay them at the foot of her bed. I turn to leave but I spy something sparkling on the floor from the corner of my eye. I walk over to her bedside table. Her tracking earrings are between her bed and the table; I leave them where they lay. Back out of the room and close the door. Sasha had come here *after* she left me with Corwin.

It's almost ten and I need a shower. I have to be at Sempers by noon. I can't be late.

I go to the bathroom, undress, and get in the shower.

Why hadn't I seen it all sooner? *U*ncle had asked me to take on more responsibilities weeks before my parents' accident. I'd said no. My dad wanted me to go to college. My mom wanted me to become an accountant like her. My dad said I should be a lawyer like him. *U*ncle said he'd make sure I made more money, but still, I'd *refused* him.

That is always a mistake.

Those days were different, though. I worked with *U*ncle when I needed money for things my parents wouldn't pay for. When I wanted a little extra cash to buy weed and get high with my friends. If there was a new bag that my mom wouldn't fork money over for, all I'd have to do is give *U*ncle a few massages, or hand-jobs and then I'd have enough cash.

Could it be true—am I the reason my parents are dead? Did Fitzroy do it? I... I just don't know.

I do know that I never told my dad anything, though. I'm dizzy as everything floods my mind. Watching the water flow down the drain, all I can see is red. Like the blood pooling next to S... that girl's head.

I don't have time for any of these thoughts.

I shake my head, clearing the red vision in front of me and get out of the shower. I dry my hair, the noise from the hair dryer makes it easier to block things out. Bruises mark my neck and sides from Collin holding me under the water. I smear concealer over those as well as the ones on my face.

After I am dressed, I look myself over in the mirror. The bruises are all covered. My makeup has done a good job. I realize I have a few extra minutes and decide to go see my brother before Ana gets back to take me to my appointments for the day. I run down the hall and through the fire doors.

My brother answers on the fourth knock. "To what do I owe this pleasure?" he says, yawning.

"I missed your face." I grab him and hug him. He's taller than me by almost a foot. He looks a lot like my dad. Tall, a bit of a belly, dark hair, and blue eyes. He is also the sweetest guy I've ever known. My brother has never—in our entire lives—hurt me. Not even by accident.

Trent hugs me back. "Want some breakfast?" he asks as he pulls away. "I've got some bagels and jam."

"Sure, but we gotta eat quick. I have to leave for work soon." It will be nice to eat with no one watching or knowing.

"Is that why you're all dressed up?" He waves a hand toward my clothes. "Your dress is pretty, but I didn't know personal shoppers had to dress so well."

I smile and follow him to the kitchen. My brother either refuses to see what I do or is in fact, clueless. I'm not ashamed to tell him; he doesn't *need* to know though. I get paid well for what I do. I feel like it might be dangerous for him to know more. I never knew why either. Until last night, I'd never been in danger before. I'd seen other girls in danger, but I'd never been... Well, there was that one time with Rachel and...

My lungs burn as images of Collin holding me under the water flood my mind. Danger lurks around me. I rub my chest trying to soothe the burn that lingers.

"Are you okay?" Trent slides a prepared bagel across the counter.

"Sorry. I was trying to remember what I'm

supposed to buy for Sempers today." I've always given my brother the names of the people I *shop* for. It's a dangerous thing to do now that I think about it, though. I should have known better. I'll need to stop doing that. "No, it's not Sempers. Geez, I'm all outta whack today. Sempers doesn't even live here anymore. It's Smith today." I lie. I feel guilty the instant I lie to him, but it seems necessary.

"Does another rich guy need more silk panties?" he laughs. "Or will this one need a ladder? You get into some weird places when you work."

"How would you know where I go when I work?"

"Ehh, I track your locations on Snapchat some-times. You never turned that feature off even after I told you to." He arches a brow at me. "You go to the home improvement store a lot more than I'd expect."

"All part of the job." I smile and take a bite of the bagel. The strawberry jam is sweet. "Thank you." I take another bite. I am okay with Trent tracking me. It's his way of worrying about me.

Trent laughs and pours me a glass of apple juice. "Drink this, too. You look pale."

"Hey." I swallow a bite. "I might work late again tonight, but could you call me and check-in before you go to bed?" I'm not sure he'll remember. "Set an alarm if you think you'll forget."

"Anything for you, sis." He grabs his phone. "Hey, Siri, set an alarm for eleven tonight. Remind me to call Alyx."

"Your call Alyx alarm is set for eleven p.m.," the phone responds.

"There, all done." He smiles at me and pops another bagel in the toaster.

"Okay. I needed to see your face. I have to go now." I shove another big bite of bagel in my mouth and head toward the door.

"Wait," Trent calls to me. The fridge door opens and closes. Trent comes over to the door. "Take this with you. You do look pale." He hands me a bottle of orange juice.

"Thanks, bro." I kiss his cheek and leave. How can I tell my brother that I might be responsible for our parents' deaths? *How* can I tell him? I walk back to my apartment, fidgeting with the bottle in my hands. I drop it when I open my front door. Before I can pick up the bottle or close the door, a foot is in it.

"Hey, come the fuck on! It's time to go." Ana pulls her foot out of the way.

"I forgot my jacket," I lie as I hold the door open for her to come inside. "I was heading down and didn't have it. I wasn't sure how late we'd be working tonight." I can't piss Ana off any more than I already have today.

I need to get my head in the game. Sempers is always a difficult *John*. He likes to get rough. I don't mind, but today, after last night, I'll need all my focus.

"Hurry up then." She shoos me away.

I run to my room and grab a sweater.

SEMPERS

We are downtown too fast for me to think of anything but what Sempers might be up to today. I climb the stairs to his building still unsure what's in store.

"Alyx," Sempers says through his intercom system. "Come to the fifth floor, love."

I turn my head and nod to the camera in the stairwell that he watches me from. I've never been on the fifth floor. The first time I ever visited Sempers, he'd had me come to the first floor. There he'd laid me on every surface and 'fucked me like the bad girl' I was.

I'd dealt with it because I walked away with four thousand dollars that day. That was two months' worth of rent for my brother's apartment. It was also before Estelle started giving me twenty-five percent, so I have no idea what he in fact paid for me.

Over time my visits to his first floor had begun to

bore him. So, he offered Estelle more money, and we moved to the second floor. It wasn't much different than being with Jennson. On the second floor, Sempers liked to tie me up. But again, he tired of that after a while.

The third floor. I pass the entryway with the large three on the door and continue up the stairwell, remembering that's where Sempers made me fuck him while he took a dump on the toilet. It was weird, but I walked away with ten grand that day. Estelle has never told me what he pays, but I get paid enough, so I don't care. The visits after that were all bathroom-related. I call the third floor, the latrine floor.

I pass the black door with the number four on it and shiver as I keep going. I'm glad I don't have to go in there today. In there, there are no lights. I'm left to wander around in the dark. Sempers wears night-vision goggles. He rips my clothes off and tells me to run. I'd end up tripping over lots of things. I'd have tons of bruises when I left. Sempers had caught me several times. I'm expected to fight and try to get away. Sometimes I do, others I don't. When I don't, things always get awkward. After the first visit to that floor, I learned not to wear anything too high fashion to Sempers' place. The money I made from the fourth floor, however, always pays rent for my brother's place, as well as food, medicine, his cellphone, and utilities.

Today might get weird, too, but at least I'll walk away with a stack of cash. Which will help since S... my money from Monday is gone.

I come up to the fifth floor. The door is black. It's cracked open, white smoke flows out. It looks more like dry ice than dark smoke from a fire. I blow out a breath and go inside.

The lights are shades of yellow and orange. There are random black lights on the walls, too. The eclectic paintings beneath them glow. The fog billows out from a smoke machine attached to the ceiling over by the windows. At least this floor has windows. The windows on the fourth floor are all covered.

There is a red sofa—at least it looks red under the lights— a coffee table with drinks on it, and a television. It's the most normal-looking floor that I've been on. Is this the standard sex floor? The television turns on, and Sempers' upper half appears on the screen. He's wearing a leather strap across his chest, a leather mask covering the upper half of his face, and he holds a whip between his teeth.

The first time Sasha had seen him, she'd said, "There's a guy I'd let fuck me for free. He's hot," and laughed. I smiled at the memory of Sasha. Shit. I let her in my head. I need to *stop* doing that. I grab the bottle of whisky from the coffee table and pour myself a glass.

I drink it down quick and pour another for good measure.

"It's almost time, my dear," Sempers says from the television. His hair is dyed orange, like the lights. His fingernails are painted black, and he cracks the whip. The sound echoes in the room. "Have a seat, and a drink, while I prepare everything for us today." The image on the screen changes, and a song plays.

The video shows some highlights from my visits to Sempers' place. I should have known he'd been recording everything. I take my heels off and set them on the sofa next to me. The music that booms into the room is hypnotic. Some brand of techno I don't know about. I don't care to know about it, but in my line of work, there are things I have to know for different clients.

My hearing muffles for a second, so I shake my head. It doesn't help. It makes it worse. Sempers comes for me as I list to the side.

Holy shit, something was in the whiskey.

He smiles a predatory smile as my eyes close.

Grunting wakes me. I try to move my head, but I puke as soon as I do. I open my eyes. The vomit rolls down my side and into floor grates.

I'm chained to the ceiling, somewhere on the fifth floor, I assume. My legs are chained, too. There is a bar between my ankles splaying my legs apart. I am naked. The lights are still orange, but it is a different room. I am centered, and there are heat lamps all around me. I feel as though I am baking in an oven. "Sempers," I yell.

Enter Sandman blares over the speakers. Water splashes down from above me. I gasp as the water takes over me. I lean forward to try and keep it out of my face. The puke washes down my body. Someone grabs my hair and pulls my face back upright. The water pours over my face.

When the water stops, I gasp for breath and choke out what went into my mouth. I silently pray that this is not some type of water boarding floor.

"Hello, Dear," Sempers says from behind me as he releases his grip on my hair.

"What the fuck!" I yell. "Let me out right now!" I thrash against the chains.

"Not today," he smiles. Sempers wears leather pants, the strap across his chest covers his nipples, and he holds the whip he'd had in the video in his hands. The mask is gone. He dances around flashing the whip, feigning he will hit me with it. "Today, I finally get what I want." He cracks the whip.

The leather straps thwack against my wet legs. I scream out in pain. "Stop it!" I yell as he continues his attack.

Sempers gets close to my face. "Today, you're mine. All… mine." He bares his teeth.

Fuck.

Sempers leans down and bites my breast, then he shoves his fingers inside me. "Let me get you nice and wet." He pushes a button on the strap that is on his chest.

More water rains down from the ceiling. He holds his whip out, letting the water fall on it. He smiles a crooked smile then turns the whip over in his hand. He uses it as a dildo. I thrash and try to get free, but it worsens the pain—which he likes. The lamps are heating up as well.

Sempers laughs and unzips his pants. He jerks off while he fondles me with the whip. He pulls the whip from me and puts it in his mouth. He stares into my eyes while he licks and sucks the leather. A trail of drool comes out the side of his mouth. "You taste… so fucking good…" His body trembles.

I can't decide if I am unimpressed by his new tactics or frozen in terror. How crazy is this asshole? He comes towards me to kiss me, and I turn my head. He grabs my chin, but as he does, my earring scrapes against my arm. Shit! He hadn't taken my earrings off. Thank fucking god! If I can somehow press them, it will alert Ana that I'm in trouble.

All of Fitzroy's girls wear a pair of tracking earrings.

Each set is equipped so that if we are ever in danger, all we have to do is press the diamond toward the back of the earring. It will send an alert to our drivers. How the fuck will I reach them with my hands tied?

I'll need to play along if I'm going to get out of this. "Do it again, *d*addy." I look right into Sempers' eyes. He always liked it when I called him *d*addy while we were on the third floor. Maybe he'd like it here, too.

Sempers looks at me. "Do what again?" He puts his hand between my legs. "You want more leather, or?" He puts a finger inside me.

I moan and move my hips around on his hand. I let spit run out of my mouth. "Yeah," I say as the dribble runs down my front.

Sempers lowers the chain I hang from. "I'm going to give you something else you want." He flashes a wicked grin, pulls me down, and lays me on the ground. He flips me over and lays on top of me. He holds my arms above my head. He inserts himself into me and bites my shoulder.

I scream out so he'll think I'm enjoying myself. Sempers lets go of my hands—which are still chained together—to hold onto my hips. He grunts and moans as he fucks me. I pull my hands closer and closer to my face. Hoping the movements won't alert him. He leans away from me to grab the leather whip he'd dropped— all while still gyrating like a rabbit.

As he grabs the whip, I grab my right earring, and press it down. Fucking praying that Ana isn't mad enough at me to ignore the alert.

I turn my head to press the other earring down, so she'll know I'm in trouble, but Sempers grabs my hands again. He thrusts himself inside me a few more times before he pulls out and gets up. He reattaches the chains to another hoist. My body rubs against the ground as the chain tugs at my arms and pulls my body forward.

My body goes past the heaters. I'm covered in water and sweat—thank fuck; otherwise, my front side would drag across the ground like eggs in a pan with no butter. The air is cooler away from the heat lamps. Sempers laughs as my body rises into the air. The chain raises me up. My shoulders ache. How long had I been hanging before I woke up?

Sempers retrieves the whip and comes toward me again. He lashes out with it, and the tips strike my flesh. A cry escapes my lips. Holy fuck, this guy is insane.

"You want more of… *daddy*?" He comes closer to me. He forces the whip's handle inside me then walks away. Sempers is back moments later, dragging a chair behind him.

He places the chair under me, pulls the whip out of me, and grabs my ass with both hands. His fingernails dig into my flesh. Sempers moves me until I hang above him, then he presses another button, and my body lowers.

He unhooks the bar from my ankles and tosses it to the side. The metal sings out as it bounces against the floor. He pulls me on top of him, so that I can mount him; my feet can now touch the ground. Sempers licks my underarms while he fingers me. "Daddy's turn." He positions me atop him. The chain lets my arms fall, and he puts my arms over his head. The chains and my hands are now behind him. His member is inside me, and he moves my hips the way he wants them to go. Lifting me up and down as he grunts. Having his way with me.

I lean my head to the side so that I can press the other earring. He bites my arm as I move. I moan, trying to keep him busy. A burst of light comes into the room. It takes a moment for my eyes to adjust. Before I can see, Sempers is no longer inside me, and I'm on the ground.

"Alyx!" Ana's voice sounds next to me.

Loud grunts come from the other side of the room as my vision comes back. Ana is releasing me from the chains, and Felix is punching Sempers. "Fucking shit! Ana! Estelle is going to kill Felix for that!"

"No, she won't." Ana helps me up.

Sempers laughs. "The briefcase is by the door." He rises to his feet.

Felix punches him, and Sempers falls back down. Ana finishes freeing me, and we walk to the open door. Ana picks up the case as Felix comes up next to me. He takes his jacket off, wraps it around me, and picks me up.

"Thank you," I say.

Felix nods.

I lay my head on his shoulder.

He carries me down five flights of stairs without losing his breath once.

CHAPTER THREE - WEDNESDAY

DAY OFF

I'm not sure how Ana managed it, but she was able to get Blake to agree to a change of pace yesterday. Ana had taken my place for that appointment. Which was okay, even though she'd had surgery, because all Blake ever wanted was for someone to finger her and fuck her with a dildo. I always thought of Blake as the no shower required kind of sex. Still, she'd yell out some kinked-up shit during our meetings. Blake was a 'mommy' kinky fuckery person.

Trent had called me last night, while I ate my fruit plate. Just like I'd asked. He sensed that something was wrong, but I told him that I was tired. He'd hesitated but let me go so I could get some rest. Trent is such a good brother.

He deserves a better sister.

I roll over in my bed and stare at the door. Felix is

in my apartment somewhere. I know because every now and again, I'll hear the fridge open and close. The television is on in the front room, too. Playing football, which Ana hates, so it isn't her in there.

Wednesdays are always my day off. Not because Estelle cared that I had a day off, it's that a lot of people had church on Wednesday nights. Clients had families they had to spend time with, too. The sole meeting I'll have today will be dinner with Estelle. I'm not sure how that will go with everything that went wrong at Sempers yesterday.

I reach past the plate of leftover fruit to grab the glass of water someone had been kind enough to leave on my bedside table. My shoulder pops as I pick it up, and I drop it. "Fuck!" I say as I try to raise up.

My bedroom door opens as I sit up. Felix stands in the doorway.

"Would you like some help with that?" He comes into my room and grabs a towel off my chair. He lays it over the spill and steps on the towel to sop up the water.

Watching the towel soak up the water makes me thirsty. "I'd like an ice bath. Fuck, I'm sore today." I don't know how to thank Felix for what he did yesterday. I'd said thank you to him as he carried me down the stairs, he acknowledged me by nodding his head.

Maybe he worried how much trouble *he'd* be in when Fitzroy found out what happened.

Felix turns and leaves the room. I get out of bed. My entire body is on fire. It must have been the heat lamps. It's like I have a bad sunburn, yet my skin isn't red, even though it feels a little crispy to the touch. I still have no idea how long I hung there before Sempers woke me.

Felix walks past my bedroom and goes into the kitchen. I follow him, taking careful steps to not cause further pain. There is a glass of ice water on the counter waiting for me when I walk in. He arches a brow at me as I take a drink. He opens the freezer, grabs the ice bucket and leaves the room.

I wander down the hall. Water runs in the bathroom. I go in and Felix is preparing an ice bath. He goes over to the linen closet, sets some towels out, and then escorts me to the tub. "Do you need any help?"

I set my glass of water on the counter. "Could you help me get my top off? It feels like it's stuck to my back. I think I used too much aloe last night before I put the shirt on."

He nods. I watch him in the mirror as he removes my shirt. He doesn't look at my body, only the clothes. He helps me get out of my shorts, too. Holds out a hand for me while I get into the tub, then leaves the room, closing the door behind him.

Who the hell is this guy? He is so different than Collin. Collin wouldn't have helped me without touching me or asking me for a blow job while I 'rest.' Being Fitzroy's bodyguard must be different than being Estelle's. Collin and Felix are as different as night and day. No, they're as different as myself and Sempers.

Two different worlds—entirely.

The water feels good against my skin. I sink down into the tub as far as I can go. I notice a bottle of aloe sitting in the corner. Felix must have done that, too. Of course, Fitzroy had trained him to take good care of the merchandise. Maybe he's doing his job, hoping not to get into too much trouble for hitting a client.

I rub some aloe on my face and shoulders, close my eyes, and lay there. After a while the door creaks open, but I don't feel up to moving. The door closes again. When I look over there is a fresh glass of ice water in the corner of the tub.

I take a drink and then stare at the glass as the condensation runs down the cup.

Could it be true? Could I be responsible for my current situation? Had I been the reason my parents were killed? As the water soaks into my skin, I can't help but speculate… What will Trent do when he finds out? I don't think he'll hate me for it, but I can see him not talking to me, or shutting down again.

I don't want that to happen.

I need to talk to Trent. We have lunch together every Wednesday. I'm not sure if I'll be up for it until I figure everything out though.

Ana said that Peter was the reason she'd met Collin —who led straight to Fitzroy. She'd said that Fitzroy spotted me outside of school one day as he picked her up. That she'd been required to take me over there. I remember the first time I went to Fitzroy's house. It was the pool party.

IT WAS two weeks until summer break started. We'd be freshmen in high school so soon! We were so excited to grow up. One day after school, Ana took me to her Uncle's house for a pool party. She was so excited to introduce me to girls from her old school. She said there'd be all kinds of kids there. Some from our soon to be high school, and more from other schools in the area. If we did well at the party, we'd have the best social lives of any freshman, *ever*!

When we arrived, the event was full of underage girls, as well as three well overaged men, and one woman who looked to be in her mid-thirties. The woman caught my attention before the men because she was a *high-class-woman*. Even poolside there wasn't a hair out of place. Her skin was sun-kissed, and her hair was brunette with highlights in all the right places. She wore a solid white two piece—though there wasn't enough material to make a dishcloth from— and a pair of large framed sunglasses.

The men however, took no notice of her at all. Even though she was by far the most beautiful female at the party. They all sat off to the side, in their lounge chairs, drinking their long island iced teas, talking about sports, and every now and then staring down one of the girls so hard I thought the girl might burst into flames. None of the men paid any attention to me or Ana, though. It was odd, because of how much they ogled the others.

I didn't mind that they didn't look at me, they were all creeps. It just seemed weird. Ana stayed close to me at that party, we had a good time.

There weren't any boys our age, but that meant that we could act a little crazy. When we'd slide down the slide into the pool we didn't have to obsess if we got a wedgie—we could pluck it out. We could jump from the balcony, doing cannonballs, not worrying if the water rose too high that someone would think us fat. Even if our hair looked a mess, none of it mattered because we had no one to impress. Of course, had any boys our age been there, they'd have drooled over the woman by the pool anyway.

There was lots of food and lots of wine coolers. Her

*U*ncle wasn't home that day, so we had the run of the mansion he lived in, too. Ana showed me the entire place. Everything was pristine. Expensive. This man was nothing but *money*.

Ana showed me the tower. I hated that I couldn't hear the waves crashing from the room though. It would have been perfect if I could've. The view of the water from the window was amazing. I could see cruise liners headed to and from port. The private beach at the back of the lot was surrounded on two sides with large stone walls. It was a one way in kind of deal. The exits were either the ocean, or back to the pool. One of the older gentlemen followed a couple of the girls out to the beach.

"Can we go swim in the ocean, too?" I'd asked Ana.

"Maybe next time we come." She grabbed my hand and dragged me down the spiral staircase so we could get back to the party.

THAT'S how it all began. A simple meet and greet. What I hadn't known at the time was that I'd been there as a gift. *U*ncle had been there, hiding, watching me, the other men hadn't been allowed to look at me. I was there for Fitzroy. Like those girls headed out to the beach were for the man who followed them.

Ana and three other girls from my school shared the same *U*ncle—but I hadn't caught on to that. Not by blood of course. Fitzroy had been Ana's handler, while the other girls had belonged to Estelle—the lady by the pool.

*U*ncle got first pick of any newcomers. Everything was done at his behest. Estelle belonged to him as much as the girls did. He was in charge. I learned the hierarchy and the rules in a flash. Every girl did, because if you didn't Estelle would beat the crap out of you and then deny you pay. She'd also set you up with the creeps from out of town when they'd come in—so you wouldn't cross her again.

Those first three years of high school were busy. Having straight A's while learning the ropes of sex work took its toll—I was fortunate that I'd had uppers to help me.

I lay in the bath and try to decide how I will tell my brother any of this.

LATER

"No, Felix. You can't go to The Island and take her. Fitzroy would have you killed. What legitimate reason do you have to take her?" Ana says.

"I'm her fucking uncle first of all," Felix says. "Fuck Fitzroy. I've worked with him long enough that I could convince Rissy to let me take her. I'd say I was bringing her to Fitzroy in the city."

"Rissy knows that Everleigh is my daughter, Felix."

"But she doesn't know that I'm your brother. She only knows I'm with Fitzroy."

"It won't work, dumbass. All you'll do is get your-self—and possibly Everleigh—killed."

I'm slow as I sit up in the water. I don't want to disrupt Ana and Felix's conversation. I am *certain* they don't know I'm listening. I can't believe it. I'd never met Ana's brother. He'd lived with his father—oh shit...

he'd lived with his father in New York—while Ana and I grew up in Florida.

I knew Ana had a brother; they'd shared a father. He'd left when Ana was in fourth grade. The year *before* I met her. I had forgotten about him. I get out of the bath. Trying to make some noise so they'll know. I open and slam the cabinets. Ana shushes Felix. I flush the toilet and their footsteps retreat down the hall.

I go to my room and get dressed. The long soak had helped my aching body. Though my skin is still a little too sore to wear a bra or panties. I dress in a t-shirt and shorts, then go into the living room.

Ana sits on the sofa while Felix stares out the sliding glass door to the balcony. I get right to business.

"Ana, did Peter bring you into this?" I chew on my bottom lip.

"Figures you'd still be on that." Ana shakes her head.

"Sorry." I look down. "I didn't know." It is my fault that Ana is in this. My fault that she ever met Fitzroy. "I don't know how to apologize."

"Jesus, Alyx. You didn't do anything to me. Get out of your head." She rolls her eyes. "I was pissed yesterday. We're good."

"Doesn't seem that way." I look away from her. "Does Fitzroy have your daughter on The Island?"

Felix's head snaps up. "You told her?"

"Shut up, Felix. Alyx and I grew up together." Ana leans forward and nibbles on her nails. "I know her better than I know you."

That throws me. Does that mean that Ana trusts me, still? "I'll take that as a yes—Fitzroy does have your kid there."

"Listen," Ana shifts in her seat and turns towards me. "I know it's not your fault. Your parents' deaths aren't your fault either. I'm tormented about Everleigh. I've got to get her off that island. Her birthday is soon. Fitzroy has used girls as young as seven before. I'm worried he'll decide to use someone younger, too. Because she's available to him, with no interference from anyone else."

"Do you think he'd use his own daughter?" I ask.

"He adores you, and he sent you to Sempers," Ana says.

"Knowing full well what Sempers is," Felix adds.

"What do you mean knowing what Sempers is?" My right arm twitches so I massage it. "What do you mean Fitzroy adores me? He doesn't like me at all."

"Alyx, you can't be this naïve, can you?" Ana rubs her head. "You realize on the sixth floor he kills you? That's what Sempers does anytime someone makes it to that floor."

"It's just so much." I knead my temples. "Are you sure *Uncle* knows what Sempers is?"

Felix comes over next to me, and sits on the coffee table. "He knew what Sempers was when he sent Rachel there."

"No," I twist my head. "Rachel was a driver, she never had sex with the clients. Plus," my eyebrows rise, and I turn my hand palm up, "Collin told me. They took Rachel back to Idaho. Dropped her off in her hometown."

Ana jiggles her head. "Rachel… went to Sempers. After Sempers had his way with her…" Ana swallows hard. "Sempers sent her body to the Chewies."

Felix shivers his shoulders and lets out a groan. "Blech."

"The Chewies?" I cock my head to the side.

"Cannibals pay a lot for fresh bodies, Alyx." Ana stares at me unblinking. "What better way is there to rid yourself of a bad employee?"

"Holy shit! You're serious." I lean back against the sofa.

"What did you think they did with the bodies?" Ana asks.

"Bodies? As in more than one? How many bodies?" I can't understand what she means. Like the information won't sink into my brain.

"Anyone who doesn't do as they're told or goes too far like Sasha did." Ana's brow rises.

"It's not like they don't value their investments. But

they make damn sure their investments pay out." Felix goes back over to the window.

"Like Hannibal Lecter *cannibals*? Like people eating people? The Silence of the Lambs, type shit? Are you sure?" Saliva fills my mouth as my stomach roils. I don't need an answer. Fuck, I don't want one.

"Yes," Ana says, giving me the response I don't want.

I jump up and run to the bathroom. Barely making it to the toilet before I vomit. Ana comes in behind me and holds my hair. "Shh, shh." She rubs my back.

I stop hurling. "Rachel?" I wipe my mouth with a washcloth. "She's really dead?"

"Why is that so hard to believe? Has she contacted you at all?"

"Well, no, but I never hear from you and you're okay." I wave a hand in Ana's direction. I grab the cup of water on the corner of the tub and take a drink.

"I'm okay because I do what I'm told. I don't buck authority. Or, well, I didn't before yesterday." Ana's brow shoots up.

"Will you get in trouble for Blake?" I worry for Ana now. My stomach flips and I dry heave. There is nothing left in my stomach. I set the cup back on the tub.

"No. I messaged Estelle and told her. She was fine with it." Ana leans against the wall.

"What about Felix? He hit Sempers."

"Yeah, but that was part of it. Sempers knew about the earrings." Ana waves a hand in the air, like this should be common knowledge. "Fitzroy must've told him at some point because his request said, 'Send one with earrings. Let someone try and save her. Make it real.' He knew what he was doing when it all started."

Sempers planned on killing me then—and *Uncle* knew? "How did Felix get back into the city so fast? Wasn't he at the manor when we left?"

"No, he left before we did. Fitzroy sent him on an *errand*." Ana looks down at the ground. Her hair falls into her face. I can see through the faded purple that she is biting her lips.

"What authority did you buck then?" I get up and lean against the sink.

"Well, I haven't done anything yet. My thoughts are consumed with getting back to Everleigh." Ana tucks her hair behind her ear. "I haven't seen her in six months."

"I'm sorry." Though what can *I* do? "What are you going to do?" As soon as I ask, I wish I hadn't. I'd been mostly spared because I didn't *know* what Sasha had planned. Would Ana also get caught doing something? I know she worries for her daughter, but I worry for my brother, too.

"I have no idea. I asked Fitzroy to take me back to

The Island last week, but he said he couldn't. He needed me here. I assume because he wants me to be your driver."

"If they knew what Sasha had planned, why didn't they stop her? Why kill her?"

"Alyx." Ana scratches her head. "They get a million a pop from the Chewies. Sasha was worth more dead than alive as far as Fitzroy is concerned."

"Fuck." I lean over the sink and rinse my mouth. It isn't enough. I grab my toothbrush and brush my teeth.

"Are you okay?" Ana asks.

I shrug.

"I'll be in the living room. Come out when you're finished."

I nod. Ana leaves.

I stare at myself in the mirror. How could I have not *seen* any of this? Rachel had been given to Sempers... so he could what... torture her and then kill her? That I could believe because I've spent so much time with him. I know what a sadist he is.

Sasha they'd sent to... the Chewies. Had that been Felix's errand Tuesday morning? A shiver rolls down my spine. But hadn't Sasha said as much that night she got shot? 'Yeah, you fuck them and then give them to your *cannibal* clients.' After that Sasha spit in Fitzroy's face. Had Sasha known where she would end up, but risked it anyway?

I look in the mirror and see red in my mouth. "Fuck." I spit into the sink. I'd brushed too hard. I rinse my mouth with cold water to slow the bleeding.

I lean there with my head hanging over the sink for a few minutes; trying to figure out how any of this could be happening.

I give up and rejoin Ana and Felix in the living room.

"Rachel, Sasha, my parents, and now your daughter, too." I flop down onto the sofa. "Ana, I can't tell you how sorry I am that I didn't see any of this before."

"Hey, we all cope the only way we know how. For some of us," Ana motions a hand toward me, "denial is how we survive."

I chew on that for a minute. Have I been in denial?

Yes, I have. It can't be anything else. When did I shut my brain off and ignore all the signs?

Felix comes over and sits on the sofa between Ana and I. He pats Ana's knee. "We'll figure something out."

"Something that won't get anyone else killed," Ana says.

Felix nods. "Until then, I have to pick up today's drop for Fitzroy. I'll be back in a couple hours."

"Okay," Ana says. She kisses his cheek.

Felix looks over at me. "You should put some more aloe on your face, or some moisturizer. You have dinner with Estelle tonight."

"Thanks, I will." I nod. I can't argue with it, he's right. I do have dinner with Estelle, and Estelle will complain if I look bad.

I go to my room to take care of my face. As I apply the moisturizer the front door closes, and Ana appears in my doorway.

"I thought you knew about Peter." Ana comes inside and sits on my bed.

I look at her in the mirror as I rub the cream into my skin. "I don't know how I didn't." How many times had Peter rubbed my back a little too long? How many times had his hand gone a little too far up my leg when he sat next to me? How often had I thought I had a crush on my dad's cute friend and his cute friend had a harmless crush on me?

My stomach rumbles again.

"Don't beat yourself up. I needed the job." Ana shrugs. "I guess we all did."

"You said that Peter told you that I'd told my dad about Fitzroy?"

"Yeah." Ana nods and then lays back on the bed. "After the accident. Remember when the police showed up at your place?"

I turn in my chair. "I called Peter to come over because the police asked if there was an adult at home. When I said no, they told me to call one over."

"Right, well. Do you remember when the police left?"

"Yeah, you were in the kitchen on the phone with your mom. You stayed the night with me that night. Your mom wanted to come over after she found out what happened."

"Fitzroy had told me to stay with you that night." Ana rolls onto her side and looks at me.

"Did you know what they were planning?"

"No." Ana pulls at her shirt. "I knew that Fitzroy adored you. He was always making sure that you were happy, perky." Her brow arches. "I'd convinced my mom not to come, and after I hung up the phone that's when Trent had his breakdown."

I look up at the ceiling to stop the tears from flowing. That night had been so awful. We didn't have any other family. Our parents were our entire world. Everyone hated their parents every now and then, but not us. We loved ours. Our lives were being taken from us. I'd never seen Trent cry so much in my whole life. His body trembled in my arms. His tears made mine so much harder to control. Trent and I huddled together on the living room floor bawling.

I held him, but there was no one there to hold me.

How could we survive without our parents? The police had told us they hadn't even found their bodies yet. Would we ever get them back? While the police and Peter worked out what to do with 'the kids,' our world shattered.

"Yeah, we were on the floor for a long time." I blink the tears away. I grab a tissue from my vanity and dab the water from my eyes.

"Well, while your lives were falling apart, Peter came into the kitchen telling me that you'd told your dad about Fitzroy. That Fitzroy had called Peter and told him he'd need to be ready to go over to your house."

"Why would Peter need to come to my house though?"

"Do you not remember what Peter did for a living?" Ana's voice goes up an octave.

"I remember that he worked with kids." I smear more cream under my eyes.

"Peter worked for the state department placing kids in foster care, and stuff like that."

"But that still doesn't explain why he'd need to be at my house."

"Fitzroy wanted him to be there so that the police wouldn't send you and your brother into the system. Peter would be there to handle the situation. He'd show his credentials so that the police would walk away, since someone from that department was already on the scene."

"That's why we were never put in foster care?" I turn in my chair and stare, mouth agape, at Ana.

Ana nods. "Peter was good at his job."

"But what did Peter tell you? Why did he think I'd said anything to my dad?"

"Peter said that your dad had approached him. He'd forbade him from ever coming near his kids again."

"I remember that." I gasp. "It was a few days before they died. My dad was furious with Peter, but he never told me why."

"He'd seen Peter with me one night and soon after he spotted us wearing the same clothes. Peter said that Fitzroy had called because a client—who happened to be a judge—told Fitzroy that an attorney by the name Beck was looking to track down people associated with Peter."

"Dad didn't know the judge was a client." I rub my forehead.

Poor dad.

"The judge explained that Beck wanted to get an investigation going but wasn't sure who Peter was connected with. Beck was certain that it was sex trafficking though. Beck had said that his daughter was involved, that he'd confirmed it with her. The next night your parents died, Alyx."

I can't stop the tears anymore. Ana comes over and

wraps her arms around me as I realize I *am* responsible for my parents' deaths.

LUNCHTIME

Ana's phone rings from her pocket. I dab at my face with a tissue then add more moisturizer while she leaves the room to answer her phone.

All this time, Peter knew. My dad had figured it out all on his own. Fitzroy had believed the judge and assumed that I'd told my dad. That must have been why he kept me so close after they died. He wanted to see what I'd do. When I behaved like a grieving child, and never did anything to try and leave... he began to trust me.

Maybe Fitzroy has been testing that trust ever since.

"Hey," Ana says from the doorway. "Felix's errand is taking a little longer, but he'll be back later." My phone vibrates on my nightstand. Ana picks it up. "Trent is texting you. He says lunch is ready. Why would your brother tell you lunch is ready? Isn't he still in Florida?"

"No," I shake my head and take the phone so I can text him back. "He lives in the next building."

"Look at us. Both hiding our brothers from Estelle. We're a lot alike." She smiles. "But why don't you use a secret phone? You know Estelle reads all the texts."

"Yes, but Estelle also thinks that I FaceTime my meals with my brother on Wednesdays."

"Clever girl," Ana bounces her head up and down. "I leave my secret phone in the box of Fudgesicles in the fridge." She laughs.

I reply to Trent. *"Be there in a few."* I look up at Ana. "I should go."

"Of course." Ana steps to the side. "I'll unpack my bag in Sasha's room since I'll be living here for now."

"Yeah, anything you need. Make yourself at home. I don't have Fudgesicles, but there's a box of Drumsticks." I slide on some sandals. Ana laughs and I leave for my brother's.

Trent pulls me into a bear hug when he opens the door. It feels nice. I have to be careful though. If I'm not, I'll burst into tears and tell him everything. I need to know more before I do that. I need to calm down. My heart flutters in my chest like hummingbird wings.

"I made chicken parmesan for lunch today." His brow waggles up and down. "With garlic bread… extra garlic, extra butter, extra toasty!" He points his fingers like six-shooters and says, "pow, pow, pow." Trent knows how much I love garlic bread.

"That sounds amazing." I smile. Though I'm not sure I'll be able to eat anything at all.

"Come on, I've got everything ready." He pulls me into the kitchen.

I sit at the bar. Everything looks great. Trent has two plates ready. He set place settings and everything. "You went all out today." I take a sip of cola.

"You've been working late hours. I figured you could use a good meal," Trent sits next to me and turns the television on.

"Thanks, bro." I lean over and bump his shoulder.

I stare at the TV on the opposite kitchen counter. It's a small television, but it serves its purpose. Trent gets fidgety if his mind isn't constantly occupied. We watch the local news every time we have lunch. Trent always wants me to know the weather for the day so I can dress accordingly—it is his way of taking care of me. I take a deep breath and another sip of soda.

The smell of the food tickles my nose and my stomach growls. Maybe, a little bite won't hurt. I am careful though. I use the knife and cut a small piece. The saliva in my mouth prepares itself for the first bite. The tomato sauce is warm, the breading on the chicken is crispy, and the cheese is gooey. "Oh, damn," I say, "mmm," I use my fork to point at the food, "so good, Trent."

Trent smiles and nods. "I know," he waggles his brow and tucks in to his own plate. "I've been watching YouTube videos on how to be a better cook."

"It's working." I take another bite.

By the fourth bite I am hooked. My stomach is also happy to not be empty anymore. I drink my soda. Trent refills my cup. We watch the weather girl talk about how sunny it will be today. I'm on my second piece of garlic bread when the story on the news changes.

"Local authorities are asking for your help to find a local missing couple." An image appears on the screen. It's Sasha, and a man I've never seen before. "The man shown here," the image zooms in on the man, "is Dorian Hedley. He was reported missing when he didn't show up for work yesterday afternoon. It was later discovered that his girlfriend, Sasha Belmont, is also missing."

I drop my fork.

I had seen him before. In a black ball cap after I left Jennson's on Monday.

Trent pauses the television. "Hey, isn't that your roommate?" he asks while his mouth is full.

"Fuck, fuck, fuck!" I say.

Trent looks over at me. "Do you know where they

are or something?" Trent's brow goes up but I can tell from his expression that he doesn't realize how serious this is.

I need to protect my brother. How can I protect my brother?

I have to tell him the truth.

"Trent." I take the fork from his hands and set it down. I grab his hands in mine. "I need you to listen to me, okay?"

"Of course, why are you being so weird?" He tilts his head down.

I'll start at the beginning. "I'm not a personal shopper."

"I know," he says.

"What?" It's my eyebrows turn to shoot up.

"I'm different, I know, but I'm not stupid, sis." He chuckles. "No personal shopper makes as much money as you do. You turn tricks,"—he shrugs his right shoulder— "but you seem to do it safely. Why do you think I follow your locations on Snapchat? I'm not a creep." He takes his hands from mine and returns to eating.

"Well shit, Trent," I shove his shoulder playfully. "You've been playing dumb with me this whole time! I have to say, I'm impressed."

"You can't help that you think I'm slow. Mom and Dad were Ableist, they taught you how to be one, too.

It made y'all leave me alone most of the time though, so I never said anything. I liked playing video games instead." He takes another bite of food.

"You're a sneaky little rat!" I tease. "I didn't mean to be Ableist," I say. "I never thought of it that way. But I can see… that's exactly what I've been doing, isn't it?" My brother is right—I just haven't recognized it. At least this is one thing I can fix.

"No worries." He shoves another bite into his mouth. "I still love you," he says around his food.

"Well, then I guess at least telling you everything will be easier."

"Telling me what?" Trent takes a big drink of his cola.

He turns in his chair so he can face me and then, for the first time in my life, I tell my brother the whole story.

I start with our thirteenth birthday party.

When I finish Trent looks at me for a moment and then he turns back to his food. He takes another bite, then another drink. Turning his head, he looks at me. "So, this Fitzroy guy, he really killed mom and dad?"

I nod. "I think so." I wipe a tear from my eye. Telling my brother that I am responsible for our parents' deaths has been difficult, but Trent hasn't turned on me yet. "I'm sorry."

"Why?" he shrugs.

"If I hadn't gotten into this mess, they'd still be here. You'd still have both of them. You wouldn't be wondering when the money will run out. When your meds will run out. You wouldn't have to worry about playing the same games over and over because you can't afford any new ones. You wouldn't have movie lines memorized because you have to watch them on repeat. I bet you get so bored you want to scream!" I throw my hands in the air. "I'm so, so sorry! I'm so mad at myself." I put my head on the counter.

"No," Trent puts his hand on my back. "I mean *You* didn't kill them. You have no reason to be sorry."

I look up. His eyes are clear. There is no hurt lurking in there to make me tear up even more. His jaw isn't clenched. No tight shoulders. He isn't mad at me.

My brother... so astute.

His lack of anger at me does not dissuade my guilt though. "I feel responsible for it." I take a drink of my soda.

"You do that to yourself. You aren't responsible, Alyx. You were a child when that happened. You aren't responsible for any of it. It's all those other people who are responsible for it." Trent twists his head side to side. "If I ever see Peter again, though, boy is he in for a world of hurt."

"You stay away from Peter. I mean it. I forbid you to go anywhere near him. He's as dangerous as Fitzroy."

"Is Fitzroy that guy who kept coming over to the house after the funeral? He'd come over and hand you an envelope every now and then." The way Trent cocks his head to the side looking through his memories makes my stomach protest the food.

"No." I rub my stomach. "That was Collin. He always brought my pay."

"All that money and they didn't even care that we were starving." Trent's shoulders shudder. I can tell by his tightening jaw that it is anger, not the fear it should be.

"You can't do anything stupid, okay? I can't lose you, too."

"You won't. But," Trent looks to me, "Alyx, you need to get out of this. How are you going to get away from these people?"

I sit there, unmoving. With everything that has happened. Rachel, Sasha… my parents… I still haven't thought of that.

I need to leave. I need to get out before *I* die.

But more than that… I need Trent to get away so he will be safe, while I try to find a way to get out.

"I can't do anything until you're safe."

"Sis, they think I'm in Florida. I'm safe."

"It won't take them long to figure out the truth

though. Hell, they might already know." How close had they been watching me? How could I know? Hmmm, maybe Felix would know.

"If they knew, they'd be knocking on the door."

We both look toward the door. Luckily no one knocks on it—my heart would have exploded. I have a lot of information that I need to process. I won't be able to do any of it with Trent so close to my apartment. I can't process much of anything if Fitzroy or Estelle think anything is up either. I'll need to be careful. I can't change my schedule. I'll have to figure everything out, while maintaining everything else. "How about this… I have to go to dinner with Estelle tonight, but I don't want you in the apartment today. I want you out somewhere safe."

"Is that safe? Going to dinner with them?" Trent scratches behind his ear a little longer than necessary. Like his brain is itching and perhaps he can scratch it.

My brother is worried about me.

"I'll be okay. I can't let anyone suspect anything." I pat his knee. "I have to go. I can't change anything until I know more." Trent gives me a half smile. "I need you safe."

"You know how much I hate it outside." His foot bounces on the stool's footrest.

"I know, I know," I rub his knee. My brother's anxiety is about to kick in. He doesn't like crowds. He doesn't like new things. But he does like movies. "What about if you go to the movies though? They have the arcade, and you *love* movies. You could see that new superhero movie."

"We don't have the money for that," Trent runs a hand through his hair.

"We have enough for you to be safe for a day. I promise." I assure him. "Go get dressed."

Trent nods and goes to change. "Don't forget deodorant, okay?" I holler down the hall. Trent waves a hand over his shoulder and groans. Even though he is three minutes older than me, he needs reminders like that. He has a difficult time with self-care, no matter how astute he is.

I clean up our lunch and rinse the plates before putting them in the dishwasher. There is so much I need to do. How could I accomplish it? Why hadn't I ever thought to leave before? Trent groans and throws something. I think it might've been a shoe. He hates wearing anything other than his slippers.

I haven't done anything before because I have no other way to take care of us.

I need more information.

Rachel and Sasha had both attempted to get away, and it cost them their lives. They were both smarter than I was.

How could *I* do this?

I grab the remote and rewind the news feed so I can hear the entire story. I'd gotten distracted by Trent, but I need to know more. Fuck, what will Fitzroy do now that this news bulletin is out?

"Local authorities are asking for your help to find a local missing couple. The man shown here is Dorian Hedley. He was reported missing when he didn't show up for work yesterday afternoon. It was later discovered that his girlfriend, Sasha Belmont, is also missing. The couple was last seen near the river. Officials are concerned that the couple may have gotten into an accident on the water. They are asking everyone to be on the lookout. If you see this couple," their image flashes in the corner again, "please call 911 immediately."

Trent comes into the kitchen. "I'm ready," he huffs.

I look over. Trent's wearing his favorite Iron Man t-shirt, the pair of jeans I got him last Christmas, and a pair of Sketchers. "Looking good, bro." I smile. I can't do anything about the clothes and shoes, my brother's comfort level about those things can't be changed. He will only wear what he is comfortable in.

I open the freezer and pull out the credit card that I stashed months ago.

"Where on earth?" Trent asks as he sees the card.

"It's a prepaid credit card. I put it there a while back for emergencies. I knew you wouldn't find it under the peas." I put my hand out so he can take the card.

"I hate peas." His fingers wrap around the cold plastic.

"I know and you're too lazy to throw them out even though you hate them. I knew it'd be safe there." I pat his shoulder.

"This isn't a real emergency though. Shouldn't we save the money for something important?" He holds the card back out for me to take. "Like food."

"Trent," I meet his gaze. "Your life *is* important. I've got a lot to do today." I push his hand down. "I might end up calling you from a new number, too. I think I'll need to get a burner phone." How had it come to this? "So, if you get a call from a number you don't recognize, it might be me. If you don't answer, I'll call right back. That way you'll know it's me. Okay?"

"Sure thing." Trent puts the card in his wallet. "Or you could text me from the number then I'd know it was you."

"I can do that, too. You leave now. Go to the theater. If the movie doesn't start for a while, play in the arcade. Stay there until you hear from me. If for some reason you don't hear from me, go to a hotel for the night."

"Geez, sis. How much money is on this card?

Hotels are expensive." Trent grabs a hoodie from the coat closet.

"Eight-thousand-dollars," I sigh.

Trent's mouth falls open. "That's so much money." His eyebrows raise high as his forehead creases. Trent has never had access to so much money. I pay all of his bills. Trent makes some money doing odd Photoshop jobs online. Occasionally he'll get a check for his YouTube channel. But nothing substantial. I let him use his money to get things he likes—he pays for the things he wants; I pay for the things he needs.

"It's okay. I got it after a…" I stop talking. I'd gotten it from a night on Sempers third floor. "Don't worry about it. Keep it on you. Don't lose it. Stay at the theater. Have popcorn, or pretzels. Play games in the arcade. That way I'll know you're safe. But don't like text me anything that will let anyone else know where you are, okay?"

"My Snapchat locations aren't on," he eyes me. "I'll be fine."

I pull Trent in for a hug. "Stay safe."

Trent's arms wrap tight around me. "I will. Will you do the same for me?"

"Of course." I hold on a little longer and pray that this won't be the last time that I hug my brother.

Trent grabs his keys and a charger for his phone. I

walk him to the elevator in his own building. He gives me a half smile as the elevator doors close.

He hates going out alone.

He hates going out at all.

I make sure the elevator makes it to the first floor before I leave. I double check that he locked his apartment door as I pass and head back to my own apartment.

I need to talk to Ana.

Maybe we can both get out together.

VISITORS

I go inside and lock the door behind me. I lean my head against the doorframe. I'm glad Trent will spend the day at the movies. I'm still shocked how well he took the news. He'd known everything the whole time. Ana's right. I have been in denial—in more than one way.

A can of soda pops open in the kitchen. "Hey Ana," I say. "I'm back. You wanna go for a run before dinner tonight?" I turn to go into the kitchen. The food at Trent's had been good, but I'll need to exercise today, too.

"No, I don't need a run." Collin strides out of my kitchen.

I take a step back as my brow goes up. "What are you doing here?" I try to smile. To hide my shock. It doesn't matter what happened yesterday. It doesn't matter that Collin had held me under the water, punched me in the sides, or bruised my ribs. I know him. He's shared a bed with me from time to time, too.

Collin came around a few times when Sasha lived here. I shouldn't be shocked to see him. Or, I shouldn't appear shocked anyway. I try to let the tenseness fall from my shoulders. I walk over and flop down on the couch, grab the remote, and turn on the television. "Wanna watch something on Netflix?"

Collin comes over and stands next to the sofa. He sneers down at me. "No, I'm here on business today." He reaches his foot out and kicks mine. "Ask me why."

I meet his gaze. He must have asked Estelle for a run between the sheets. He knows today is my day off, so I bet he figured Estelle would say yes. Day off is a strong term—it's the day that I use to keep my body, nails, hair, or otherwise in pristine condition.

He smiles and takes a drink of his soda.

"Why?" I flirt. "Oh, do I have a new client?" I lean forward pulling my shoulders back, accentuating my breasts. Hopefully showing my excitement for whatever is to come.

He swallows his drink then smiles. "No," he shakes his head.

"Collin, get back here!"

My head snaps up. Fitzroy yelled for Collin from down the hall. Fitzroy is... *here*?

Collin waggles his brow at me, sets the soda down on the table and then walks down the hall.

I get up and follow him.

Collin passes my bedroom and heads for the bathroom. Why would Fitzroy need Collin in the bathroom? Why would he be here at all?

Collin goes inside. I follow him still. Fitzroy looks himself over in the mirror. He has a mark on his neck, he's dabbing it with a cotton ball. "Take care of that will you?" He says to Collin as he motions his head toward the tub.

Collin moves to the side and that's when I see her.

Ana is in the tub.

Face down in the water.

The water that I'd forgotten to drain.

The cup I'd left on the corner of the tub is on the ground, spilled, ice melted long ago.

Ana isn't moving.

My heart rate accelerates. I try to keep my breath slow and even. Fitzroy notices me. "Alyx, my sweet." He smiles and turns toward me. "Can you help me with this, dear?" He points to the mark on his neck.

"Of course, *Uncle*," I say. "Come in my room, I have some Band-Aids in there." I give him a sweet smile and hold out my hand. Just because everything that has happened to me recently is known to him, or caused by or ordered by him, doesn't mean I can snub him at all. I can't pull away from his touch. I can't react to Ana, either.

He takes my offered hand with a smile. *Uncle always likes it when his girls treat him like this. Caring for him like he is important to us. All the girls do it. At least all the ones who start out with him as their handler.*

I lead him to my room and sit him down at my vanity. "Ouch," I say as I tilt his head to the side. "Are you okay?" I pout my lip then turn to get supplies to clean the scrape.

"Yeah, little accident with Ana."

I can feel his eyes boring into the back of my head. I steady myself and find my first aid kit. "Oh, no. I'm sorry. Let me see what I can do." I smile as I open the kit and prepare a cotton ball with peroxide. *I can't seem like I feel bad for Ana. I can't react for her at all.*

"It seems as though you keep having trouble with drivers, Alyx." His brow rises as I turn toward him. I dab his neck with the swab. "Why do you think that is?"

This is where I need to shine. "Jealousy." I shrug one shoulder while I dab. I pull the cotton ball away and blow on the tiny injury.

Fitzroy shifts in his seat. The blowing is awakening his desires. No reason I can't further those. Perhaps take his mind off this line of questioning.

"The drivers are always jealous. Especially when they think the clients are hot." I exaggerate an eye roll while letting my mouth drop open—making sure no teeth are too exposed. I have to try to get his mind going in a different direction. "I've been thinking about it, you know. Since Tuesday." I throw the cotton ball in the trash and prepare another one. "Sasha always rolled her eyes when she'd drop me off with Jennson." I dab at his neck again, blowing between my words. "I mean, Jennson is okay," —blow— "he's not tall like you though." —blow, dab at neck— "He does like the kinky, though." —blow— I pull back and arch my brow at Fitzroy.

I turn and toss the second swab in the trash. I have Band-Aids in the first aid kit, but I need to distract him further. His toes are bouncing up and down, so he is almost distracted. Geez' it's a good thing I remember all my clients tells.

I walk over to my bedside table; certain he is watching me. I bend over at the waist, leaving my legs as straight as I can, so my ass will pop out. I pull open the bottom drawer, before I can pull the box of bandages out, Fitzroy's hands are on my waist.

I jump up and giggle, like I'm surprised. His right

hand slides forward as he stands behind me. I press my butt against him. He leans his head down and breathes heavy on my neck. I trail my left hand into his hair and down his neck as he nuzzles against mine.

His right hand slides past my waistline and into my shorts.

"No panties?" he says and a low growl grumbles in his chest. He nibbles my ear, and his fingers find a home inside me.

I pull at his hair and let out a soft moan. Biting my lip and stretching onto my tiptoes, giving him my pleasure. It does what I want it to. It distracts him. He pulls his hand from my shorts, turns me around and lays me on the edge of the bed. He smiles a crooked smile then gets to his knees.

"No panties, Alyx. You bad girl." His face plunges into my crotch. His hands go to my waist. He wiggles his head around moving my shorts so his tongue can find my warmth. He hasn't taken the time to remove them.

I grab his hair with my hands and arch my back. Fitzroy growls again, the vibration goes through my body as his tongue tastes me.

Shuffling comes from the hall as Collin passes by the door. He raises a brow and I close my eyes like I haven't seen him at all. I let out a loud moan.

The sound makes Fitzroy get to his feet. He walks

over, closes the door, and then comes back over to me. He leans over and kisses me fiercely. I wrap my hands in his hair. He tugs my shorts off and undoes his zipper.

I reach for the bedside table to grab a condom. *U*ncle grabs my wrist. "No need." He plunges himself inside me.

A gasp escapes me. *This is against the rules.* "But, *U*ncle," I say breathlessly, "the rules," I moan, hoping the cadence matches someone who is excited for sexy time, and not someone who is terrified out of their minds. I can't show him that I am only doing this because I don't want to die next.

He stops thrusting for a moment. "I make the rules, I decide," he thrusts himself hard into me "who can," he pulls out and thrusts harder "break them," he bites his lip and thrusts again. "and when." He leans down and kisses my neck. Thrusting over and over.

I moan appropriately.

*U*ncle grabs my shirt and pulls it up. He buries his face between my breasts. His right hand grabs my leg and lifts it up. I follow orders and wrap my legs around him while he gyrates inside me. He licks and sucks my nipples. I put my hands in his hair and moan like I know he wants.

He pounds into me harder, raising his head, placing his hands on either side of me. His hands grip onto the blankets. There isn't enough for him to hold on to, he reaches out farther and holds onto the edge of the bed, grunting and moaning.

I play along. "*U*ncle, oh, *U*ncle," comes out as breathless as I can manage. "Fuck me hard!" I scream.

This is my job. The first thing I was ever trained to do. When *U*ncle is about to *climax*, utter those words. You'll make *U*ncle happy and in return, *U*ncle will make sure you're safe.

Fitzroy's hips work hard as he accomplishes his task. A loud moan comes from his lips as he forces his last thrust inside me. His body trembles as he lays down on top of me. His task finished.

"Oh, Alyx." He raises up on one elbow. "I forgot how warm you are." He kisses my breasts. Nibbling each nipple with his teeth.

"I could never forget how you feel." I bite my lip. "I always remember *you*." I run my hand through his hair, rest my hand against his ear, and then pull him in for a kiss.

Flattery is what got you to your next client. I'd known that. In all actuality though, flattery is what has been saving my life this entire time.

He kisses me back hard, *wanting*. His hand is behind my head, holding me there. Not letting me leave the kiss. Not that I would pull away from him, I know better than that. I wrap my legs around him again. I feel his member pulse. It isn't enough to make him hard, he'd just finished, he'd need a little bit before he could fuck me again. But it is enough that I know I've done my job.

Fitzroy has no idea what I am planning.

Though to be honest, neither do I.

RUN BEFORE DINNER

"Don't forget your run." Collin looks me up and down.

I lean against the wall and bite my lip, staring right at Fitzroy as he takes a swig of his drink. I need to look aloof, and in love.

Fitzroy sets his drink down and notices me staring. A smile plays in the corner of his mouth.

I lick my lips, slow and deliberate, letting my bottom lip catch against my teeth.

Fitzroy rolls his shoulders and comes over to me. He puts one hand on my hip, and the other holds my face. He leans in and kisses me. "Thank you for today, Alyx. It was most surprising." He leans his forehead against mine.

"For me, too." I inch closer.

Fitzroy puts his hand down the front of my shorts

again. He plunges his finger inside me. I moan and tilt my head back.

"This is mine. Do you understand?" His breath is heavy against my neck as he fondles me.

I move my hips against his hand.

"Mine." He removes his hand from my shorts.

I gasp and open my eyes as wide as I can. I let my mouth fall open a smidge—not enough to show my teeth—and nod my head.

"Good girl." He kisses my forehead and then holds my chin in his hand. "Now, since I know you're a good girl,"—he smiles at me— "I know it's not necessary for me to tell you that you are to leave Ana alone. But I will anyway." His fingers squeeze a little tighter. "Do not touch Ana. The *movers* will be along shortly." He looks over his shoulder to Collin.

"Within the hour." Collin nods.

"Within the hour. They will collect Ana. Let them in, go to your room, and close the door." Fitzroy bobs his head up and down. He moves my chin up and down when I don't speak.

"Sorry. Of course. Let them in, go in my room, close the door," I repeat.

"That's my, Alyx." He smiles. "They'll lock up behind themselves."

"Okay," I smile back.

"I'll see you later for dinner." Fitzroy drops his hand

from my face, licks the middle finger he'd had inside me, smiles, and walks over to the front door.

Collin opens the door for him and *Uncle* leaves.

"I don't think you listened before." Collin holds onto the doorknob. "Don't forget your run before dinner." He waves a hand to my face, "and use some more moisturizer." He closes the door behind him.

I fall to my knees the instant the door closes.

How close had I been? If I hadn't gone to Trent's for lunch, would I be dead, too?

"Ana," I say as tears roll down my cheek. I pull myself from the floor and walk to the bathroom.

Ana is rolled in a blanket; ice is in baggies on top of the blanket. My body slumps to the floor. The tub is empty. The entire room smells of bleach. Collin had prepped her body to be moved. And the ice...

Oh, my god... the Chewies.

I sob. Were they prepping her for the cannibals she'd told me about? What could I do? What had happened while I'd been gone? What had Ana said that caused Fitzroy—or Collin—to kill her?

I lay back. The upper half of my body is in the hall, while the lower half is being cooled by the tiles on the bathroom floor. My mind is shutting down. I can feel my body go slack. I have nothing else to give.

After a few minutes, I turn to my side and try to tuck my feet under myself. My toes clip the end of the blanket and I feel something cold against them. Colder than the tiles, but… oh my… I'd touched part of Ana. Part of *dead*, Ana.

My stomach grumbles. I get up and run into the kitchen.

I puke in the sink.

After my meal is out of my body, I do the only thing I know to do. I open the freezer and grab the box of Drumsticks.

It's there, Ana's extra phone. It's a flip phone. I open it and search for the text messages. There are no messages or contacts; everything has been deleted. How can I contact Felix without a phone number? Fuck.

There is a loud knock on the front door. "Oh shit." I stuff the phone back in the box and put it back in the freezer. The movers are here to get Ana. I wipe my eyes and straighten my clothes. "Just a second," I holler as I make sure I look… *appropriate?*

I throw my hands in the air. It doesn't matter what the *movers* think. They'll be in and out. I'll answer the door and go to my room. I'll do as I was told.

I take a deep breath and open the door.

Two bright blue eyes meet mine; they are framed by long light blonde hair hanging down. "Hello, ma'am," the woman says. "I'm Agent Shwetz, this is," she points over her shoulder, "Agent Payton." Agent

Shwetz is wearing a pair of dress slacks and a black shirt. Her shoes are polished. The man that is with her, Payton, wears something similar, but his shirt is red.

I lean in against the doorframe, pulling the door closed as I do. "What can I do for you?" I offer a sweet smile.

"We've been told this is the home of Sasha Belmont. Is this correct?"

Fucking hell. "Yes, she left a few days ago. She went on a trip with her boyfriend. I'm sorry, I don't know when to expect her back." Jesus why hadn't I prepared myself for this? I should have fucking known after that damn newscast.

The agent bobs her head. "Has Ms. Belmont contacted you?"

"No," I shake my head. "We live very different lives." I laugh. "I work, she plays." I roll my eyes hoping that I look as though I don't have a care in the world. Hoping that my eyes don't reveal that there is a body on my bathroom floor.

"Well, if you do, could you have her give us a call?" Agent Payton hands me a card.

"Of, course. Not a problem." I smile and take the card. "Is everything okay?" I tilt my head to the side. I need to appear ready for gossip.

"Well, have you seen the news?" Agent Shwetz says.

"No," I arch a brow, "why?" I tilt my head to the side.

"Mr. Hedley."

"Oh, Ana's boyfriend?" I interrupt her. The agent looks back at her partner. "Did he do something?" I put my hand over my heart. "Is she okay?"

"We aren't sure," Shwetz says, turning her attention back to me. "Mr. Hedley didn't report to work yesterday afternoon. We can't find him. We also cannot locate Ms. Belmont. Which is why we came here."

"Oh, phew," I let out a breath.

"Why does that relieve you?" The Agent's eyes widen.

"I thought someone was hurt." I wipe a finger across my brow. "They went off on a little trip. I'm sure he forgot to call into work or something. With as irresponsible as Sasha is," I roll my eyes again, "I'm sure that's all it is."

"Well, if you hear anything. Please let us know." Payton smiles at me when he finishes.

"Of course. If I hear anything I'll call you myself." I give a genuine smile.

"Ma'am," Agent Shwetz says, "if you're in any kind of danger, all you need to do is say something. If you can't say something, maybe you could look down at your toes?" she whispers the last part.

"What would make you think I'm in danger?" I scrunch my face up like I am clueless.

"Just a feeling. Are you sure you're, okay?" she reiterates.

"I'm fine. I'm late for my run. Time got away from me." I smile and make sure my neck stays straight. I don't need to look at my toes and have them both come crashing into my apartment.

The elevator doors open and two people in coveralls step off. I glance at them as they pass up my apartment and go down the hall.

"Thanks for the card," I say. "I'll be sure to have Sasha call you as soon as I hear from her." I smile.

"Have a good day, ma'am," the officers say.

I close the door.

Fuck, fuck, fucking, fuck! Wait, they'd introduced themselves as Agents, not Officers. My brow pinches together. Why had they done that? I look at the card and it says FBI. Seriously… fuck.

There is another knock at my door. Fuck, the *agents* are back. I open the door, "Look," I begin to say, but the agents are gone. It is the two men in coveralls.

I open the door and step out of the way. They both come into the apartment. One goes over to the sliding doors on the balcony, the other closes the door and stares at me.

"This will take a few extra minutes." He nods his head upward once, telling me to go down the hall.

I turn my head and go to my room. I close the door like Fitzroy had ordered me to do. I go over to my bedroom window and look outside. I watch as the agents get into their vehicle. The car starts up, but they don't drive away. *Fuck.*

There is a knock at my bedroom door.

I open it. An outstretched hand holds a phone. I take the phone and put it to my ear.

"Take your run, run through the park. Take a nice, looong, run." Collin's voice sounds through the phone.

"Okay," I say. The line disconnects.

I hand the phone back, but don't look up to see the man's face. I'd seen too much already. I change my clothes, without bothering to shut the bedroom door. I put on my running shoes, grab my cell and my small wallet, then leave the apartment.

When I exit the building, I run past the Agents' car and head for the path that goes by the river. I don't dare a look in their direction. I know I am the distraction to pull them away from the building so that the movers can finish their job.

Fuck I'm so glad I had Trent leave today. Damn it, I need to tell Trent to stay away. I need Trent out of New York. Where can I send him?

I try my best to run the way I always do. Follow the

same path. Stop when the lights are red, wait for the crossing sign to say it is clear to run. Double check by looking both ways. Breathe, breathe, breathe. Nothing good will come from a freak out.

I've been in worse situations. Sempers eyes flash in my head. I can leave my apartment and pull the agents away. While everything that keeps me alive happens. I can't think about *what* is happening up there. I have to do Fitzroy's bidding. If I don't, I'll be on the next *moving* truck, and my brother will be alone.

I cross into the park. I'll let this run take me past the soccer field today—like every Wednesday. I don't look behind me, even though I want to, so fucking bad. I need to decide what I am doing. Fitzroy had been at my place.

Shit.

I stop running. Fitzroy had released while he was inside me. I'll need a plan B pill, and soon. I don't want to end up like Ana, with a child on an island. With Fitzroy as that child's father.

Fuck!

Ana's child.

I sit on a bench and put my head in my hands.

I need a pill. Ana's child needs to be saved. My brother needs to stay somewhere safe, too. How can I *accomplish* any of this alone? How can I do it and still be living and breathing at the end of it all?

Felix.

I need to talk to Felix. His number isn't in my phone. As far as Estelle's concerned there's no reason for me to speak to Felix. He isn't even Estelle's bodyguard —Collin is.

I walk over to the water fountain and get a drink. If anyone is watching me, they'll think I've tired out. I need to run up to the Soldiers' and Sailors' monument, because that's where I always run. I have to do this.

I drink another big sip and take off. I bump into a guy on a bicycle. "Sorry!" I yell as he wobbles. Get your head in the game, Alyx!

Run... Focus.

Run...

Run...

I am out of breath by the time I reach the monument, but I am happy. I've done it. I'd managed to stop thinking and run. Now that I've stopped, ideas flood into my head. First things first. I need a phone so I can contact my brother. I also need a plan B pill. Those work better if you take them within twelve hours of unprotected sex. The pharmacy might even have a few of those disposable phones, too.

There is a pharmacy on the way back to my apartment. I walk over to a food cart and buy a big bottle of water. I drink while I walk. It is getting hot in the city. I notice it is almost three in the afternoon. It will get hotter as the summer day drags on.

My phone rings. It's Estelle. Shit.

"Estelle," I answer the phone out of breath. "What can I do for you?"

"Darling, Alyx," she yells out my name. I have to pull the phone away from my ear. "Fitzroy will be joining us for dinner. I'll need you there at nine sharp, okay?"

"Of course, Estelle. Anything you say." There isn't another way to respond to Estelle. You do what you are told.

"He'll be bringing an old friend. I need you to look spectacular. I'll be bringing Misty along, too. She's going to be wearing red, so you wear another color. Okay, dear?"

"Absolutely. Do you care what other color?"

"No, as long as it won't clash with red, anything will be fine. Heels as well," Estelle says. She pulls the phone away from her mouth to say something to someone else. "No, Deidra, I'm on the phone, stop talking to me, I'm busy." She huffs. "So sorry, new ones are so difficult to manage. I wish they all behaved as well as you."

"Thank you, Estelle." Always thank them for compliments because you know; 'you don't deserve compliments.' How many times have those words grazed my ears since I turned fourteen? Too many, that's how many.

"Alright, see you at nine."

"Wait, Estelle. Where are we having dinner tonight?"

"L'appart, dear. But don't worry, Collin will pick you up. I must go," Estelle says, and she hangs up.

Shit. L'appart is as *fine* dining as you can get. Fitzroy must have wanted an upgrade. Estelle and I prefer places like CUT or Majorelle. Without a doubt very upscale dining, but L'appart is a place you expect someone to take you if they were proposing marriage or something.

If my stomach weren't in knots, I'd be excited to go.

Before all that, I'll have to get to the pharmacy.

Danny's pharmacy has everything I need. They also have a bathroom. I go in with my purchases, tear the packaging open and swallow the pill before I can drop it. I take a deep breath. I've taken plan B pills before. Just in case. There were times I worried that the condoms broke but the *J*ohns hadn't been honest with me about it. You can never be too careful. I am lucky that I haven't had many pregnancy scares.

I open the phone package. The phone is ready to go right out of the box. Thank god. One less thing for me to worry about. I dial my brother's number. He doesn't answer so I send a quick text. *"Hey bro, it's me. Call me back as soon as you can."*

He is at the movies, maybe his phone is on silent. I purse my lips. I toss my garbage in the trash and decide I'd better use the restroom while I can. As soon as I am sitting the phone rings. I answer it before the second ring.

"Hey, Alyx. Is that you?" Trent whispers into the phone.

"Yeah, buddy. Are you still in the theater?"

"Walking out," he whispers again. "There we are," he uses his regular volume. "Sorry I missed you. You, okay?"

"Yes. Listen. I need you to book a hotel for the night. Pick one close to the theater—the Franklin maybe." I hold the phone against my ear with my shoulder and wipe. "Use your phone and make a reservation online. Do it right now."

"Franklin will work, but should I do it while we're on the phone?" He asks.

"You know what I mean. As soon as we hang up, but before you go back into the theater. Use the card I gave you."

"I don't have my computer though," Trent whines.

"It's only for tonight." I hope. "I don't want you anywhere near the building."

"Fine," he huffs. "Are you sure you're, okay? You don't sound okay."

I flush the toilet. "Yeah, I'm fine. I still have a lot to do. The cops, or maybe even the FBI showed up at my place looking for Sasha, too."

"Shit. What did you do?" Trent's breathing picks up.

"I did what any smart girl who loves breathing did. I lied." I exit the stall and wash my hands.

"Alyx, isn't it bad to lie to the cops?"

"How the hell do I know that they're cops? They introduced themselves as agents. They showed me badges, but how would I know if they were real or not?"

"That's easy," Trent scoffs. "A legitimate police badge will always have a photo ID attached, that is signed by the Chief of Police. The badge will identify the holder as a commissioned law enforcement officer. FBI badges will also have a photo ID, but the badge should be gold, and about three-inches-by-three-inches in size."

"How the hell do you know that?"

"YouTube," he answers nonchalantly.

"That's helpful Trent. Thanks. If I run into them again, I'll take a closer look. Hopefully I won't, but if I do..."

"You'll know what to do," Trent finishes for me.

"Yes." Damn it, I love my brother. He is always surprising me, but today he has surprised me more than he ever has. "Are you enjoying the movie?" I can't help but ask.

"Yeah. It's great. I'll watch the next showing, too. If you think that'll be, okay?" His tone is the same tone he had when we were five and he'd ask mom to watch Iron Man again, right before bedtime. His voice rises and I can hear his smile.

"Yes, Trent. You can absolutely stay and watch it again. But only if you make that reservation!"

"I'll do that right now! Love you, sis. Stay safe."

"Love you. You stay safe, too."

"I will. Call me when you're safe will you?"

"I promise." I wanted to hug him so fucking bad.

"Bye sis."

"Bye," and he hangs up. I close the flip phone.

I stare at myself in the mirror. The heat has taken a toll on me. My hair is a disaster. I have no makeup on, and my clothes don't match at all. If I'm going to be presentable for dinner, I'll have to go back to the apartment. The movers should be gone.

I hope.

DINNER...AND A SHOW

No one is in the apartment when I arrive. I put my phone in the freezer with Ana's. I shower in Sasha's bathroom. I can't bear to use the other—even though there is no longer a body in it. I know because I closed that door. I just can't walk past the room while the door is open. I still don't know what happened with Ana. Maybe I'll be able to fish some info from Collin tonight on the drive.

I spend time painting my finger and toenails. I linger on my makeup, making sure that every detail is flawless. I use clear lip gloss as my lips are the perfect shade for a night out on the town all by themselves. I pull my hair in a messy updo, making sure a few dark tendrils fall around the sides of my face.

I spray my Misfit perfume before I dress. I don't

wear a bra, but I do put on a thong. I'm not sure Fitzroy will handle seeing me twice in one day without panties. I don't want him again today. I've had enough.

I force the images out of my mind. I have other things I need to do.

First... my shoes. My Louboutin mule pumps will do. They are classic black, red on the bottom, open toe. The shoes will look great with my... I run a finger across the many dresses in my closet... the black satin slip dress will hug my curvy form. My satin black clutch will complete the look.

Misty will wear red, so I'll wear black. That will make Estelle happy. I check myself over in the mirror. I turn making sure that everything is in place. This should impress whoever their special guest is.

Collin knocks on my door at precisely 8:30. I answer without hesitation. I don't need any bad reports to Estelle or Fitzroy. I must be compliant.

"Shit, Alyx. If I'd have arrived fifteen minutes early." He shakes one hand out and to the side and makes a 'tisss' hissing noise. "I'd have taken you for a spin before I dropped you at the restaurant."

I turn in a circle. "Yes, but you'd have messed up my hair." I smile and run a finger across his chest as I exit the apartment. "Let's go, we can't be late. There's a special guest," I tease.

Collin smiles and closes the door to my apartment. He holds out his arm for me to take. I smile and accept. I hold onto him all the way to the car. I do this for two reasons. The first is out of necessity of life preservation. I have to behave normally. Any time Collin has ever offered his arm to me, I've taken it. If I am off, in *any* way... I might die. I cannot be out of sorts.

The second reason is another kind of necessity. I'm not sure I can go with him. My body wants to stay. I am too stressed. If I don't let him lead me to the car, I might not go. Which let's face it. At that point I *will* die.

I sit in the back seat of the sedan, while Collin drives. It is a twenty-minute drive from my place to the restaurant. If I want to find anything out about Ana, now is my chance.

"Collin?" I ask as I stare out my window.

"Yeah," he peeks at me in the rearview mirror.

"What happened with Ana today?" I've always been straight with Collin before. "Was she jealous of Jennson like Sasha was or was it someone else?" I know I have to follow the same story I'd told Fitzroy though.

"Oh, so before the movers, not after?" he laughs.

"Yeah," I snort a pshaw. "I can't believe she'd give Fitzroy any grief over Sempers. But who could it have been?"

"Alyx." Collin doesn't give any of us girls any credit

in the brain department. "Ana," he tilts his head to the side a couple of times like he's trying to decide how to dumb down what he's going to say next. "She didn't have the... Ana, wouldn't stop asking for Fitzroy to take her back to The Island. She just wouldn't stop. You know how much he hates being badgered."

I laugh. "Why would she want to go there? I thought you didn't get paid at The Island. Seems like a waste of time if you ask me."

"You don't get paid there. She wanted to go for... *other* reasons."

"What other reason could there be? Is it like grand or something? Oh, does it have a beach?" I sit up a little straighter in the seat and eye him in the mirror. Not letting on that I know why she wanted to go.

"Alyx, have you never been?"

"No," I reply.

"Maybe I'll see if Fitzroy can take you when he goes again. He's going soon. There's a celebration event."

"Cool," I say. Fuck. I've invited myself to The Island. I've never been, but stories from some of the other girls have never made me want to go either.

Ruby was the first one to ever tell me anything about it. On The Island, you don't get paid. You wear a bikini at all times. Depending on the day and the clientele will depend on if the bikini bottoms were crotchless or not. Hell, some days you were required to be nude the entire day. She had said though, that food was aplenty—as were drugs. Anything you wanted you could get.

Collin opens my door when we reach the restaurant. He helps me exit the vehicle and walks me to the door. Fitzroy and Estelle are walking up at the same time. Misty behind Estelle, and... oh, wait... Ruby walked behind Fitzroy. Ruby wouldn't be considered a special guest. Not because she was Ruby. I adore Ruby, but Fitzroy would never consider one of *us* a special guest. We were cannon fodder as far as he was concerned—at least that's what I am learning.

"Alyx." Fitzroy's eyes rake over me. He wraps one arm around me, letting his hand trail down the side of my dress. He traces his fingers over my panty line. "Oh," he lets out a breath, "so close." He leans down to my ear. "Today was fun, perhaps we'll have another round in the restroom," he nibbles my ear.

I give him a sweet laugh and arch a brow. "Anything, for you *U*ncle." My stomach ties itself in knots as the words leave my lips.

"Alyx." Estelle leans in and air kisses each of my cheeks. "You look lovely dear. Exactly as I imagined you'd look. Isn't she such a good girl, Fitzroy?"

His eyes are glued to my skin. I have to hold back a shiver.

"She is." His lips form a sneer that soon turns to a lustful smile.

"Felix, dear!" Estelle turns.

I hadn't even notice he was there. Fuck I should have prepared myself for him being close. Does he know about Ana?

"Yes, ma'am." Felix comes up beside her.

"We've reserved a separate table for yourself and Collin. Please make sure Collin doesn't drink too much. We'll need him to drive later, too."

"Of course," Felix says.

Fitzroy and Collin are having a private conversation near the car. I have no idea what they are talking about, but I hope it has nothing to do with me going to The Island.

Felix nods to me then shifts his head in Collin's direction. I know he's asking where Ana is. She was supposed to be my driver. He doesn't know anything yet. I can't tell him here. I put my hand on my neck and move my head side to side. To everyone else I look as though I am rubbing a sore neck. Felix will see it as the answer it is. 'No, she's not here.'

"Alyx, have you met Deidra?" Estelle asks me as she grabs the girl's hand and pulls her closer to me.

Deidra is a beautiful young woman. I feel like a wretch standing next to her flawlessness. Jesus she is gorgeous. Dark skin, silk dress, no panty lines. She is slim and tall. I have no idea how old she is. Young, that's all I can tell. "Hi." I offer a hand.

"Hey," she says with a smile and instead of taking my hand she hugs me. "We're all sisters now." She whispers in my ear.

"Yeah," I smile. "You're stunning." I tell her outright.

She nods. "Thanks. I tried." Deidra shrugs. "It's my first night out since I came to the manor." She seems excited.

"How long ago was that?" I ask hoping to get a timeline of her arrival. Did she come before or after the Sasha event? Had she been at the manor when *everything* happened?

"Long enough," is all Deidra says. She leans over. "Want any molly? I've got some."

"Not yet, though ask me later," I laugh. I know I won't be doing anything tonight because I have to keep my wits, but I can't tell anyone else that.

"Alyx." Ruby comes over and air kisses each of my cheeks, so we don't ruin each other's makeup. Ruby's wearing a white slip dress. Her hair is the fabulous afro she always wears. Ruby always looks like she's stepped out of the seventies ready for a party. She looks *fine*! Her dark skin glimmers with body glitter. "How are you, Love?" Her words are light, but her eyes say. 'I know what happened, are you good?'

I want to grab onto her, hug her, and say 'let's run away!' I know that wouldn't work. I know that option doesn't exist. I look down at my feet for a minute. *If only those agents were watching me now.* "I'm well. How are you?"

Ruby grabs my hand and squeezes it. "I'm happy to see you. You do look well." She nods.

Fitzroy comes up behind me and wraps his hand back around my waist. His finger rolls over my panty line. "Alyx," he shoos the other girls away. They all run to Estelle's side. Felix goes into the restaurant. I'm certain he is informing them that our party has arrived. "My special guest is here for you," Fitzroy whispers into my ear. "But you're still mine. If you'd left your panties behind, I'd have a difficult time not taking you right here on the spot."

"Of course, *U*ncle," I look over my right shoulder and up. Fitzroy is so tall I have to lean to the side a bit to do this. "Who's this guest?" I say as I let my hand brush against the front of his pants as I turn around in his arms.

Fitzroy is eager as he smiles at me and then nods over his shoulder.

I look behind him and my mouth drops open. My heart rate speeds, and I take a step back, bumping right into someone. I turn and it's Felix. His brow shoots up and he cocks his head to the side.

"I knew you'd be happy," Fitzroy says. "Come on over. Join us, Peter." Fitzroy motions a hand for him to walk over.

It is *him*, too. It is *Peter*. The man that I always thought of as family. That is until I found out that he is the reason that my brother and I have no family. He is older now. His hair is graying. It gives him a distinguished look, well if you don't know what a horrible lying wretch he is. He's wearing an expensive suit, but in the darkness, I can't tell which brand it is. His cologne is so strong I can smell it from where I stand.

It is the same cologne he always wore. Old Spice.

Felix clears his throat and bumps my back a little with his arm. He passes me up so it will look like a mistake, but I know what it means the instant he does it. I haven't yet greeted the special guest.

"Peter!" I run over and wrap my arms around him. "I can't believe it's you." I pull away but don't let go of him. "It's been so long." I run my hand down his green tie, stopping at the last buttons on his suit jacket.

Peter's brow shoots up. "It's a pleasure to see you again, dear." He looks me up and down. "My, my, how you've grown." He grabs my hand and holds it up so I can do the showoff spin.

As my body spins my parents' faces flash in my head.

"You look amazing, and not a day older than seventeen." Peter winks at me.

"That's the plan." I wink back. My father would be proud that I'm able to keep my composure under all this pressure. He always told me, a good attorney knows how to keep their cool in any situation, a lady should be no different. Fuck, I missed dad right now. He'd kick Peter's ass on the spot for looking at me like this.

Something awakens in my mind. I know what it is right away. This is it. It is the flash of a thought, one that I've been dreading. In this moment... I know without a doubt... I will get away from these people. I *will* figure this out. I *will* get away. I *will* do everything I can to do it, too.

"Aren't you so happy to see him?" Fitzroy asks. Though I can see the twinkle of jealousy in his eyes.

"I've got my two favorite men in the world with me," I say as I pull Fitzroy over so that I stand between the two of them. "What more could I want?" I look up into Fitzroy's eyes, and then lick my lips slowly.

"Table's ready, sir." Felix comes up beside us.

Fitzroy orders a caviar service for the table. Estelle insists that we have the cheese course as well. Fitzroy nods once and agrees with her. He insists that everyone at the table have the tasting menu. The tasting service lets you try everything the restaurant offers. He insists on the wine pairing because the wine will change based on the sommelier selections according to our meals.

Ruby is seated with Deidra over at the table with Collin and Felix. Misty and I are on either side of Peter at the circular table in the center of the room. Fitzroy is on my right, and Estelle is on his other side.

Estelle, Misty, and Peter are talking about Florida. Peter is filling Estelle in on some of the drama from the country club that he still attends. Fitzroy's hand is on one of my legs—Peter's is on the other.

Fitzroy leans in to speak to me after the waiter leaves the table. "Peter is in town for a few days. He'd like to meet with yourself and Misty privately," he squeezes my thigh, "before he leaves."

"Anything you say, *U*ncle." I smile.

"His status is upgrading to *U*ncle soon, too." Fitzroy winks at me.

I smile back but my heart pounds in my chest. Is this special dinner about Fitzroy giving me as a gift to my new *U*ncle? Would he do that? Will I have to fuck Peter?

I know I will.

But I can't think about it now.

Drinks and food come and go from the table. Peter keeps touching my leg, or my shoulder. He places his hand on top of mine if I set it on the table. I smile, like the good employee I am. I don't jerk my hand away and smack him. I don't get up and scream that he killed my parents' as much as Fitzroy did. I don't smack either of them over the head with the wine bottle that Estelle insists stay on the table.

I don't do any of that. I charm them both. I have someone I have to protect. I don't have another option.

"Corwin!" Estelle shoots up out of her chair.

I look over my shoulder and sure enough. Corwin Thwaite is there. He stands alone, wearing his designer suit. Looking as handsome as ever. I smile. It is the first real smile I've had all night. I stand up to greet him as well.

"Mr. Thwaite," I wink.

"Ladies, how lovely to see you out and about." Corwin smiles.

"Come, join us." Estelle pulls him over to our table.

"Oh, I can't. Not tonight." Corwin looks to me and then back to Estelle. "I've got some packing to do."

Oh, shit. I'd forgotten about Corwin. "That's right," I say. Perhaps I could use this to my advantage. "I'm so glad you showed up. Estelle, Corwin asked me Monday evening if I could help him go through Rita, and Becca's things. He's sold the house. Is it okay if I go with him?" I look at Corwin and hope that the expression on my face makes him understand. Makes him know that I *need* to come with him.

"It would help me ever so much," Corwin puts his arm around me, "if this sweet young woman could come home with me." He smiles.

Estelle's eyes light up. I nearly pass out in shock. Some-fucking-how—Corwin knows what I need.

Estelle's head shoots to Fitzroy. Fitzroy's jaw tightens but he nods once to Estelle. "Of course!" She says happily. "I'm so glad you'll have Alyx to help you out. She's a fine girl. Quite good at," Estelle tilts her head to the side, "so many things."

"It's settled then. Alyx, thank you. Gentlemen," Corwin nods to the table, "it's been a pleasure, Estelle, as always."

Estelle kisses Corwin's cheek. She looks over her shoulder and nods in our direction. Ruby gets up from her table and takes my place next to Fitzroy. Peter's hand goes to her leg. Fitzroy leans back in his chair.

Corwin puts his arm out for me to take. I glance back at Fitzroy. He motions for me to come over. "Once second, Gramps," I smile at Corwin.

Words are important when I am near Fitzroy. I can't call Corwin *Grandpa*, because that term is used in the hierarchy, but I can refer to him as Gramps with no one batting an eye at it.

Corwin laughs, and I do as I am bid. I lean over and Fitzroy whispers in my ear. "*Mine*, can go with Corwin tonight, and you can bring back some gold.

Because that's what *mine* is worth... pure gold." He nibbles my ear. "Understood?" he says as I pull away.

"Yes." I nod.

Fitzroy mouths the word 'mine' one more time.

I join Corwin and we leave.

I don't even glance at Peter.

CHAPTER FOUR - THURSDAY

KNIGHTS

"Ms. Alyx," Corwin says as we exit the restaurant. "I feel as though I may have saved you from a terrible date." He laughs as he takes my hand and wraps it around his arm.

I take the offered arm happily. Honestly, I'm not sure how much longer I'll be able to stand. But I know I have to. "You did." I nod my head. "You're my knight in Armani armor." I raise a brow as I look over his suit.

Corwin laughs. "Well, I'm not sure which one you were with, but I can say they were both old enough to be your father." He walks slow as he holds his hand over mine. "If that were my Becca, I would have punched them both square in the nose."

It is my turn to laugh. "That would have been

funny. But I doubt their bodyguards would have thought so."

"They had bodyguards?" He asks as we cross the street.

"At the corner table."

"Ah," he says. "Can I ask you a personal question, Alyx?"

"Corwin, after what you just did, you can ask me anything at all!" I squeeze his arm. "Really, you saved me back there. It is appreciated." I blow out a quick breath.

Corwin chuckles. "Why did you agree to go on a date with such an older gentleman?"

"Most of the men I date are older than me." I answer honestly.

"How," he holds onto the word for a second, "often do you date?" The tone of his voice is concern, not judgment.

"I go out a few times a week." I look over. "But don't worry, you're still my favorite dinner date." I say, again honestly. Corwin is my best date. He never wants anything from me other than my time and conversation.

"Well, excuse me while I offer some fatherly advice. Feel free to tell me to shut up if I overstep." Corwin laughs. "Becca would've already told me to hush."

"I'd be happy to have some." I say as we cross

another street. "I haven't had any fatherly advice in a long, long time."

Corwin nods his head. "Don't give *anything* away to them. A good man will not take what isn't deserved or granted by a lady. Please, don't ever feel like you owe them anything, no matter how much they spend on dinner." He pats my hand while we walk.

"That is the sweetest advice anyone has ever given me." It really is. "I'd also like to apologize to you."

"What on earth do you have to apologize for?" He asks as he looks both ways before we cross the street. City traffic requires constant attention.

"I forgot about meeting you tonight."

"There is nothing to apologize for. Though, can I ask why you think you forgot? It's not good networking skills to forget meetings." He smiles as he falls back into his role as tutor.

"Monday got a little crazy when my driver never showed up."

"Estelle called me about that. Did she ever arrive?"

I know I can't tell Corwin the truth. "No, she left with her boyfriend and forgot to tell anyone." I hate lying to Corwin. It feels wrong. I never mind when I lie to anyone else. Well, I don't like lying to Trent either.

Corwin nods and we continue. It's a seven minute walk to Corwin's place. When he opens the door, I gasp. His apartment is on the twentieth floor of the building. The walls are white. The ceilings are high, and even though it is dark outside, it is bright inside. There are beautiful pink flowers in the vases that sit next to the door. "Corwin, your home is stunning."

"Well, it's not mine anymore. The new owners take over at the end of the month." He closes the door. "Bedrooms are this way." He ushers me to the right and down a small hall.

Everything is stylish and polished to perfection. "The closets are here," he says. "This one is mine, this one Rita's. Becca's room is here." He turns back around and leads me across the hall to his daughter's room. "The boxes," he holds onto the word as he takes me on a mini tour of his home, "are in the guest rooms."

He leads me back into the foyer and points down the hall. "Past the kitchen, there," he says. "Would you like anything to drink?"

"Water, please." I smile.

He walks into the kitchen and grabs two bottles of Voss. Corwin hands me one and takes the other into the living room. The windows are high, and the view is astonishing. "Corwin, really. Such a beautiful home. This view." I let my mouth drop open.

"It was Rita's favorite view of New York." He smiles. "Is it okay if we sit for a minute? I'd like my dinner to settle before we get started." He opens his water. "I think the realness of everything is setting in, too. You being here… to help me… pack." He looks down at his feet.

"Of course, no need to rush. I have no where I need to be."

"Would you like to sit?" Corwin motions to the sofa.

I smile and take the offered seat. There are gray throws draped in a few places. One looks like Corwin uses it often. There's a pillow on the sofa as well. Corwin must sleep here as opposed to his bedroom. I know how much he misses his family.

Corwin leans over the table and turns on the small television that sits there. "I bought this after I lost them both. I was never much for television. But the house was too quiet with them gone." He half smiles at me. "Now it's background noise, but I'm used to it. Helps me relax." He takes a sip of his water.

"I understand that. After my parents died my brother and I always left the television on when we were going to bed. The noise provides a level of comfort. A … not aloneness… level of security."

"I'm sorry, Alyx. I didn't realize your parents had passed. You always speak of them with such admiration. Which of your parents is Estelle's sibling?"

I'd let the charade fall for a second and shoved my foot in my mouth. "Estelle is my great Aunt." I lie. "She was my mother's aunt." I lie again. Though, it isn't like I can tell him the truth.

Corwin nods and takes a sip of his water. "Well, I guess we should get to it." He gets up and I follow him down the hall. "The movers left me some extra boxes here." We enter the guest room.

The boxes are banker boxes for files. Most of the boxes and lids are already folded into shape. Corwin goes over to the stack and grabs a few. I follow suit and grab two as well. "Markers are here." He grabs one of the many markers off the table next to the bed. I take one, too.

He leads me back to Becca's bedroom. He sets the boxes down and opens her closet up. He inhales deep then swallows hard. Corwin doesn't have to tell me what is happening. I already know. He hasn't opened that closet since she died. Her scent is still there. "I'll be in the next room if you need me," he says without looking toward me. The way his shoulders fall forward I think perhaps a few tears have escaped him.

I leave Corwin alone with his sorrow. I know from personal experience that he needs someone here, but he doesn't need them to comfort him. He needs to *feel* this.

I grab a box and set it on Becca's vanity chair. I pull the chair over to the closet. There are so many nice things. All brands that are high end. I run a hand along the clothes. I have a nice set of clothes, but nothing as grand as this. As I push some of the dresses to the side to peruse them. There is a set of drawers behind the clothes.

Might as well start there first. More than likely things in there can be gotten rid of. I was right. The first drawer has socks and underwear. I toss them in the box, and label it, 'undergarments.' I'm not sure if those can be donated or not, but someone might want them.

I open the second drawer. Everything is folded neatly. I smell her perfume in this drawer as well. It smells similar to the Misfit perfume Estelle got for me. I take out the first layer and add them to the second box. I go back to the drawer to pull the other items out and clasp both hands over my mouth.

Holding back a scream.

There right in front of me is the pink halter top, with the black FG below the left strap. Next to the shirt is a pair of black sweats. My mind whirls. Had Becca been one of Fitzroy's girls, too? I look over at her vanity. Her jewelry box sits atop it. There is one way to find out.

I open the box and rifle through it. I don't see anything. I soon discover the top section is a tray. I pull it up. I stare as my mind registers what my eyes see. The little diamond earrings. I pick one up to see if they are the same as the ones I have. I press the diamond toward the back of the earring. They click as the tracker engages.

I pull the earring apart, to disengage the tracker.

"Holy shit," I say.

"Did you say something, Alyx," Corwin asks from across the hall.

Footsteps clank against the tiles and I place the earring back in the box and return the tray. As Corwin comes in, I admire her jewelry. "Corwin, Becca's taste was so beautiful," I say as I try to breathe at a normal rate. "Such amazing pieces." I smile.

"Becca, and Rita, were always shopping." Corwin smiles. "They'd come in with bags and spend hours going through their purchases. Sorting them, deciding where to put them in their closets." He chuckles. "Wait till you see Rita's. It's packed."

"Thank you, for trusting me with this Corwin." I'm honored that he does. "I know how hard this can be."

"I'm certain you do, dear." He gives me a sweet smile. "How about, I help you in here, and then we'll tackle Rita's things."

"Sounds great." I go back over to Becca's closet and pick up the top and the pants that are absolutely Fitzroy's uniform for his girls. I'm placing the items in the box when Corwin sees them.

"Oh, my goodness. I forgot about those." He takes the items from me. "I meant to return these to Estelle."

"Estelle?" My brow arches a bit too high, but Corwin doesn't notice.

"Yes." Corwin's head bobs up and down. "Becca had left a note. She wanted to return them when she got home for spring break."

"Why would Estelle need Becca's clothes?"

"I'm not sure. The note was found in Becca's dorm room. You know, after the accident at the school."

"A note?"

"Sorry, yes. I'm being vague. The note, of course, Becca didn't know she would die in that accident. It was more of a list. 'Things to do and items to return,' was scrawled across the top. Becca's roommate, Ruby, gave the note to me when I went to pick up her things."

Holy fucking hell! Ruby… Ruby was there? Could it have been the same Ruby? Could it have been the Ruby I'd had dinner with tonight? What had she been doing at Becca's? "What else did the note say?" I try to keep my voice even. I'm certain Estelle never planned on telling me anything about Becca. She'd never let on that Becca had worked for Fitzroy, *ever*.

"It was a list of things to do when she got back home for break. She wanted to return some things and buy a bike for school." Corwin smiles at me. "Becca hated all the walking on campus. It took too long. She wasn't one to waste any time." He laughs at some memory that he doesn't share with me.

"How did her roommate come to give you the note?" If it had been Ruby, I know Ruby isn't in college —she's never been. She is at The Island more often than she is anywhere else. If it were the Ruby that I know who gave him the note, she wasn't a student.

"Funny story. I almost ran the poor girl over. I'd packed everything into the trunk of the car. The school had told me they'd mail her things. But I wanted to lay my eyes on her things, you know. The accident had been so… unexpected."

"As accidents go," I say.

"Yes," Corwin nods. "It was odd, though. I'd unenrolled Becca from the school and gathered her things after I received a letter stating that I had to do so. But afterwards as I backed out someone smacked the back of my car. I got out, worried that I'd run over some student."

"I'm certain they understood that you were stressed." I pat his arm.

"Yes, the girl was very nice. She introduced herself. 'Mr. Thwaite, I'm so sorry for your loss. I was Becca's roommate. I found this on our cork board and thought you might like to have it.' She smiled and ran off." Corwin shrugs.

"Do you still have the note?"

"Yes, I do." Corwin walks out of the room.

I know he is hunting for the note, but I have to see

it. I'm not even sure why I want to see it, but I have to. Had the note been written by Becca? What had Ruby been doing there?

Corwin comes back in. "Here it is." He holds out the paper.

I'm gentle as I take it, showing the item respect. I know it means a lot to Corwin if he still has it. He believes it to be his daughter's unfinished tasks. I look it over. At the top of the paper words are spelled out in loopy letters. 'Get a new laptop. Buy a new desk lamp. Return clothes and earrings to Estelle—pink FG halter top, black sweats, and diamond studs. Buy a bike for school.' But at the bottom, there are words scrawled in a different hurried hand. I stare at the words.

'To Have Essentials: Inhaler Sandals Lanyard Aquarium Noodles Donuts.'

I can't believe my eyes. There it is. It *is* the Ruby I know. The words mean nothing. It's what they spell that means everything.

The Island.

"Corwin, may I ask *how* Becca passed?" I knew there had been an accident, but was Becca dead, or was she at The Island? Had Ruby been leaving a message for Corwin, hoping he'd see it? Or had Fitzroy killed Becca? Maybe he killed her because she left him and went to college. How could I know? I'll have to speak to Ruby to know everything.

"I got the call early on a Wednesday morning," Corwin says as I hand the note back. "It was someone from the University's staff. Informing me that there had been a fire in one of the science labs. The fire department had shown up and put out the fire, but they wanted me to come to the University." Corwin rubs his neck. "I was too busy. There was a merger that day. I asked if they could please tell me over the phone because I had things to do."

Corwin runs a hand over his hair. It looks as though he is trying to pull the guilt out of his head. "The woman paused for a long time, and I have to admit I was rather rude. 'Could you please get on with it? Why do you need to inform me of a fire, if the fire department has taken care of everything?' I asked in a rush.

"'I'm sorry to inform you this way, but since you insist. Everyone is accounted for apart from one student,' she said. That's when I dropped my phone. I quickly picked it up as she went on, 'no one has seen Becca, and she'd been in that class before the fire.' I don't know what I missed.

"I'd lost Rita seven months prior, you know," Corwin says looking to me. I nod and let him continue telling me the story. "When I arrived on campus a few hours later, the fire trucks were still in the lot. The chief came over to speak with me. 'Mr. Thwaite, I presume,' he said it with such respect. I knew right away that he would tell me my daughter had died. His tone was the same as the doctors who'd told me of Rita's passing in the night." Corwin sniffs as tears form in his eyes.

"I'm so sorry, Corwin." I hug him.

He pats my back gently. "Thank you, Ms. Alyx. It has been hard."

I pull away. I hate to do it, but I still need more information. "Can I ask a hard question?"

"Of course," he says.

"Did they find her in the ashes?"

"There wasn't enough left of her to return." He looks down solemnly. "They did however find her bag, and one of her shoes. The fire chief said it was possible that the explosion threw her from her shoes, and that's why they found her bag, one shoe, and not *her*. The fire had roared more violently nearest the chemicals in the lab. They believed she'd been thrown across the room and possibly into the shelves where they were housed." Corwin looks up and blinks.

"I'm sorry to cause you pain of remembering. I know it's a lot. It was hard when they finally found my parents' bodies, too. They showed us one area on each of our parents. A piece of skin on my mother's right shoulder, and my father's left ear. Their bodies had been in the water too long. I asked them to show us areas that were relatively untouched."

"You lost your parents tragically then?" Corwin asks.

"An accident. They said my father had been drinking and lost control of the car. Went off the bridge and into the ocean."

"I'm so sorry," Corwin says. "Is this why you so readily agreed to help me?"

"Shared trauma, right?" I smile.

Corwin laughs. "Thank you, Dear. It does mean a lot to have someone who understands help me with this great task."

"I understand why you don't want the items to go to waste. They mean something." I turn back to the closet. I run a hand over the clothes. "I don't have much from my parents. My brother and I couldn't afford to stay in the house. We lost most everything."

"I'm sorry to hear that. You'd said your father was an attorney, and your mother an accountant?"

"Yes." I nod.

"I can't believe they wouldn't have set things up for their children."

"They had. That's the worst part. Florida sued their estate, due to the cost of the recovery of their bodies." I shrug and run my hand over a blue dress that looks similar to one my mother had owned.

"Hmm." Corwin makes the noise. I look over and he is rubbing his chin.

"What?"

"It seems odd that the state would do that. But it is Florida. Some of their representatives are idiots." He rolls his eyes.

I laugh. "They certainly are."

Corwin and I spend the rest of the evening packing up the closets. At one point he decides to change out of his suit and into a pair of sweats and a T-shirt. He offers me some of Becca's clothes to put on, but I decide to stay in my dress. Worried if I smell like Becca and wear her things, that this will be even tougher on him. I do, however, slide my shoes off and place them at the foot of Becca's bed.

By the time we're finished Corwin has ten boxes designated for me. He writes my name in bold letters on the side of each box. Not wanting them to be mistaken for donations. He also gives me the stud earrings that Becca was supposed to return to Estelle. I put them in my purse so as not to lose them.

"Alyx," Corwin yells from the kitchen. He'd gone to get us more water.

"Yes, Corwin?" I call back from Rita's closet as I dust off her shelves. Trying to make everything easier on Corwin.

Funny how something as simple as dust can hurt you so much. When our parents died, we didn't dust or clean. We were alone. After so much time the dust became a reminder of how long they'd been gone. Each layer meant another week without them. If anyone came by and touched it, Trent would get angry and storm off. I'd find something from a tall shelf, then blow that dust wherever they'd touched. Trying to replace the dust so he could calm down.

Dust was a reminder of what we'd lost. I didn't want that for Corwin, too. He doesn't need to see the dust to be reminded of how long his family has been gone. There is a constant reminder in the silence he lives in.

"Where shall I have the boxes delivered?" He asks as he comes in and hands me another water bottle.

"I'll text you, my address." I smile.

"That will be wonderful. I'll have everything delivered." Corwin sits down on a small bench and tells me his phone number.

"Thank you, Corwin." I grab my phone. I begin to type my address and realize that I don't want Becca's things to go anywhere near Estelle again. Corwin thought it'd been too long, and it would be rude to return the things to Estelle, so he placed them in one of my boxes.

I shoot off a text to Corwin that contains my brother's address. I don't need to text Trent because he isn't at home. I'll put the boxes inside Trent's place myself after my appointments are over for the day.

Corwin's phone chimes and he retrieves it from his bedside table. "You're near the park then?"

"Close enough." I smile. "I run a lot. It's nice to be close."

Corwin nods and gives me a sweet smile. "Alyx." He looks at me. I stare back with a matching smile. "I cannot thank you enough. I can see that you understand my sorrow." He pats a hand over his heart. "I appreciate your kindness."

"Corwin." I walk toward him. "I'm always happy to help someone who is so kind to me." I hug him.

Corwin hugs me back. A bear hug.

He'd needed this more than he knew.

And so did I.

BOXES

"Alyx," Corwin says as I reclaim my shoes from Becca's room.

"Yes, sir?"

He comes into the room. "How much do you get for a night out like this?" He looks down at his hands while I slip into my first heel.

"Usually about twelve grand," I answer as I slide my second shoe on.

Corwin's eyebrow shoots up.

"Oh my god!" I stutter. Corwin has asked me if I am a call girl, and I've answered *yes*. Fucking hell what is wrong with me? "I didn't mean that," I laugh trying to play everything off. I look around for my bag, but I can't see it anywhere. Fuck, I left it in Rita's closet. "I was joking," I smile, and walk past him heading toward my bag.

"Alyx," Corwin says a little too kindly for someone who has asked *that* question. "It's okay. I figured it out a while ago. I wanted to confirm it," he says it so casually as he follows me.

I round on him. I don't know if I should scream or cry. "Is that all this was? A ruse to get me to your house so you could ask me what I do?" My brow tightens.

"No," Corwin puts his hands up in submission. "I like you, Alyx. I trust you. I'm exceedingly good at reading people."

"Like you read, Estelle," I say under my breath.

"Estelle is a complication from my past. We attended college together. I always thought something was off with her, different." Corwin lets out a deep sigh. "I kept convincing myself that I was wrong. But when you were out tonight with those older gentlemen. Well," he lets the word hang in the air.

"Corwin," I say. "Please don't say anything to Estelle. Please?" I beg. This information can get me killed. Estelle wants me to land Corwin, but she doesn't want him knowing *she* is behind anything.

"Not an issue, Alyx. Your secret is safe with me. But, is this something you want to be doing?"

"Are you judging me now?" I'm shocked. Corwin has never judged me before. Of course, he's never *known* what I do. But he's made assumptions.

"Of course not!" He sighs again, this one is more

laugh than sigh though. "I'm curious what will happen to you if you arrive with nothing." He rubs his thumb and his first two fingers together. "I'm assuming that Estelle believes that tonight is the night that you accomplish your task of landing me as a *client*."

"How could you know that?" I ask mystified.

"As I say, Estelle is a complication from my past. It's less that I figured you out, and more that I know Estelle. I could tell she wanted something from me." He shrugs a shoulder. "I can always tell when someone wants something from me, and they don't ask for it outright."

"I'm sorry, Corwin. I don't want anything from you."

"I know, Alyx. Don't worry. I won't say anything." Corwin walks over to his side of the closet.

"I hope not. Corwin, this is the only way I can take care of my brother and myself. If you do anything to mess this up." I stop myself. What else can I say? I've spent the evening helping him, and I've ended up killing myself in the process. I've let my guard down. How could I be so foolish? I pick up my purse and head for the front door. My heels click against the tiles as I walk away.

"Alyx," Corwin calls from his room. His bare feet patter against the tiles as he comes up behind me.

I turn to look up as my hand grips the doorknob.

All I can do is stare. How have I fucked everything up so incredibly in one night?

"Here." He holds out his hand to me.

I look down at his hand. My brow shoots up. "What?" I ask as I stare at the stack of cash in his hand.

"Twelve thousand. That's what you said right? Do you need more?"

"What?" I ask again. Corwin is offering me *money*? "Why?" I say mystified, yet again.

"Alyx, I can't send you empty handed. I don't know what might happen if I do."

"I'm confused here, Corwin. Estelle knows that you and I don't have that kind of relationship."

"Ah, but she is expecting us to eventually have that kind of relationship. Or at least she's hoping that we will." His head bounces up and down a bit.

It is almost four in the morning. I am too tired for all of this. I'm drained, but it's more than that. I feel exhausted in my bones. Corwin's hand sits there, outstretched, filled with cash. Waiting.

Corwin grabs my hand and places the money in it. "I know this business can be dangerous. I wouldn't want to encourage a dangerous situation for you, Alyx. Please. Allow me to help." He lets go of my hand.

I meet his gaze once more. "How can you *know* any of this?" I am weary. Everything is crashing down on me. My knees are about to buckle.

"Alyx," Corwin lifts my chin so he can look into my eyes. "One does not get where I am today, without coming across people who like to take advantage of others."

"Is that something you do often?" I ask—though I can't ever imagine Corwin doing anything like that.

"I try my best not to take advantage of anyone. However, I can see when others are doing this." He arches a brow. "Before tonight, I hadn't seen you *with* Estelle. Please, come back inside, let's talk," he says. He backs away and encourages me to follow him to the sofa in the living room.

My steps are barely my own. I've been sapped of everything. Corwin—a person I don't want to know *who* I am—now knows everything. The ruse of me being a college student is gone. That is a fantasy life I enjoyed living, but now… it is gone.

"The look on Estelle's face tonight, I could see the true shock. I knew my assumptions had been right. When I asked you about the older gentlemen," Corwin stops.

"I answered honestly and then you knew everything," I say as I sit down.

"Yes." Corwin sits next to me. "I do have another question for you, though." Corwin's gaze is fierce. I nod. I already know what's coming. "If my daughter knew Estelle… Does that mean that she *worked* for her?"

I look down at my shoes. I stare at the black satin straps crossing my feet. How can I answer this? How can I tell her father? I'd never want anyone to tell mine.

"Ah," is all Corwin says.

"Mr. Thwaite." I look into his eyes. "You cannot, please, tell anyone that you *aren't* a client." My self-preservation kicks in. The need to keep my brother protected. My mind begins to wake. "You'll have to tell them how *well* I did this evening. How much you enjoyed my company. You'll have to ask for another appointment with me."

"First one's never free in business." Corwin sighs. "It won't be a lie though; I do enjoy your company." He smiles.

"A second appointment is required, if I want to,"— I stop myself from saying *live*— "keep my job."

"Do you *want* to keep this job?"

"I don't have another way to take care of my brother, Corwin. He'd lose his apartment and his medicine if I stopped paying for it. There's nowhere else for either of us to go."

"Alyx, I have a friend that can help you."

What on earth can he mean by that? "I don't need help Corwin. I need clients."

"It seems to me that help is exactly what you need."

Corwin gets up and goes into his room. He comes back in a few moments and hands me a card.

Holy fucking hell. The card looks similar to the one I'd gotten earlier from Agent Payton. However, this one is from the other Agent—Shwetz—and it says FBI on it, too. I steady myself. "FBI?" I question as innocently as I can manage.

Corwin nods. "Yes, they did an investigation at the school. After the fire. Customary I suppose after an incident like that." He looks toward the window for a moment. "Anyway, Agent Shwetz said that if I ever needed anything I could call her. I suppose this would be as good a way to use that offer as any. Tell her that *I* gave you the information."

I chew on my bottom lip. What can I tell him? He seems to know more than he is letting on. I need to think of Corwin like my other clients right now. I need to wake the fuck up. I've lost my edge in a matter of hours. Being with Corwin at his home is familiar. It dawns on me—Corwin is a lot like my dad. My parents had kept a wonderful home for myself and Trent. Our house was always welcoming… safe. I haven't had safety for such a long time that I've sunk into it without realizing that I shouldn't.

I pull my phone from my small bag. I scroll through the photos. I need to know. I pull up a picture of Ruby, Ana, and I from a few months back. We'd gone with Estelle out shopping, and then for a carriage ride. It was a happy day for Ruby. Estelle never treated Ruby too well. At least she hadn't until after that day. Ruby had proven herself in some way to Estelle.

"Is this Becca's roommate?" I hold the phone so he can see.

Corwin looks at the picture. "Yes, there in the middle." He points to *Ana*.

"She said her name was Ruby?" Ana had started a long time ago trying to help other girls. I'd never even known. No wonder she is… *was*… so pissed at me. She had every right to be. How much had Ana known about Sasha? I know there must be more than she ever told me. I need to see Felix.

"Yes," Corwin's brow rises. "Is that not her name?" he guesses.

"I'm not sure I should say more," I say.

"These girls work for Estelle, too?"

I shake my head. "Not exactly." I can't get into the ins and outs of this business with Corwin. He doesn't need that information.

"The man that was at the table this evening?" Corwin makes his guess.

"I shouldn't say anything else." I get up and walk back toward the foyer.

Corwin exhales, but then he follows me. "Alyx." He positions himself between me and the door. "I can tell you're holding something else from me. Please," his eyes beg me, "please let me help you."

"You have," I say as I hold up the cash. "More than you know."

"Well, you have my direct number now. Please Alyx, call me anytime. Day or night. I will help you."

I nod. "Thank you." I kiss his cheek. "I should go."

"As you say," Corwin says, and he opens the door.

REARRANGED SCHEDULE

My phone vibrates. It's a text from Estelle. I click the message as I exit the cab. I'm glad I am home, and betting this text is my schedule for today. It's Thursday. But my schedule has been rearranged so I'll probably spend my day like I would my usual Tuesday.

"*I canceled 2:00 AM since you were with T. I sent D at U's behest. Please be at Mr. O's by 1:00. C is on the way to your place to see that you arrive swiftly. Blue has been requested for this week. Prepare yourself for M's limo as well. As well as dinner with K. Our special guest will need to see you soon, too.*" Estelle always codes her texts. Can't let anyone know anything. Names are never used. Texts and things like that can be tracked. Fitzroy wants no trace.

"*Of course.*" I reply and put my phone back in my bag.

Marcus opens the door to the building for me. He tips his top hat at me as I pass him; I smile. The elevator opens to my floor and I'm glad. I need a shower and a nap. My phone vibrates again as I enter my apartment. I close the door and check the text. It's another text from Estelle.

"How did it go?"

"Everything you dreamed would happen, did happen." I reply.

"Fantastic," she replies. *"Will there be another?"*

"Definitely. Once walking can recommence." I know that Estelle loves to make men weak. She loves it when a girl fucks a man so hard that *he* can't walk.

Estelle replies with five, star shaped emoji. She is happy with me.

"Hello, Dear," a voice says. I look up and Fitzroy stands in the entrance to my kitchen.

Instead of screaming or running, I open my purse and pull the cash out. I walk over to *U*ncle, kiss his cheek, and hand him the money. "Good morning, *U*ncle," I say.

"I see you had a good evening." He smiles wickedly at me. "How did *M*ine do last night?" His grin widens. "Did it take a *licking*?" He strokes his tongue across his bottom lip.

"Not everyone knows how to use their tongues." I pass him and grab a water from the fridge.

Fitzroy laughs then stands at the counter counting out the cash. "I still owe you for Monday." He lays what I assume is four grand on the counter. Since the event at the manor, the pay for Monday has been forgotten. "For last night," he holds onto the word as he lays another three down. "You know what?" He stares at me. I know not to respond. He smiles when I say nothing and raise my brow. "You are such a good girl. Why don't you keep the lot of it." He lays the remaining cash down.

"*U*ncle, that is too generous." He won't catch me doing anything I shouldn't. I can't allow that. "Please, I know the trouble you go through to make sure my clients are clean and respectable. I'll take my pay, from Monday and last night. You already pay me well enough. Please, keep the rest." I smile and kiss his cheek. "So thoughtful," I add as I pull away.

"I insist. Besides, you'll be coming with me later. I'd like you to go out and do some shopping. On me." He winks at me.

"*U*ncle," I gasp. "Truly?" I tilt my head down. Compliance is my only option.

"I'll need you to buy several bathing suits. In four colors."

"Which colors?" I lean into him and sigh. The sigh signifies that I can't think properly with him being so close. The pressure of my body against his, drives it home.

Fitzroy chuckles. "Alyx, you are one of my best girls."

"You flatter me." I let pink flood into my cheeks and bat my eyelashes. "Sorry, I'm getting distracted. Which colors did you need me to get?"

"Something stringy and orange. Another tiny and white. A full piece blue suit, and a red top, no bottoms." He tucks my hair behind my ear. "Some of the other girls will have green, but you won't need anything green." He grabs my chin and pulls his face down so close to mine that his lips rub against mine as he continues. "Because you're all mine." He kisses me.

My lips part as his tongue traces them. His breath is hot as his arms wrap around me. I have to keep my breath less than measured. I heave my chest to show my excitement. I have to *fake* it all.

"Boss." Collin comes into the room.

Fitzroy puts one hand out to stop Collin as he kisses me. When he finishes both his hands are on the sides of my face. "Such, a good girl." He smiles wickedly and then turns to Collin. Fitzroy turns my body and pulls me against him, wrapping his arms around my front and rubbing a hand over my left breast.

Collin ignores Fitzroy's fondling hand and continues. "I tossed Sasha's room. I didn't find anything. Neither of them kept any cash there."

The front door opens and slams closed. There is a wall blocking my view, but Collin looks over. "Find anything in the storage area?" Collin asks whomever it is.

A hand lays on the bar before the person comes into view. I have to stop myself from gasping with joy. It's Felix. I don't think he'll let anyone kill me while he's here. At least not without a fight. "No." He balls his hand into a fist. "Those bitches hid that money good. I can't believe Sasha picked up Ruby and Deidra's takes on Monday, too. Why would they give her their drops?"

This is another time I can shine. "Oh my," I gasp, happy to let a shocked gasp escape. "That's against the rules. You give your money to your own driver. Never to another one." I try to be as aloof as Collin and Fitzroy believe me to be.

Fitzroy's hand goes up to my shoulder and he pulls me into him, in a kind of half hug. "So smart." He kisses the top of my head and then releases me and leans on the bar. "You checked everywhere?" he says to Felix.

Felix nods. "Yes. I checked every area that was open, as well as a few that needed the lock picked. I was thinking of the best places to hide that kind of cash, too. If it were in the basement, I'd have found it." He slams his fist down on the counter. "100K will fit in a bag about this big." Felix holds out his hand showing the size of a small bag. He knows all the top clients pay with large bills.

A stack of a thousand bills is 4.3 inches in height. I know because I've held that much money in my hands so many times over the years. Only a portion of it was mine, but you get to know how much cash is in a stack of bills when you handle and count money as often as I do.

"Did you check the vents, Collin?" Fitzroy looks at Collin.

Collin nods. "Guess it's time to check everywhere else then." He opens a cabinet.

Fitzroy nods to Felix. Felix nods once and then heads down the hall. Collin begins throwing things out of the cabinets and into the floor. Fitzroy pushes me into the corner of the kitchen. I'm not sure what he's going to do. I've never seen this look on his face. It's a mixture of lust and anger. I try my best to smile. My chest heaves up and down. I am scared of him, but he doesn't need to know that.

Fitzroy must take the heaving as wanting. A sly grin spreads on his face. I pull my hair behind my ear and look down. The bulge in his pants is large. Shit. He's going to fuck me in the kitchen while Collin tears it apart. Felix is making noises down the hall and in the bathroom and my room. But I feel as though those noises are superficial. Cabinet doors open and close. Things are shaken, but I'm not sure if he's tossing the house the way Collin is.

As Collin flings a box of cereal into the floor, Fitzroy's hand goes up my dress and he gets on his knees. He pulls my panties down my leg. I hold onto his head as he lifts my foot to pull them from one leg then the other.

Collin drops the glass coffee jar into the floor with a smile on his face. Fitzroy puts my panties inside his jacket pocket, then puts his head under my dress. He pulls my right leg up and puts it over his shoulder and his tongue finds the treat it desires.

This will be the most concentration I've needed since Sempers. I have to ignore Collin destroying my apartment and focus on giving Fitzroy the show he anticipates. I let a soft moan leave my lips and my fingers grip onto his hair. I move his head back and forth. Not in a forceful way, that would get me slapped, but in a wanting way. I want you to do this to me. I want you to want me.

I gasp as his fingers find their way inside me. His left hand finds its way to my breast as Collin opens the freezer. *Fuck!* He's going to find the phones if he keeps going. Fitzroy's hand pulls my dress down so he can play with my nipple.

"*U*ncle," I moan. Collin looks over and watches us. So, he wants a show, too. I stare and lick my lips. *U*ncle goes to town on my southern route as Collin watches him fondle my breast. I put a hand to my hair and then trail it slowly down my front. I close my eyes for a moment while I let go and allow my warmth to flood into Fitzroy's waiting mouth.

He growls with delight and his tongue sops up every drop of me. Fitzroy licks up and down my legs, not letting anything escape him. When he rises, his face is wet. I smile and then wipe my hand across his mouth. "I'm all over you," I say, then lick my hand. I reach out and pull Fitzroy's face close to mine. I lick myself off his face then pull away.

"Fuck," Collin says from behind Fitzroy. "That was hot." His brow shoots up.

Fitzroy turns on him, then punches him square in the jaw.

Collin didn't expect that. But Collin had stolen Fitzroy's moment. Collin lets out a yell and Felix comes running into the room.

"What the hell?" Collin rubs his jaw.

Fitzroy goes for him again, but Felix jumps between them. "No, Boss!" He stops Fitzroy. "You're meeting."

Felix looks over his shoulder and stares at Collin. "Wouldn't want any blood on your suit."

Fitzroy rolls the anger from his shoulders and looks at Collin. "Do that again, and you'll find yourself with Sempers. He's been wanting a change of pace." His jaw clenches.

"Sorry, boss." Collin looks down.

"I'll finish with the kitchen," Felix says. "You go check the living room closet." He points for Collin to leave.

"I wanted to search the fridge." Collin sidesteps out of the kitchen, not daring to pass Fitzroy or me.

Fitzroy watches Collin, and I share a quick glance with Felix. I hope my eyebrows convey that there is something in the freezer. Felix rolls his head and then opens the freezer.

Fitzroy comes back over to me. "Excuse that minor distraction." He pushes himself against me.

I giggle and let myself fall into the wall. Fitzroy laughs. "So," he says, "how would my tongue be graded on your scale?"

I let my eyes grow wide and I tilt my head. I lean in and whisper in his ear, "I can still feel you tasting me." I let a small shiver roll through my shoulders.

"When you sampled your own flavor, from my lips," —he nuzzles my neck— "how did you taste?" His gaze finds mine again.

I stare raising one brow and opening my mouth. I let a hot breath out and then lick my hand, tasting myself again. Fitzroy's eyes rake over me. "Like pineapple," I answer. I eat sweet fruits every day before bed, for this exact reason. What you eat plays a role in how you taste. I've had too many *Johns* who smoked like freight trains. They taste like ash, and tar. Vegans taste better than the meat eaters, and those who eat tons of fruit taste the best. I am high class; I have to taste as good as I look.

Fitzroy grabs my face with both hands and kisses me fiercely. I dare a look at Felix, he's found the ice cream. He nods and I close my eyes. Collin slams the closet door.

"Fucking Cows!" Felix mumbles, so as not to disturb Fitzroy.

Fitzroy pulls away from me and turns to look at Felix. "Everything okay?"

"Fucking ice creams in the freezer." Felix smashes the box down into the trash can. "Estelle is going to be so mad."

Fitzroy turns to face me. I lean closer to his ear. "Do I taste like I eat that garbage?" I suck on his earlobe.

Fitzroy's head moves into me. I put my hands around his waist and continue tracing my tongue down his neck. Fitzroy pulls me away as his phone rings. "I hate that I'm going to have to leave, now." His head twists side to side. He smiles at me then answers his phone and walks away.

Felix looks at me and then down at the garbage can. I nod and walk out of the room. Collin follows me down the hall and into my bedroom. I sit on the edge of my bed. Collin leans against the doorframe.

"I'll be taking you shopping. You should dress for that." He stares at me.

I nod and grab my toiletry bag. I need a bath before I can go out. "I'll grab a quick shower," I say as I pass him.

Collin lets a hand trail across my front as I exit the room. I ignore it and go for the bathroom. It's a good thing Fitzroy is distracted by his phone call because I know—if Fitzroy sees Collin touch me, there will be a brawl.

SHOWER

As I walk into the bathroom, I know this is going to be difficult. I can't take a shower in the other bedroom because that will be odd behavior. Fitzroy will know that I'm upset about Ana's death if I don't use *this* room. I open the closet and grab a towel. Collin stands in the hallway watching me. His reflection is in the mirror; his eyes are tracing me. I don't look at him when I close the bathroom door.

I undress and get in the shower. Doing my best not to look down at the water going down the drain. Even thinking about seeing it makes blood flash in my mind's eye. I scrub my body. Before I can get to my hair the bathroom door opens.

"Alyx," Fitzroy says. He comes in and closes the door behind him.

"Yes, *U*ncle?" I reply a little timid.

Fitzroy walks over, his shoes clacking against the tiles. He pulls the shower curtain back a bit, peeking inside. I turn my head but not my body. His gaze is on my feet, working its way up before his eyes meet mine. "Jesus," huffs out of him. "I hate that I have to go." He bites his lip.

I smile before I turn back to washing my body. I put more soap in my hands and then lean down to wash my legs. Letting him watch.

Fitzroy clears his throat. "I'm going to leave Felix with you. Collin has a little lesson he needs to learn."

I nod as I rub soap in between my legs, working my way up to my abdomen in slow fluid movements.

He licks his lips. "Do you remember the list of things I told you to get?"

"Yes, *U*ncle," I say as I wash my breasts.

"I also need you to prepare a bag. Bring things you'll need for a weeklong stay." Fitzroy rubs a hand on his chin as his eyes explore my soapy form.

"Of course." I nod and let the water run over me. Rinsing the soap away.

Fitzroy bites his lip. "I'll see you soon."

I smile and turn to get some shampoo. Something grabs my elbow. No, *someone* grabbed it. I turn and Fitzroy has that same look as in the kitchen. Fury and lust—it's like he's a spider and I'm his prey. He forces me closer. My feet slip but he holds me upright. His fingers dig into my arm. "No one, and I mean, *NO ONE*, touches you." He puts his other hand on my face and squeezes my cheeks. "Do I make myself clear?"

I don't pull away from him. I don't yell out when I almost fall. I nod my head and meet his gaze. "No one, *U*ncle," I whisper back through smooshed lips. I let my body get closer. I put my hand on his neck and pull him toward me. He leans into it and his breathing picks up. I trace my tongue along his lips before forcing it inside his mouth. I kiss him deeply. Not letting my body get any closer. I know I can't ruin his suit. He has a meeting.

"Fuck it." He squeezes my elbow more and pulls me from the tub. He stands me on the rug in front of the sink. "They can wait a few more minutes, this won't take long," he says with fervor. "On your knees, Alyx."

I do as I'm told. My body is dripping with water. Fitzroy undoes his belt and drops his pants to the floor. I grab the towel from the sink and cover them, so they won't get wet, too. His phallic is at full attention. He grabs ahold of my hair and shoves himself inside my mouth. I do my best not to choke as he goes all the way in.

I learned years ago to control my gag reflexes. Some men love a good gagging girl, while others hate it. They want you to accept all of them without your body trying to fight them. It's offensive if your body fights them.

Fitzroy is someone who doesn't like a girl to gag.

I suck and lick his cock while I play with his balls. I let my finger trail around his asshole, another thing he loves. I put a finger inside him, and he moans. After a few more thrusts he ejaculates hard into my mouth. His fist tightens in my hair while he finishes. He grunts his happiness.

Tar, salt, and … bad whiskey. The taste lingers on my tongue as he retrieves his pants and buckles his belt.

"Finish your shower." Fitzroy smacks my ass hard—I'll have a bruise there later. He opens the bathroom door and leaves. Leaving the door open behind him.

"What the fuck? Why can't I stay?" Collin yelps. Fitzroy must've punched him again.

The front door opens and closes.

It's safe to close the bathroom door now. I close it, then spit what remains of Fitzroy out of my mouth and into the sink. I grab the bottle of mouthwash, pour a large serving into my mouth, and gargle until his taste is gone.

I get back in the shower and finish bathing.

Felix doesn't disturb me once.

I go to my room and dress. I put on a halter top and a miniskirt, with a pair of flats. I slip my hair into a ponytail.

Felix waits until after I have finished dressing before he even approaches me.

"So, when did they do it?" Felix asks as I come out of my bedroom. He goes into the kitchen and pulls the box of ice creams from the trash can. He retrieves the two phones inside the box. Handing one to me and putting the other in his pocket.

"That was close. I'm so glad you knew where she kept that," I say as I take the phone.

"You were pretty quick on your feet, too." His brow arches. "I mean; I guess I can say *feet*."

"A girl only has so many tools she can use." I pick up one of the cereal boxes from the floor. Cleaning the kitchen will be a good distraction.

Felix pulls a trash bag from under the kitchen counter and holds it open for me. I clean and he waits for me to answer his question.

"It was Wednesday. Shortly after you left. I went to get lunch and when I came back." I lean over the sink. I can't keep vomiting every time I picture someone dying again and again in my head. I need to get control over this.

I need control or I'll be next.

Felix rubs my back. "It's okay, Alyx. I know you had nothing to do with it."

"I'm sorry," I say. "If I'd have been here, maybe…"

Felix stops me. "Maybe you'd be dead, too." He looks down at the floor.

"Do you think they'll ever stop looking for the money Sasha stole?" I kick what remains of the glass jar that has coffee grounds in it. "Or will I have to hire someone to keep cleaning up after them?"

"She took over one-hundred-thousand dollars. They're going to do their best to find it." Felix looks away. "They won't find it though." He shrugs.

"Why do you say that?"

Felix reaches around to his back. His hands go under his jacket and then reappear with a small bag in them. "Because Ana found it and hid it." His brow goes high.

"Holy fuck, Felix. You're going to get us killed!" I push past him and go into my room.

"Alyx." He comes after me. "You're not going to die."

"How can you be so sure?" I turn on him. "You've got stolen money in your hands, and you've shown it to me. When they find out that I knew about it, I'm as good as dead." My body shakes.

Everything I've tried so hard to hold onto is splintering. Everything almost shattered with Corwin last night, but now, I'm not sure I can keep it together. I need to get my brother to safety. I need to. I take a deep breath and hold it. Felix begins to speak but I block everything out. I listen to my breath.

In.

Out.

In.

Out.

The breath unwilling drags from my body. When I open my eyes Felix's hands are on my shoulders. He's so close, concern on his face. "I'm sorry, Alyx. I don't want to scare you. I didn't mean to. I understand how you could be scared. But I have to tell you. *You* are in no danger."

"How can you *know* that?" I ask him, keeping myself calm by focusing on the air in my lungs.

"Fitzroy, *fancies* you. More than anyone else." Felix's head bobs up and down. Assuring me that what he says is true. "He told me before he left, that I was to cancel all of your appointments until further notice. That while you were with him, no one else was allowed to touch you." He looks at his own hands and then drops them from my shoulders.

"So, you're scared enough of Fitzroy to not touch me, even when he isn't around, but *I'll* be, okay?" I say baffled.

"Trust me, he wants to keep you around." Felix clears his throat. "I'm trying to make sure my mission gets accomplished. Collin already pissed Fitzroy off, I don't want to add to his frustration. Besides," his head cocks to the side, "maybe he'll put Collin on newbie duty and take me with him to The Island, then I can finish what Ana started."

"That's why he wants me to get the bathing suits?"

Felix's brow shoots up. "What do you mean?"

"He told me I had to go shopping to get several different colors of bathing suits. That I needed to pack a bag for a weeklong stay. I assume that means he's taking me to The Island, too." I rub my neck. "I inadvertently invited myself while asking Collin about Ana."

"Did he ask you to get a green one?" Felix clenches his jaw.

"No, he told me other girls would have green, but that I wouldn't need anything green."

Felix takes a deep breath and blows it out.

"Why?" I ask as I make him look me in the eye. "Why is green bad?" I know by the look on his face that it isn't a color I want to be associated with.

"Those who wear green on The Island," he swallows hard. "They're for sale." His eyes bore into me.

"How do you know that?" I was sold once to Estelle. Being sold means you get a new handler. Doesn't it? Fitzroy wanted to keep me close though. I'm not sure if I should be upset by that or not. At least I know how to distract him.

"Ruby," is all he says.

We stare at each other for a few moments. I nod and go over to my vanity to finish getting ready. "We need to go shopping."

"I'll go clean up while you get ready." Felix pauses as he exits the room. He puts his hand on the doorframe. I look at him in my mirror. "Don't even pack green undergarments, okay? Like, nothing green. No eyeshadow, lipstick, socks… nothing!" His head bobs up and down.

I nod and get back to my makeup.

"Neman Marcus, okay?" Felix asks as he opens the car door for me.

"Of course," I say as I get out. Felix doesn't even offer me a hand to exit. He's on edge more than he even realizes. "I'll be inside." I look at him and he nods.

After I'm inside the building I look back. Felix gets into the driver seat and drives away. He'll be inside following me after he parks. We are never allowed to be alone while out and about for too long. Felix may be planning on stealing money and one girl from Fitzroy's Island, but he knows how to stay off the radar.

Just like I do.

SHOPPING

I find everything except for the red bikini top that Fitzroy requires. I decide to try the women's section since there aren't any in the junior's area. The glass walls along the escalator always serve me well. In the time that I've been in New York, I've never left this store without a new client.

That always makes Estelle happy.

With Fitzroy saying I'm off limits to anyone else; it makes the ride up easier. I don't have to look longingly at the men who bend down as they ride past me—their gaze drifting under my skirt as I go up and they go down. I'm not for sale today.

It's oddly freeing.

Felix hasn't found me, but maybe he knows I don't need him for this. Shopping I'm good at. I find the bathing suits and a display with red tops. I exhale sharply and look for one that's skimpy enough to please Fitzroy's taste.

"Can I help you with that Ms.," a voice calls from behind me.

I turn my head without looking at them, "No, thank you." I go back to my shopping.

"Are you certain I couldn't interest you in anything else?" The woman says again and clears her throat.

I look back at her and try to hide my shock. The woman wears a zip-up hoodie, and her blonde hair is in a ponytail. I take a step back. It's Agent Shwetz. I glance around. Where is Felix? "Umm, do I know you?" I arch a brow. "You look familiar to me for some reason." I pretend to still be shopping. If I need to, I can go to the checkout and leave. I grab a red top with tiny triangles that will only cover my nipples. I have everything I need.

"Ma'am," Shwetz says. "I know you are in a predicament. I can assist if you'd like." She looks over her shoulder. I can't tell if she is looking at another agent, or if she's making sure the coast is still clear.

How long has she been watching me? Had Corwin fucked everything up and called her? "I am in no such predicament thank you." I pass her and head for the escalators.

"Ms. Beck, please," she says.

How does she know my name? How am *I* going to

get out of this? "Listen, I don't know what anyone told you, but my roommate is gone. I'm not sure when she'll be back. If you could not follow me around looking for her because I have no idea where she is." I step onto the moving stairs. She follows me.

"Alyx, I know more than you think I do. I can help you. You don't want to go wherever he's taking you."

"Where *who* is taking me?" I lean to the side. I glance at her over my shoulder but turn away at once.

"I'm not sure. I know he's male. I know he's in charge. Though, that's all the information I have."

I step off the stairs and walk at a brisk pace toward the counter. The agent grabs a scarf from a display and follows after me. Feigning that she too is shopping. "I'd appreciate it if you stopped stalking me. I'd hate to have to call security." If Agent Shwetz is having to lie about being in line, then she doesn't want anyone to know what she's doing either. A threat might get her to back off.

"Sasha didn't have time to tell Agent Hedley his name," Shwetz says in a low tone. She meant that information to be mine alone.

I play her words over again in my head. Hedley had been the name of Sasha's 'boyfriend' from the newscast. I straighten my shoulders and move up a few paces in the long line. It seems even the news lies around here.

"Dorian hasn't reported in since his last conversation with Sasha. Sasha was supposed to meet him at the river after she dropped off her trackers."

Collin had said that people drown in rivers every day. I suppose that's where Collin found Hedley. Fuck, what will Fitzroy do when he finds out that Sasha had been working with the FBI. For that matter, why had Sasha been working with them?

The agent is so close to me I can feel her breath. "Like the trackers in your ears."

It's my turn with the cashier. I ignore the agent's words about my earrings and step forward. If she wants to, she can arrest me. There must be a reason she hasn't done that yet. I just don't know what it is.

"How are you today, Ms.?" the cashier asks.

"Fine, thank you." I set my things on the counter. Shwetz doesn't say anything while I complete my purchase. She peruses the items sitting near the register. Shwetz isn't as good at blending in as she thinks she is.

I pay with the cash Fitzroy gave me, take the bag, and walk away.

"Oh, dear, this is the wrong one, sorry to waste your time," Shwetz says from behind me, and her shoes click against the tiles as she speeds away from the checkout.

I exit the store. Felix is nowhere to be seen. I need to get his damn number in my phone. Perhaps I can get it and tell Estelle it's necessary while I go shopping.

Since Fitzroy trusts Felix more than Collin it should be okay. *I hope.*

The store's doors open and close behind me. "There you are," comes a brisk voice.

I turn expecting Shwetz, but it's Felix. "Fuck, where have you been? That damn Agent found me and wouldn't leave me alone."

Felix's eyebrow tightens. "Agent?" he asks.

"Same one who came looking for Sasha yesterday." I grind my teeth. "Where's the damn car?"

Felix inclines his head over his shoulder. "Come with me." He puts out his hand, then pulls it back. He's not allowed to touch me, he hasn't forgotten. He lifts it so that he can place his hand behind me, without touching me.

I walk alongside Felix while he leads me to the car. I'm happy the windows are tinted close to black. At least Shwetz won't find me inside. Felix takes my bag then opens the door for me to slide into the back seat. I stare past Felix hoping she hasn't followed us. I see no one.

Felix closes the trunk, but instead of getting in the front, the back door opens.

"Excuse me," the voice startles me.

I turn to see Agent Shwetz getting in the back seat.

"What in the actual fuck. Are you trying to get me killed?" I say, pissed.

Her brow shoots up. "Who is trying to kill you, Alyx?"

Fucking, fucking, fucking, *Fuck*! There are so many things I can handle, but why my grip has been loosening so much can only be explained by my stress. I need some damn weed or some molly to calm me the fuck down. I have to stop speaking out of turn or I'll get myself and my brother killed.

I look around. Felix is behind the car, the other agent is holding him. Keeping him from getting in.

"No one," I answer her. "Could you please leave me alone. I have places to be. My driver has nothing to do with any of this. I don't know where Sasha is." It isn't a lie. I don't know physically where she is. I can't give the agent an address. If she is in fact an agent and not someone who works for Fitzroy. He has been testing me a lot lately. I have an idea that Sasha is with some cannibals. Sempers is the closest thing to where I know to look, but that's it. Why would I give that information to some random stranger?

"Listen, Sasha and Ana—they're working with us. If you could help us, too." The Agent stares at me.

"If they're all working with you, ask them," I say. I'm not going to risk my brother's life. If these agents were any good at keeping people alive, Sasha and Ana wouldn't be on a cannibal's table right now.

"I thought it would be best if I asked you away

from prying eyes. Which is why we're here. Dark windows, no one can see." The agent motions her hand around. "Felix chose a good spot so we could talk."

I clench my jaw. "Felix? What are you talking about?" Has Felix involved himself in this, too? "What makes you think I'm going to talk to you?"

"Felix parked in a good spot. That's all I meant. I know you cared for Ana. Sasha told us you did."

"Care*d* for?" I question her use of the past tense. Maybe Felix doesn't have anything to do with anything. I can't tell if the agent is trying to trip me up or what.

"Don't play coy, Alyx. I know you are aware that Ana is also missing."

So, the agents don't know she's dead. "I have different drivers quite often. How would I be aware of anything?" I say. "Can you please leave now?"

Felix knocks on the window. "Get the fuck out of the car ma'am," he says.

The Agent turns and looks behind the car. Her partner is on his phone, no longer holding on to Felix. Payton—I think his name is—heads for the front door. "Listen Alyx," she begins. "I know you know this is a dangerous game you're playing. I can't keep you safe if you don't help me out."

"Like you kept Sasha and Ana safe?" I stare. "Seeing that they are *both* missing now." I make sure to not give away anything with my expression. I can't let the images of their bodies... *no stop*.

"They are missing because they refused to listen to me. If you girls would listen to me, no one would be missing. Not even Hedley." Shwetz stares me down.

The front doors open, and Felix and Payton get in.

"What the fuck, Felix," I say as he turns toward me. I motion to the agents and stare at Felix. At least Corwin wasn't the one who called.

Felix stares back at me confused. His head tilts. "They cornered me when you got in, Alyx." He smacks the steering wheel.

I look down at my feet.

"Shwetz," Payton says. "They found Hedley."

"Where?" her word rushes out. "Did he get Sasha out?"

"No. They *found* him," he swallows hard. "His body washed up onto some rocks near Craig Road."

"On Governors Island?" Disbelief fills her tone.

Payton nods.

"Then the girls are dead, too." Shwetz says. She punches the back of the driver's seat.

Felix's body bounces forward from her outburst. "Could you not?"

I sit in silence. I can't risk my brother's life. I don't want to risk my own. I hate that this risks Felix's life, too.

Felix's phone buzzes. He takes it from his pocket. "Who lives in apartment 3D in the building next to yours, Alyx?" he asks as he rubs his neck.

Holy shit. That's Trent's apartment. "What?" I stare forward not really seeing anything.

"Your *friend* texted. Said you gave…" Felix takes note of the two agents in the car before he continues. "*Gramps* a weird address. See," he turns his phone. I'm glad he didn't use Corwin's name.

I want to smack myself. Last night, I texted Corwin from *my* cell. The cell where Estelle reads the texts. The text had given my brother's address because I didn't want Becca's things near Estelle. I'm so bad at protecting others. Tears fall down my cheeks. Another text comes through. Felix's phone is no longer in my line of sight. "What does it say?" My tone is as defeated as I feel.

"They're," Felix doesn't use any pronouns that will give anything away, "going to send R and D. They think you have a secret boyfriend like Sasha did. Some newscast has been playing on repeat," Felix says. "Alyx, if you're finished with your friends, I think they should leave."

"My friends?" I huff. "I didn't invite them here."

"Why won't you tell us, Felix? Say the handler's name," Agent Shwetz says.

"Agent Payton here,"—Felix waves a hand toward

the agent sitting in the front— "said that Ana spoke to you about getting someone safe. When they're safe, maybe I'll tell you what she wouldn't," he says. "Safe like you promised, *Ana.*"

I know he means Everleigh, but Felix doesn't seem to trust these two anymore than I do. The agents must've been watching me to have caught up to us while we shopped.

"We can get them to safety, if you tell us," Payton chimes in.

"You want to take the big man down, that's all you care about," Felix's brow furrows. "Someone else will replace him in an instant." He snaps his fingers. "Until they're safe, you get nothing."

"Why are you helping them at all?" I question Felix.

"I wasn't. They told me that *you*, Ana, and Sasha were." Felix locks his phone.

"I don't even know these people, Felix." I glare while my jaw tightens.

"What the fuck!" Felix stares at the agents. "You said Alyx was helping you."

"No, I stated that Ana, and Sasha were." Agent Shwetz shifts in her seat.

"Get the fuck out," Felix hisses as his gaze flares.

"It's not my fault that you made assumptions, Felix. If you want the same person safe that Ana wants safe, you've got to help us. Fucking give us something to work with," Shwetz says.

"Why would I help you if you think m… Ana is dead." Felix points to the doors. "For the last time, get the fuck out." He waves a hand toward the doors. Maybe the agents don't know Ana is…was… Felix's sister.

Agent Shwetz puts her hand on the door handle but turns back to me as Payton exits. "Listen, I know you don't know me from Adam, but I can help. I've been working this case for years. I've saved a fair share of people. But I'd love to save all of you." Her gaze is fixed on me. "You have no reason to trust me, but it seems as though your brother might be in need of some help. If that is in fact who lives in 3D. I can help, Alyx."

I stare back. How does she know about Trent? My head tilts to the side. Of course, she's with the FBI. Maybe they know a lot about me that I've never shared with anyone else. They probably know a lot about Felix, too. I'm glad that Trent isn't at his apartment. I'd be worried if he were.

"Fine," Shwetz scoffs. "We have a line set up. It's untraceable. It won't even show up as dialed from any phone you call from. It won't show up on a phone bill. One hundred percent *untraceable*! Dial 5212 and press the star key, from any phone. It will lead you directly to me. It will also signal me to your exact location. Repeat it back, both of you," the agent requests in a harsh tone.

"5212 star," we both reply.

The agent gets out of the car.

"Felix, what the fuck?" I say as the agents walk away.

"I had no idea, Alyx. I'm sorry. I thought..." He looks down for a moment. Felix starts the car and backs out of the parking space. "Ana started it. I thought I might need their help to get Everleigh. I haven't determined if they're useful yet," he says.

"Why bring me into it?"

Felix turns right out of the garage and heads back toward my apartment. "They asked me about you directly while I put your bags in the trunk. They said they'd been to your apartment before. I assumed you must be talking with them, too. I figured out that you weren't after I got inside the car."

"Fitzroy will kill both of us when he finds out," I say.

"Then don't tell him." Felix looks at me in the rearview mirror.

I clench my jaw.

TROUBLE

Felix carries my bags up to the apartment. I set the bags on my bed and then decide I need to go to Trent's. I use the disposable phone to text my brother. I tell him to stay at the hotel a while longer. He's reluctant but agrees. It won't be long before he gets frustrated and goes home to get his laptop. I purse my lips while trying to think of a way to get him safe.

I hide the phone under my mattress then go into the kitchen. "Felix."

Felix is sweeping up Collin's earlier mess while trying to fight frustration of his own. "What?" he asks as I come into the room.

"I need you to come with me. Don't ask me any questions. But come."

Felix drops the broom and motions for me to go.

I run down the hall to the emergency doors. Felix

behind me the entire way. When I get to my brother's apartment Felix follows me inside and closes the door, locking it behind him. He'd seen the number on the door, he knows where we are. "Find any kind of electronic and put it in this box." I tip out a box full of old DVDs that my brother watches over and over.

Felix moves swiftly around the apartment while I head to my brother's bedroom. I grab the things I know he can't function without. His laptop, headphones, backup drive, and his light blocking glasses. He may be a computer nerd, but he protects his vision. I reach under the bed and grab the box I stashed there when he moved in. It's covered in dust.

It's all we have left of our parents. Their wedding rings, and a family photo. I don't open it; I know by the weight of the box that everything is still inside. I pull open Trent's dresser drawer and pull the envelope I taped there—months ago—free.

This envelope has ten credit cards inside. Almost $80,000 worth. I've been stashing my bonuses as often as I can. I spread it out on different cards hoping that we'd have enough if I ever got fired or if Trent ever needed any kind of medical procedure. Of course, that was before I knew that getting fired meant you ended up on someone's plate.

I double check the rest of the apartment. I think we have everything Trent needs. Besides clothes. But he can buy more of those. Trent will have to go on a Walmart run to get the comfortable clothes he likes. I put everything inside the box. Felix did a good job finding various gaming devices, and games. The box is full by the time I add my load to it. I write Princess Heidi on the side of the box. Trent will understand.

"Take this to the basement of this building. Put it out of the way, but somewhere noticeable."

Felix nods and leaves.

I set about cleaning up Trent's place. I already know what I'll say to Estelle. 'My brother moved.' 'How wonderful!' she'll say in return. She'll get on me for texting Corwin. I'll have to say he insisted, but that I didn't want him to have *my* address. That I hadn't thought quickly enough on my feet to send the items elsewhere. I'll explain that I'd let myself get too close to Corwin.

This bit of truth might protect me from her anger.

There is a rapping at the door. I look through the peephole. Ruby and Deidra have arrived. "Ruby." I'm cheerful as I open the door. "What a wonderful surprise!" I hug her as they both come inside.

Deidra moves past me and begins checking the apartment. She's eager to please Estelle. I've been eager to please her before—I know what it looks like. I also know what it feels like. If I please my handler, I might eat tonight. I might bathe tonight. I might be able to sleep in a bed instead of on the floor. Starting out is hard on every girl or boy who works for a new handler. But when you need Estelle, it works in Estelle's favor, not yours.

"Chick," Ruby hangs on the word as Deidra goes into Trent's room. "What is this place?" Her voice carries just enough. She wants Deidra to hear everything. Her stare gives her real question away. 'Are you insane? You can't keep a secret from Estelle.'

I nod. "Oh, my brother moved to town." I motion a hand around the room. "He surprised me." I laugh loud enough that Deidra overhears.

Felix comes back inside the apartment. He looks from me to Ruby. We both nod our heads down the hall. Felix's head bobs up once and then he goes to the fridge. Pretending that he's been here before. Like it's no big deal at all. Felix is smarter than I give him credit for. "Want a drink, Ruby?" he asks.

"Sure, whatcha got?" Ruby takes a seat at the bar.

I follow next to her and sit down, too. Deidra must've gotten the information she wanted because as she returns, she's texting Estelle I assume.

"Mountain Dew." Felix sets two drinks on the counter. "Oh, hey, Deidra. Want a drink?"

Deidra glances at Felix then walks over to the window. "No, Estelle will be up in a minute. I don't need any extra calories."

Ruby pushes her soda back across the counter. "Water?"

Felix gives a half smile and returns the drinks to the fridge and replaces them with waters. I look at Felix and blow out a breath. His brow pulls together. He understands I want something, but he doesn't know what yet. I look at Deidra. Felix nods.

"Deidra, why don't you come with me. We can wait for everyone at Alyx's. No need to be in the way." He puts his arm out for her to grab ahold of.

Deidra nods and takes his arm. She looks more scared than anything. "Perhaps, Estelle could take care of Alyx better if there were no one else here." Deidra leaves with Felix.

"Alyx," Ruby says in a rush. "Do you know where Ana is? She was supposed to call me. She hasn't checked in. I'm worried." I look down at my feet. "Fuck!" Ruby pounds her fist against the counter. "Did they find out what she was doing?"

"I have no idea."

"We were almost all ready to go, too." Her head shakes. "Is this your brother's place?"

I nod.

"Guess I'll be headed back to The Island, then." Ruby's shoulders fall.

"I'm sorry I don't know more." I rub her back.

"It's okay. I'll figure something else out." Ruby

smiles at me. She opens her water and takes a drink. Someone knocks on the door and Ruby starts laughing. "Oh, Jesus, Alyx, you're so funny," she says loudly as she gets up to answer the door.

Ruby looks at me and nods her head a few times. I catch the message. I chuckle loud enough to be heard through the other side of the door. "Only when I'm with you Rubes," I say as she opens the door.

Estelle comes inside the apartment. She's wearing a white pantsuit. Her gold earrings are so long they drape over her shoulders. Sunglasses push her hair back and the scowl on her face lets me know she's upset with me.

Luckily, I expected this. "Estelle," I'm zealous as I say her name. "What a pleasure."

"Stop it, cow," Estelle hisses. "You'll need to explain yourself." She looks around the apartment. Holding her arms close to herself like she's afraid if she touches anything she'll get a disease. Her nose curls up in disgust. This is no luxury apartment.

"Oh," I say with a smile. "My brother moved up here. Isn't that great!" Ruby smiles and bobs her head. "He surprised me."

"Where is he then?" Estelle's head tilts to look down the hall.

"Oh, he had to go get more stuff from the storage facility. He shipped everything to the wrong place." I laugh.

"New York is difficult to understand if you've never lived here before." Ruby joins in on my laughter. Assisting me with my lies. Whether she knows that she's assisting in lies or not, I'm glad she does it so well.

"Ruby, please retire to another room," Estelle says.

Ruby gets up without another word and goes into Trent's bedroom.

Estelle snaps her finger and then points downward.

I jump up and take my place in front of her. Estelle is a few inches taller than I am, I know not to look up. She wants her girls to be less than her. We aren't allowed to look at her when she's angry, not until she tells us otherwise.

"To your knees, cow," she says through her teeth.

I obey and get down.

"All fours, now!" She stamps her foot.

I do as I am told and put my hands on the floor, too.

"I don't know if you've forgotten because I've been so good to you, but Alyx." Estelle places her foot on top of my hand. I don't pull away. If I try to pull away her heel will tear into my skin. "You are not allowed to keep things from me and then give the information to your clients." Her heel presses firmer into my hand. She hasn't put her weight behind it yet.

"I'm sorry, Estelle. I didn't know." I lie again.

"You knew enough to give Corwin this address." Her heel digs further into me.

I try not to clench my teeth, but her heels are sharp. It hurts. "Only because I didn't want to give him *my* address."

"Why on earth would you do that?" She twists her foot.

I concentrate on my breath, not the pain. "I helped him pack, remember? He wanted to send me some of the stuff he wasn't going to donate." Estelle's foot twists back so that my skin is no longer pulled. "He insisted that I text him right then. I knew that if I did as I was told that he'd ask me to bed. You know how well I read men." Estelle grabs my hair and yanks my head back.

Her eyes shift between mine rapidly, looking for the lie. She moves her foot and uses my hair to get me to a standing position. "Corwin did text me and ask if it would be okay if you came to his house for dinner, instead of going out. Do you believe this is him trying to find a way for you to come over again?"

"He enjoyed himself a great deal, I would assume that is what that means." Estelle slaps me so hard that I fall down.

"You should assume nothing, cunt," she hisses at me then kicks me in the ribs.

"I'm sorry." I lay on the floor. I know better than to try to get away from her—that will make things worse.

"Get up, fucking *cow.*" Estelle looks at her nails. She's checking to see if she's damaged any when she hit me. If she did, I'll be in for another hit.

I stand. Estelle finishes checking her nails. They must be free of damage because she doesn't strike me again.

"You'll go see him tomorrow," Estelle sneers at me.

"I can't do that," I say. "Fitzroy…"

Estelle strikes me on my right cheek. My head flings so hard to the side I'll need to check to make sure I don't have any loose teeth later. She'd used her left hand to see if she could damage any of those nails. I know Estelle as well as I do my *J*ohns. Her breathing picks up. Estelle gets off on dominating her girls. "How dare you speak for Fitzroy!"

"I'm not trying to do that. I'm explaining that Fitzroy told me I couldn't earlier today," I say as I turn toward her. Both of my cheeks are on fire.

"When did you see Fitzroy?" Estelle's brow furrows.

Holy shit. He hadn't told her he was at my apartment today. Estelle always shoves it in our faces that Fitzroy tells her everything. That has been a lie of its own. "He was at my apartment when I arrived home from Corwin's."

Felix comes into the apartment. "Fitzroy would like you to come to Alyx's," he says looking to Estelle.

Estelle nods and shoos Felix away. "Ruby," she calls.

Ruby comes out of my brother's room. "Yes," she says.

"I would like you to stay here and wait for Alyx's brother to arrive. He deserves to be welcomed to the city." Estelle gives me a wry smile.

I offer her no response.

"Certainly," Ruby says, pulling Estelle's gaze away. "I'll let you know when he's been welcomed." Ruby laughs.

Estelle wraps her arms around Ruby, hugging her. This is Estelle letting me know that I am no longer her favorite. I got a pay cut. Ruby looks at me and mouths 'don't worry, I won't touch your brother.'

I nod.

Estelle lets go of Ruby. "Lead the way, Alyx." She waves a hand for me to leave the apartment.

Felix is outside the door. We walk in silence other than Estelle's heels clicking as she walks.

Felix opens the door and I walk in first. Fitzroy stands next to the door to the balcony. He turns as we come in. His head shifts to the side. Felix snaps a finger at Deidra telling her to exit the apartment. She gets up from the sofa and walks out. I glide over to Fitzroy. I know my face is still red from where Estelle slapped me because my cheeks still burn.

Estelle comes inside and Felix closes the door, staying outside the apartment.

Fitzroy wraps an arm around my shoulder and then puts a hand under my chin. "Alyx, what is it?" His question is sincere. When I don't look, he curls a finger and pulls my eyes to meet his. Anger flares as he takes in the redness of my cheeks. "Who did this to *my* girl?" His gaze is fierce. "Who *touched* you?"

I can do two things with my answer. Appease Estelle, and Fitzroy at the same time. "I wouldn't want to get anyone into trouble, *U*ncle. I'm fine. I made a mistake. It's okay."

"Alyx." Fitzroy shakes his head. "What did I tell you before I left?"

"That no one was to touch me," I answer.

Estelle gasps so low that I'm not entirely sure that I've heard it.

"Did you allow this person to touch you?" He looks in Estelle's direction before looking back to me. "Or did they do this of their own accord?"

I look back. "I'd rather not say, if that's okay." I let my hand wrap around his back. Seeking shelter in his arms. At least that's how he'll take it.

"Alyx, my love," Fitzroy says. I try to hide the absolute shock. He's never used that word around me before. *Love.*

"Yes," I smile.

"Please, go to your room. Finish your packing.

Don't come out. I'll be in to get you soon. Understand?" His hand rubs my back.

"Yes, *U*ncle," I say.

He leans down, kisses my forehead, then gently
pushes me away from him. Telling me to leave.

I do as I am told and *walk* to my room. I close the
door. The screaming begins as Fitzroy lays into Estelle
for touching his property. I run to my mattress and
retrieve my burner phone.

*"Corwin, I have no time. This is Alyx, please go to The
Franklin on 87th, ask for Trent Beck. When he comes
down tell him that Alyx sent you to get him. Use the word,
Princess Heidi. That's our family's secret word. He'll know I
sent you. There is a box in the basement of the address I
gave you yesterday. It has his important things in it. Please
don't let him come back to the building but please have
someone get it. Please keep him safe! I can't tell you more.
Only that I'll be gone for a while. Please, please, keep him
safe!"* I click send.

I pull up a fresh message. *"Trent, I love you. Princess
Heidi is coming for you. Go with him! He'll keep you safe."*

The phone alerts me to a text. I click it. Corwin has
written back. *"Alyx, are you safe? I'll get your brother. I
promise."*

I delete the messages. I don't have time to text him
back. I turn the phone off because the screaming stops.
I don't have time to hide it, so I throw the phone inside

my makeup bag. In a hurry I toss my makeup bag and some clothes in a duffle bag. I grab my purchases from earlier and shove those inside, too.

My bedroom door opens as I look over the dresses in my closet. I look over and Estelle has some red marks on her own face this time. Her sunglasses are no longer on top of her head and one of her long earrings is missing, too.

"Alyx, dear," her voice wobbles. "I'd like to apologize for my outburst. I understand that Fitzroy had you under orders. It was not my right to know them. He has reclaimed you. Do you forgive me?"

Part of me, the part that has been hit more times that I can count, wants to say no. I want to condemn her to the fate she's brought upon herself. The other part of me, the part that sometimes thinks of Estelle as a protector, as another mother, wants to free her of any punishment. I'm not sure which side will win.

Fitzroy pushes Estelle into my room. She's in his way. He tilts his head in her direction.

"Do you forgive me?" Her eyes beg me to agree.

I take a minute to decide, glancing up at Fitzroy then back to Estelle. "Of course, *Auntie*." I use her official title now that she's no longer my handler. I don't want anyone's blood on my hands.

Not even hers.

"That was easy, was it not, Estelle," Fitzroy says.

Estelle bows her head.

"Now, get the fuck out of here. I don't want to see your face anymore. You're not welcome at The Island this month, either."

Estelle nods her head but doesn't speak. She turns and leaves.

"Are you about ready?" Fitzroy comes toward me. His gaze expecting.

"Just about," I smile. "Will I need any dresses?" I turn a hand palm up showing off my clothes.

"Only for my pleasure. You'll be mostly undressed on The Island." He licks his lips. "I can't wait for that."

"I shall select your favorite colors." I grab black and red items from my closet.

"That will be fine." He slides out of his jacket. "But before all that…" He looks at me. "I'll need you to bounce up and down on me a few times." He winks at me and undresses. He lays back on the bed. "Take off your panties. Leave the rest of your clothes on." His member stands to attention.

I do as I am told and mount him.

BRACELETS

Fitzroy smacks my ass. "Thank you for that lovely bounce." He wipes himself clean with a wet-wipe. He reaches out a hand for me to take it when he's finished. I take the cloth and toss it in the little bin next to my bed. He stands up and redresses. "I'm going to go down now." He slides his shirt back on. "You take a little time. Come down when you're properly dressed." He bounces up and down while he pulls his pants up. Buckling his belt, he says, "also, Alyx." He waves a hand for me to come and stand by him.

I grab his suit jacket from the chair while I do as I'm bid.

"The Island," he bobs his head side to side, "it's a bit different than the parties you are used to. I want you to know that while you are there, you are still mine." He puts a hand under my chin. "I want you to wear this."

He pulls something from his suit jacket pocket that's still draped over my arm. "This will show others that you are spoken for, by an *U*ncle. I will not be the only *U*ncle there. However, red is my color. Therefore, it shows that you are *my* girl. This is the only bracelet you wear. Do you understand, my Alyx?" He slides the metal bracelet onto my left wrist. Locking it closed with a screw.

Bracelet colors are how people are marked at events. Red is a new color though. I nod my head then look into his eyes. "Yes, *U*ncle. Thank you so much." How many others would be there? "May I ask a question?" I twist the metal on my wrist, admiring it. Hopefully the look in my eye is happiness at being claimed.

"Yes, my Alyx," Fitzroy puts a finger under my chin, pulling my eyes back to his.

"Will there be *F*athers, *B*rothers, and *G*randpas there?" The hierarchy starts with *U*ncles, then works its way down. Beneath the ones I'd mentioned were *B*oyfriend and *C*ousin. After that the *C*ousins were numbered. *S*econd, *T*hird, and so on. Girls are allowed to deny anyone who has a number before their title. I'll need to be diligent about watching for their peach-colored bracelets. Just like at all the summer parties in Florida. I don't need to worry about the female titles, *A*unt, *M*other, *S*ister, *G*randma, because women in the hierarchy aren't allowed at *these* events.

"Dear," *U*ncle pushes my hair behind my ear, "everyone who's paid the price to be at this *exclusive* event will be there." He arches a brow at me. "But you... are off the menu." He wraps his arms around me and hugs me. "You are my prize," he whispers the words into my hair as he lays his head against mine. The words were not meant for me to hear though.

I nuzzle against his chest. I can*not* falter.

Fitzroy pulls away from me. He smiles. "Make an entrance, in say, ten?" he asks.

"Of course," I smile.

He leaves the apartment and I go to Sasha's... *no...* the spare bedroom.

Collin had given it a once over. The mattress is no longer on the bed. Every dresser drawer is open. The clothes are flung out of the closet. I walk into the *spare* bathroom. Looking for the pill bag with golden sequins.

My old driver—I wanted to curse myself for not using her name now that I've mastered not doing it— *they* had a bag. The bag held emergency supplies for women in my line of work. I find the bag underneath a pile of towels that Collin had thrown into the floor. I open it to find there are indeed a few plan B pills. I take one.

This is the second one in two days. If the week continues like these past couple of days, I'll need to ask the girls on The Island if they have any there. I'm on the pill. Every girl is, but I can't be too careful when it comes to getting pregnant.

I take the golden bag back to my room to get dressed. Fitzroy wants an entrance—so I have to look amazing. I put on my black lace strapless bra and lacey panties. Find my black ruched one shoulder mindress with long sleeves, and my Gianvito Rossi Slingback pumps in tabasco red.

After looking myself over in the mirror I put my hair up in a loose bun. I look ready for a night on the town. Though I feel like I need to sleep for a week. When is the last time I slept? I can't even recall.

I grab my bag and head for the waiting limo.

Felix is in the foyer of the building. He's waiting to take the duffle-bag from me. He knows Fitzroy wants to watch me. *Uncle* always likes to watch other people eye his girls. "You, okay?" Felix asks as he takes the bag.

"Of course," I say. I don't have another option. I have to be okay. I hesitate at the door. Happy that I'm out of sight of the waiting limo.

"Those things that Corwin gave you," Felix says. Estelle must have told him. "Were there a set of tracker earrings with them?"

I stare at him and decide a nod is the best response.

"I got an alert on my phone that night. I didn't respond to it because I know that girl isn't in *service* anymore." Felix rubs his neck. "Do you have them now?"

"Yes," I reply. "They're in my bag." I hold up my black evening bag.

"No one else has access to those trackers, besides me. Keep them on you, okay?" Felix's brow pulls together.

"I thought you said I wasn't in danger." I run my hands along the front of my dress, straightening it. If anyone sees me, they'll decide I'm making sure I'm ready for the show I have to put on.

"I don't think you are, but at least this way, I'll be able to find you—*if* anything happens."

"Aren't you coming to The Island, too?" I've never had Felix around much. He is always with Fitzroy. I've been with Estelle for a while now, but for some reason, it seems that it will be easier with Felix around and not Collin.

"Yes," Felix says. "I'll be there." He nods and looks down at my duffel bag in his hands.

"I'll do this, then," I say as I reach up and take my right earring out. I open my clutch and pull one of Becca's earrings out. I place mine inside a small wallet pouch, so I'll know which is which. I put one of Becca's on. "How's that?" I ask as Felix watches me finish putting the back on.

"Don't forget which is which." Felix points between

the two earrings. "Right will make sure I get the message. Left will mean every bodyguard on The Island does." His brow arches high. "Which means *U*ncle will come along with any alert. He's ordered everyone to keep a close eye on you. *Everyone.*"

I nod and exit the building.

Felix comes around me and opens the limo door. I thank him and slide into the back seat. Deidra is nearest the driver's window, while Estelle is across from her. Fitzroy sits in the back, staring at me like the others don't exist.

He strokes a finger down my bare neck. Fitzroy always likes my hair up. "You look lovely, as always, Alyx."

"Thank you, *U*ncle," I smile sweetly.

Estelle shifts in her seat but doesn't look back at me. If Fitzroy ever decides to send me back to her, I'm going to be in a world of hurt.

The window partition comes down. Collin is in the driver's seat. "Where too boss?"

Felix slides into the passenger seat. I take note of Collin's busted lip and black eye.

"Heliport," Fitzroy says, not looking away from me.

The partition rolls up and we set off. Leaving Ruby behind at my brother's place. Fuck, what will happen to Ruby when Trent never shows up? I bite the inside of my cheek.

"Are you worried?" Fitzroy asks me.

I give him a soft smile. "No, it's just new," I say.

"You'll love The Island." He pulls me closer. "It's always warm. Especially at night." He slides his arm around my waist. "Down by the water, it's dark, hidden." He nuzzles his nose into my neck. "I'm excited to," he holds onto his words until I meet his gaze, "show you around." Fitzroy kisses me.

I have to go along, but I'm not sure what to do. He's never kissed me like this, not in front of Estelle. I've always thought of them as, *together.* They are partners. Or so I thought. Estelle sits below Fitzroy on the hierarchy. Or she did before she hit *me.* Fitzroy's hand slides down and caresses my bottom while he kisses me. I follow suit and put my hands into his hair while Estelle's icy glare trails over me.

We arrive at the heliport. Felix gets out and grabs our bags. He sets them on a trolley. Fitzroy puts a one-hundred-dollar bill in the air, and a heliport employee appears and takes charge of the cart.

"Sir." Felix puts a hand on the trolley. "I thought I was coming along. I can handle the bags."

Fitzroy turns to Felix. He leans over and whispers something I don't hear into his ear. "I want you to bring Ruby, too. I know Estelle left her at the building, but I want you to go back for her. I'll tell the pilot to return after they drop Alyx and I off." Fitzroy's head bobs up and down.

"Of course, sir." Felix lets go of the cart.

Fitzroy speaks to the employee giving them the flight details. Felix looks at me, rubs his right ear— reminding me that he'll be watching for me— then he sighs, and gets into the limo.

Felix has access to my location. I'm not sure why it is necessary to remind me considering he will be along soon, but I am glad that someone's watching out for me.

Fitzroy grabs my hand. "You're going to love The Island." We follow behind the employee who pulls the trolley.

"I'm excited." I bounce up and down a bit while we walk. I need to show the proper enthusiasm.

The employee leads us to a helicopter, its name scrolled along its side in red letters. We don't have to wait in any lines. We don't have to show any paperwork. We get into the *Airbird* and Fitzroy buckles me in. After I'm strapped in, Fitzroy does the same. The employee hands him a small bag then secures our luggage.

"Alyx." Fitzroy pulls items from the bag.

I look around the helicopter. I know I'll need a headset, but I can't find one that is meant for me.

"The Island is secret," *U*ncle says as something pinches my thigh.

I look down and Fitzroy's hand is on a needle that is pressed into my left thigh. His thumb presses whatever medicine it holds into my leg. "Secrets must be kept at all costs." He removes the needle. How many times have those words echoed in my ears? "Perhaps one day you'll get to know." He smiles wide.

There is no hole in my dress, at least not that I can see. I yawn. This medicine works fas….

CHAPTER FIVE - THE ISLAND

THE ISLAND

———

My eyes open. Dark purple velvet drapes hang in long swags above my head. My mind hums, dizzy, out of focus. It's like the hangovers I used to get after a long night of smoking weed and doing pills with other girls at the manor.

I raise up onto my elbows. There are light purple sheers hanging between the heavier velvet curtains. My shoes and gown are gone. I'm wearing the stringy orange bathing suit that Fitzroy asked me to buy. I'm not sure who dressed me. I am alone in the room.

The walls are wooden, stained a dark color. More windows are covered by the same drapes that hang from the canopy above the bed. A glass of ice water is on the bedside table and a pill. A card next to it. "Take me and drink me." Written inside.

I do as I'm told.

A pair of tall heels are on the floor next to the bed. The heels are between six and eight inches. They seem an odd height. I've never seen these shoes before. There's another card. "Wear me." I put the heels on. Someone must have an obsession with Alice in Wonderland.

The room is surrounded on two sides with curtained windows. I walk over and pull the purple velvet back.

Sunlight flashes into the room. I squint and allow my vision to adjust before I peek outside.

There is ocean as far as the eye can see. There's no doubt that we're on an island. The large swimming pool has a lazy river that wraps around the island, beginning and ending in the pool. There are lots of coves to get lost in. Men are in many of the coves with girls and boys—who wear orange colored swimwear.

I know there are boys who do what I do, too. Estelle handles only girls though, so I don't know any personally.

On one of the many poolside lounge chairs a man is laid back. A woman stands over his face, no bottoms on, while two men are on their knees—one on either side of the man. The man, who is wearing dark blue striped socks, has one hand on each of the men's backs. He presses one hand, and one man goes down and sucks on the man's member, then the other. They are taking turns sucking him off. The man himself is tasting the woman while she stands over him.

The Island lives up to its reputation. Anything goes here.

"Alyx," Fitzroy's voice sounds from the door.

I turn to see him striding in. *U*ncle wears a purple terry cloth robe, open in the front. Purple tight speedo, and a purple rubber bracelet on his wrist. Anyone in the hierarchy wears one. Purple is the color for *U*ncles. He has sunglasses in his hair.

"Are you rested?" he asks as he strolls over to me.

I smile and meet him halfway. Wrapping my arms around him, grateful for this opportunity—as far as he's concerned. "Yes, thank you so much." I raise up on my tiptoes getting my mouth as close to his as possible. He needs to *know* that I want to be here. I have to ask for a kiss, to thank him. This is the only way to ask for a kiss.

Fitzroy puts a hand on the nape of my neck. He nuzzles his nose against mine and then kisses me deep and slow. Almost like he's longed to kiss me this way.

His behavior towards me has been so oddly gentle. I can't know what to expect. I still have a part to play though.

I press my body against his and move closer wrapping my arms around his neck. I must show my desire for him, thankfulness, and happiness for all he does for me. I moan against his lips.

He pulls away. Tracing my lips with his tongue as he finishes kissing me. "It's going to be a lovely week." He grabs my hand. "I'll take you on a mini tour. Ruby will show you around as soon as she wakes."

If Ruby is here, then Felix is, too. We leave the bedroom.

Turning right outside the door we go down a long hall. As we round a corner, one wall is nothing but windows. Showing off the pool and lazy river. "This is the fourth floor." Fitzroy stands in front of an elevator. "Only *U*ncles and their guests are allowed here." He flashes his bracelet at me. "Your bracelet and mine," he grabs my wrist and waves it in front of a digital screen on the wall, "will allow elevator access to *every* floor."

The doors open and we step on. "Third floor is for *F*athers, *B*rothers, and *G*randpas," Fitzroy says as we pass that floor. "The second is for all manner of *C*ousins." The number two appears on the elevator's screen as we pass it. "The first," the doors open, "is where all of the food is."

Many scents flood into my nose as we step off the elevator. Pineapple and coconut are the strongest. However, pepperoni pizza, chocolate chip cookies, and steak are also present. As we round the corner a huge buffet is set up. Men—as well as employees wearing orange like I am— are all helping themselves to food and drink.

Fitzroy looks down at me as we pass the table with fruit on it. "Want anything?"

I take a piece of pineapple and eat it. "Juicy." I allow a small dribble of the juice to go down the side of my mouth.

Why men like to watch girls drool is beyond me, but Fitzroy smiles and shifts his junk around in his speedo, so I know it worked. I need to keep him distracted on some level at all times.

He needs to think sex encompasses my thoughts.

"Let's go." He pulls me away from the food. "The pool," Fitzroy says as we walk out a set of open doors.

The smell of the ocean breeze is nice. It reminds me of the home I shared with my parents. Fitzroy pulls the sunglasses from his head and looks over at me while squinting against the sunlight. "Oh, here." He grabs a pair of sunglasses off a girl as she passes.

Her skin is olive in tone, her hair dark brown. She doesn't stop him. She doesn't even question him. She smiles, tilts her head, allowing him to take them, and walks away. She has a green bracelet on her wrist. Hers is rubber like Fitzroy's. The girl next to her, a pale girl with red hair, has a blue bracelet. The dark-haired girl is for sale, while the other is marked for use by *F*athers, *B*rothers, and *G*randpas.

Fitzroy puts the sunglasses on my face and smiles at me. We walk out to the patio. Some people are laughing and talking. Others are involved in various forms of sexual favors or intercourse. One girl bends over a table, a man with light brown skin behind her thrusting as his hands hold onto her hips.

"The world is mine, here," Fitzroy whispers into my ear. "I can't wait for the feast." He gives a wicked grin and pulls away from me. "Follow me, Alyx." He leads the way.

I walk behind him. Other girls walk behind other *U*ncles. Each *U*ncle wears a purple bracelet like Fitzroy's. None of the girls following behind them have a bracelet like mine. Fitzroy had said no one could touch me based on this bracelet. I twist it as I follow him. I don't see *any* on anyone else, so at least I can't be confused for them.

Walking down the stairs in tall heels doesn't bother me. One new Dolly struggles in her heels. New employees are always called Dollies; they wear the colored bracelets on their wrists, marking who can partake of them. The established employees like myself are Vixens. Vixens wear white ankle bracelets, too. Anyone can ask for our time. At least while at events like this one. The summer events are usually much smaller. A total of ten *J*ohns max. There are many, many more than that here.

The Dollies are easy to spot because of their wrist bracelets. This means that the *J*ohns have a bit of free reign. They are meant to be broken in—tamed.

I know the *J*ohns from the employees because each employee wears orange in some shade or variation. This is always the case on the first day of an event. It is the *W*elcoming. The Meet and Greet.

We pass by a group of men with blue rubber bracelets. The neon blues are *F*athers. The sapphire blues are *B*rothers. The baby blues are *G*randpas. These men have to spend great sums of money each week on sex. Jennson is one of my *B*rothers, spending six grand a week. While the sum of twelve thousand like Corwin gave me the other night—to protect me—is reserved for *F*athers. *G*randpas only have to fork over two grand a week to stay in the loop.

Staying in the loop means you are granted invitations to events like this. To accept the invitation there is another fee that has to be met. *F*athers have to pay twenty-five grand, *B*rothers eight grand, and *G*randpas two-point-five grand, to be allowed to attend.

*U*ncles never have to pay to attend the events, as they are the reason the events exist in the first place. They do, however, have to spend fifteen thousand a week on their inventory. Whether that be investing in new Dollies or keeping their current Vixens in mint condition. As long as money funnels into the business, *U*ncle's maintain their positions.

I don't know what happens to *U*ncles who don't uphold their side of things. Nor do I know who decides if their sides are upheld. Maybe they have meetings. I tuck a hair behind my ear as I follow Fitzroy.

I notice a group of *B*oyfriends, with their yellow wristbands. A few *C*ousins are intermingled wearing brown ones. I turn my nose up as we pass a group of peach wristbands. Fitzroy laughs while the men groan. This is a pleasure of all the higher ups while events happen. We are allowed to turn down anyone with a peach wristband. We can ignore them if we want. They only get special treatment when they upgrade their position—for a large fee of course— or they are granted something special by anyone above *G*randpa level.

We travel down several flights of stairs as Fitzroy leads me out onto a dock, walking all the way to the end. "Do you see this, Alyx?" He pulls me in front of him. Turning us in a slow circle. I can see the roof of the mansion. The noises of the activity near the pool waft down but are muted by the water lapping against the columns that hold the dock up.

"It's amazing." I push myself tighter against him.

"There," he points down. The dock ends at a hot tub that is hidden from the sun by a blue tent. "That place is meant for *K*ings." He turns me in his arms pulling me closer. His hands grip tight onto my ass.

"*K*ings?" I question as I look up. "I thought *U*ncles were at the top."

"Only one *K*ing is allowed at events." He winks at me. "This event is my upgrade. I am to be made a *K*ing." He leans down and kisses me.

If *K*ings are higher than *U*ncles, how many are there? There are only fifteen *U*ncles in the entire world. Fitzroy's hand goes underneath my bikini bottoms as he reaches around and caresses my flesh.

"Let's get in." He motions his head toward the hot tub. He drops his purple robe and steps out of his sandals.

"Anything for you, *U*ncle." I slide off my heels and go down the ladder. "Will I still get to call you *U*ncle?"

"After tonight, you'll call me *K*ing. Then," he comes into the water, "if you are still a good girl," he reaches his hand around me and undoes the strings on my bikini top, "perhaps I'll think of allowing you to call me Fitzroy." His brow quirks up.

"*U*ncle," I say as the top slides off my body and lands in the water, "I do not deserve such an honor." I get onto my knees. Anytime *U*ncle gives you anything, it doesn't matter if it's a mint, or a vacation, he honored you. In return, you honored him with whatever he wanted. The hot tub is deep, but my head and shoulders still float above the water.

"Today, Alyx," he sits on a reclining seat in the water, "you have done well." He puts out his hand for me to take.

I accept the offered hand and stand.

"But for now," he pulls me closer, "I want you naked." He tugs at my bottoms.

I pull the bottoms off and drop them into the water. His eyes rake over my skin. I don't turn away from his stare. I have to show him that I am his, fully.

"I will not touch you until tonight," he says, then he bites his bottom lip. "It's nice to let the tension build though." He slides a finger across my midsection. "However," his lip quirks up, "that doesn't mean I can't enjoy a show." He sits me on his lap. I can feel his hardness beneath his speedo. "It's your turn, Alyx." Fitzroy takes my hand and puts it between my legs.

It's time for me to put on a show.

I mimic him and bite my lip, letting my lower lip catch on my teeth the way he likes. He nods his head and waits for me to fondle myself. I smile and comply with my instructions.

THE KING'S TOUR

After watching me please myself Fitzroy ties my top back on. "Go get some food and find Ruby. She'll be in the B1 basement. Room 407." He strokes my back. "Have her take you on the *K*ings tour, understand?" He kisses my back between my shoulder blades.

"Yes, *U*ncle." I put my bottoms back on and climb out of the hot tub. I look back and smile making sure to let my gaze fall to his crotch and then compose myself and find his eyes again. Feigning that I've been caught looking at something I shouldn't. I giggle then turn and run back down the dock. Like the good *little* girl that he wants.

It's part of the job. I have to behave younger than I am. It's part of what turns him on. It's what keeps me with income—and breathing, too. As I walk up the stairs, I realize I've forgotten my heels. I can't go back for them now. Fitzroy wants to relax alone before his big night.

I don't know what becoming a *K*ing in this business entails, but he wants to be relaxed when it comes.

I make my way back through the crowd. Several men look at me. They each turn away as soon as they notice the bracelet on my wrist. Everyone gives me a wide berth as I come through. Other Vixens and Dollies nod once and then turn away, too.

That is different.

Jesus the house is enormous. It's much larger than Estelle's manor house. I walk through the sliding glass doors that are open and go to the buffet table. As I approach everyone backs away. No one says a word to me.

I pick up a plate and look over the buffet. I choose pineapple, strawberries, and shrimp. I want to get some of the mac n' cheese, a hamburger, some of the fries, and a bowl of chili to dip it all in. I'm certain a choice like that will get me in trouble even though Estelle isn't here. I grab a small single serving bottle of champagne as I pass the table with drinks, too. I ignore the table with the weed, cocaine, and pills. I need to see what is what before partaking in any of that.

As soon as I leave the buffet, everyone returns to it and whispers. "Chosen One," are the select words I can make out from the mumbles.

I don't know what they mean, but I assume that since Fitzroy has brought me as his special guest, that I am this Chosen One. Everyone on The Island knows not to get in my way or touch me.

I'm not sure if I like that or not.

I go towards the front of the house. I want to explore a bit more on my own before I find Ruby. The entrance to the home is gorgeous. Massive curving staircases going to the second floor, another elevator in the center, hidden behind a massive floral arrangement. All fresh flowers.

The ceilings are at least thirty feet high. A large chandelier hangs in the entryway. Windows surround this room, too. The façade of the house is stone. Some of the interior walls hold the same dark brown stones. There are benches, couches, and rugs all over. Many of which hold people in varying stages of undress.

I sit on an empty bench and eat my small plate of food.

Nearby one man—peach bracelet—eats a hotdog while a woman—green bracelet, white ankle bracelet— goes down on him. Another man—baby blue bracelet —has a male Dolly pressed against the front window, giving him his pleasure.

Other's watch, some eat, but all the *J*ohns are hard or semi-hard.

After they see the bracelet on my wrist—none of them look at me twice.

I finish my meal; set the plate on a table I pass and go for the elevator. I swipe my bracelet and the doors open up. Inside the walls are all mirrored. The floor and ceiling, too. I press B1 and descend to find Ruby.

Room 407 isn't difficult to find. Everything is labeled like a hotel. Though the hallways in the basement are smaller than the upstairs ones. The rooms seem to be closer together, too. I knock and wait for Ruby to answer.

The door opens. It's Felix. He lets out a sigh when he sees me. "Thank god." He ushers me inside the room.

"Where's Ruby?" I ask.

The room is as small as the bedroom in my apartment. A single full bed is pushed into one corner. There is a dresser across from the bed, and a nightstand next to it. On the opposite wall there is a lone sink, a toilet, and a shower. Everything looks as though it has been shoved into this tiny room.

Felix points to the bed.

I look over. I hadn't known anyone was in the bed. "Oh, she's still asleep?"

Felix nods. "Drugs should wear off soon."

"So, you're allowed to know the location of The

Island?" I ask as I watch the drugged sleeping, Ruby. There is a glass of water and a white pill on her bedside table as well.

"No," Felix shakes his head. "But they don't knock bodyguards out. We're blindfolded and muffed." He mimics putting earphones over his head. "They can't have bodyguards out of commission."

"That's understandable," I say. "Why are you in her room?" I've never seen Felix touch any of the girls, but that doesn't mean he doesn't.

"I waited for you. I knew Fitzroy would send you to Ruby. My headphones didn't quite stay in place." He smirks. "My right ear wasn't covered when he called one of the other passengers."

"I see." So, Felix is planning something, too. "I haven't seen any children," I say, making sure he knows I'll keep an eye out for Everleigh. If I'd have seen any kids during my mini tour with Fitzroy, I would have thought of her sooner. I need to improve my focus.

"They're kept in the lower levels during events like this. Only *U*ncles, *F*athers, and *K*ings are allowed in the sub basements."

"How many *K*ings are there?" Felix is the sole person I can ask.

"There were four, one died," he runs a hand through his hair, "after tonight, Fitzroy will be the new number four."

"Does that worry you?" My brow tightens.

"I want to get Everleigh out. I don't give a shit about anything else. It was all Ana wanted." Felix pauses as he stares at me.

"What?"

"What's that?" He points to my wrist.

"The bracelet?" I hold it out so he can see it. "Fitzroy gave it to me."

"Well, at least no one else will touch you." His jaw drops. "Does it have elevator access, too?"

"Yes. Fitzroy said I have free reign. I could go anywhere I wanted. He told me Ruby would give me the *K*ings tour, though."

"That's fantastic! That means you have access to the basements, too."

Ruby rolls over in the bed. Felix's head snaps in her direction. He tilts his head toward the door. I follow him as he exits. "I'll find you later. Stay with Ruby as long as you're allowed, okay?"

I nod.

"By the way, a box," he eyes me, making sure I follow what he's saying, "left with a tall handsome gentleman when I picked Ruby up."

"Thank you, Felix."

He nods and disappears down the hall.

At least Corwin has my brother and his things. One thing I don't have to worry about. Maybe with Trent safe I can concentrate on The Island. I will watch for Everleigh and Becca, too. There is a small chance that Becca is here, based on the note that Ana gave Corwin. I can at least look.

I go back into Ruby's room and she's sitting on the edge of her bed. She too wears a stringy orange bikini. Her wrist bracelet however is multi-colored. That means that any John can ask for her company. At least it isn't green. Her ankle bracelet is white. Like me Ruby has been doing this long enough to be a Vixen. Which is what the white bracelet tells everyone.

"Hey, Alyx." Ruby picks up the little white pill.

"Hey," I reply as she swallows it. "Fitzroy says to have you take me on the Kings tour. But, please, take your time."

She wobbles to her feet. "I swear every time they give me whatever that shit is to knock us out, I have a harder and harder time waking the fuck back up. I need some fucking coffee." Ruby stands. "Follow me." She stretches then leaves the room.

I follow after her. She walks down the hall in the opposite direction that I came from. There's a small kitchen area. Several people are there. All of them either Vixens or Dollies.

"No Johns are allowed in the basement," Ruby says when she notices me looking around the dark green room.

"That's a relief." There are several tall tables with stools. It's like a help-yourself coffee shop. There are snacks in baskets all around. Fresh fruit, donuts, and bagels. The lighting is dim, and there is a low hum of music playing. Fresh lavender hangs in baskets along one wall.

Ruby pours herself a cup of coffee. After she drinks the entire cup, she pours another.

"Hard start again, Rubes." A white boy with pointy brown hair stands up and comes over to us. The highlights in his hair are bright blonde and he is *tan* for a white boy. He has an early nineties surfer vibe. I assume it is part of his *costume*. He must spend every single day in the sun. There is a bottle of sunscreen sticking out of the blue fanny pack he wears. "Do you need some?" He pulls the bottle out.

He is exceptionally observant, too. "Thank you." I accept the bottle and squeeze some into my hand.

"Oh." He notices my bracelet. "Haven't seen one of you in ages." He looks me up and down. "I'm Quentin," he smiles at me.

"This is Alyx," Ruby offers my name.

"You mean, Queen." He tilts his head in my direction.

"What does that mean?" I arch a brow, never having come across the title before.

"All the new *K*ings are allowed to pick a Queen, though most of them do not do so."

"Why not?" I rub the sunscreen into my legs.

"Queens," he leans forward, "are rare around here. Most of the *K*ings like to share their ladies. They like choices, lots of concubines." He smiles. "When a *K*ing chooses a Queen," Quentin makes the noise, tsk, tsk, tsk, "they've chosen one woman for their first month of ruling. No other girls are allowed to touch the *K*ings unless strictly invited to do so."

"What of the Queens?" I ask.

"Queens, oh that's up to the *K*ing. If he wishes to share her, he may. However, she's not to look at another man, or woman if the *K*ing says that as well. If *K*ing chooses, he may make the Queen wear an eye mask, so that her gaze does not take in another human for that entire time."

Well, that's that then. If Fitzroy is planning on making me his Queen, I am certain he'll choose the eye mask option. I finish applying the sunscreen and hand Quentin the bottle back. "Thanks."

"Fuck, Alyx, that sucks." Ruby's face squinches up.

"I don't know. Only having to worry about *U*ncle," I shrug, "might not be so bad." Ruby is with Fitzroy; I don't want to put her in an awkward place. She needs to believe that I don't mind being here. That I want to be here. "*U*ncle has been kind to me." I look down and smile. If anyone ever questions Ruby about my loyalty, she won't have to lie. It might keep her safer, too.

"Ah, but you don't understand," Quentin says. "That means the *K*ing is also allowed to not use any protection." He arches his brow, driving his point home.

"So, *K*ings are allowed to have *Q*ueens, so that they can… *reproduce*?" Ruby asks.

I stand there in stunned silence. Quentin and Ruby speak of things, while I hear nothing other than my own heartbeat.

Fitzroy has brought me to The Island to *breed* me.

QUEEN

I stand there unsure what to do with myself. I've been selected to be Fitzroy's *Queen*. His breeding partner. I am meant to bear him children. Does that mean my life isn't at risk? Is that what Felix meant all the times he said it wasn't? Did Felix know Fitzroy's true reason for bringing me here? Had he hidden that from me?

"Alyx," Ruby says, shaking my shoulder.

"Fuck, Ruby!" Quentin looks around the room. "Don't touch her." He takes a step back.

Ruby's hand drops from me at once. "Sorry." She looks around, too.

"It's fine," I say as other people eye Ruby. "I told you earlier that you were allowed to rouse me if I became unable. You're fine." I want to secure Ruby's safety. I don't know if I'm allowed to do that, but if I don't know then maybe none of the Dollies or Vixen's know otherwise. "Clear the room." I make eye contact with as many as I can.

Everyone gets up and exits. Quentin begins to but I stop him. "Not you."

He inclines his head toward me then smiles when everyone is gone. "You think fast on your feet, girl."

"Not always." I take a breath. "I need more. When was the last time there was a Queen?"

"It was the first year I was here." Quentin puts a finger to his lip and taps it. "The fourth King's coronation. He chose a Queen, too. That King has five children here on The Island. But since he's passed away, I'm certain they're all wearing green bracelets."

"And the Queen?" I ask.

"Oh, no, each child has a different mother."

"But what happened to the Queen he chose?"

Quentin fiddles with the green bracelet on his wrist. "I can't recall." He looks down at his feet.

"Quentin," I say as I get closer. "Please tell me what happened."

Quentin steps back. "I… I don't know." He looks at Ruby once then leaves the room.

I turn to Ruby. "What the hell?"

"I've never known of a Queen." Ruby's hands flop down to her sides. "What are you going to do?"

"I don't have any options." I look down. I can't tell anyone about the pills I have with me. Maybe I can hide them and continue taking my birth control. Fitzroy doesn't know I've already taken two plan B pills. How many more can I safely take? Will I risk any health problems if I take too many?

Ruby comes over to me. She stands so close I can feel the heat from her skin, but she doesn't touch me. "What of Everleigh? Do you think that's why Ana isn't here? Does Fitzroy want a new kid?"

Well, had Ana told Ruby about Everleigh or am I missing something else? I pull my brow together and cock my head to the side. I don't know Ruby well enough to tell her everything I know. Had she been with Ana and Sasha, or is she the reason they were busted? I have no way of knowing. "I have no idea." There isn't anything else I can say without putting myself in harm's way?

"Let me take you on the *Kings* tour." Ruby pours herself another cup of coffee. "I'm sure Fitzroy is expecting to see me show you around."

I nod. Ruby drinks her coffee, and we leave the room.

Ruby shows me each floor. Where every type of *John* stays. She shows me every secret cove of the mansion as well as the ones that are hidden outside. "Fitzroy loves it when a girl leads him to a secret spot to devour him."

She smiles wide. "He favors her when he's surprised by it, too."

"Favors her how?" The only time Fitzroy had favored me while I was with him when I was younger was with gifts. Honoring and favoring are two different things.

"Treats," Ruby's shoulder hitches. "Or a dip in the exclusive pool on the roof. Only *U*ncles and *K*ings are allowed there. Vixens are allowed up on occasion. Dollies aren't allowed *ever*."

"Before today I didn't even know about the *K*ings," I say as Ruby passes the elevator for another staircase. "Can we take the elevator?"

"I don't have a key," Ruby sighs.

"I do." I show off my bracelet. I hold it to the screen and the doors open up.

Ruby nods and joins me. "Let's get to the pool, it's almost five. There will be an announcement about tonight's feast."

Fitzroy sits at a table underneath an umbrella as we come outside. His speedo is gone, he's wearing a red polo shirt and a pair of black shorts. The heels I'd left on the dock are on the table. I walk over and stand beside him. He is speaking to a man in a hat and dark sunglasses. "Yes, but that doesn't negate our expenses inland," Fitzroy says as the man turns.

"No, but demand means our supply must increase. We need to increase our exports by at least five percent," the man says. He laughs when he notices me. "Well, well, well. If it isn't the exquisite Alyx." He slides his sunglasses and hat off.

"*B*rother," I reply as Jennson stands up.

"Have a seat, please," Jennson says.

I look to Fitzroy, asking permission. Fitzroy inclines his head to say no. I stay in my place and nod once to *U*ncle. Letting him know I will obey him. Fitzroy sets my shoes on the ground. I slide the pumps onto my feet.

Jennson sits back down and takes a swig of his long island iced tea with a scowl on his face. Jennson isn't used to not being able to tell me what to do.

A Vixen in an orange speedo comes over, leans down, and whispers something in Fitzroy's ear.

Fitzroy nods and shoos them away. He looks up at me. "It's time for the announcement." His lip quirks up in the corner. "Follow me, my Alyx." He stands.

"See you soon," Jennson says. I nod but follow *U*ncle.

Fitzroy goes over to the open doors. He stands in the entryway, motioning for me to stand behind him, but to the side. There is a microphone set up a few feet from him.

"Ahem," a voice calls from behind me.

I turn. It's Peter. Fitzroy turns, too. "Ah, there you are," *U*ncle says. "It's about time you came out. Are you ready?"

Peter nods, smiles wryly at me, then stands to the left side of the microphone; Fitzroy is on the right. Peter is wearing a purple polo shirt and black shorts. His bracelet is neon blue.

The *U*ncle from Nigeria strides forward. He wears his purple bracelet as well as a bracelet with his country's flag. Anyone who isn't from the U.S. has to show their country's flag in some way. Some wear bracelets, others wear clothing with the flags on it. It's up to them. I'm not sure why, but it's one of the rules. I met the Nigerian *U*ncle at the Spring party held in the Carolina's the year that Sasha got hurt. His name is Maduka Idowu.

He taps the microphone. The noise sounds through speakers. "Ah, there we are," he says. "We have come to this event to promote one of our *F*athers." The man waves a hand toward Peter. "The event is special because we will also coronate a new *K*ing."

The crowd of men cheer. Everyone who wears orange claps or nods. Their voices aren't to speak out at any event.

"Come *F*ather." Idowu waves Peter forward.

Peter takes his place.

"Have you the fee?" Maduka asks Peter.

"Yes," Peter's voice carries across the patio.

"You're prepared to pay the cost and the price of admission to become *U*ncle?"

"Yes," Peter says louder than before and puffs out his chest.

"Then pay it," *U*ncle Idowu says a bit smug.

Peter nods. He turns and waves someone who stands behind me forward.

A girl in a white bikini passes me. Fitzroy had me get a white bikini, so I don't tear my gaze away. I may have to do whatever she does soon, too.

She carries a briefcase, cuffed to her wrist. She strolls over to Peter, gets to her knees in front of him, sets the case on the ground, then looks up, her hands together in supplication. She wears a green bracelet and a blue one, too.

"Margaret," Peter says, "open the case." He tilts his head. Margaret obeys and the case pops open. "Two-hundred-thousand-dollars," Peter says with a wide grin. "The cost to become *U*ncle."

*U*ncle Maduka waves a hand, "Bret," he says. A man comes forward. Peter hands him a key. Bret frees the case from Margaret's arm, takes it to another table, and begins counting.

No one speaks while the money is counted. Bret returns and whispers in *U*ncle Maduka's ear. "The cost has been paid," he says. He turns to Peter. "Now pay the price of admission." His eyes leave Peter's and flutter to Margaret who still sits, knees on the ground, looking up at Peter with her hands together, as if she were praying to him; like *he's* a god.

Men stand, craning their necks to see what will happen next. Those wearing orange all go to the ground. Knees against concrete, bent at the waist, hands laid out in front of them. Fitzroy looks to me then shakes his head no again, telling me to remain standing. I nod once and look on.

Bret pulls a smartphone from his pocket. "Recording." He zooms in, to a circle that has been drawn in chalk on the patio.

Peter stands inside the circle, drops his shorts, and turns in a full circle showing his hardness to everyone present. Including the camera.

"Take the virgin," Maduka says.

Peter walks forward. He pushes Margaret down to the ground and holds a hand over her mouth while he thrusts himself inside her. Margaret doesn't fight him. She doesn't even make any noise. Her eyes are glassy. She's been heavily drugged for this.

Peter grunts and gyrates inside her. After he finishes, he places his hands on Margaret's neck. He squeezes. Her face turns from the light color it was when she stepped forward to red. Her right hand momentarily rises then falls back to the ground. Her body is unable to fight due to whatever they've given her. Her lips soon go from pink to blue.

Her feet fall to the sides as Peter finishes satisfying himself with a loud roar. She is dead before he comes inside her.

Another girl has died in front of me—and there is nothing I can do. I can't even let a tear escape. If I look away, I'll be found out, too. I have to stay strong. I watch as Peter rises from the ground and pulls his pants up.

"The price has been paid," sounds over the speakers with a squeak. "The cost has been collected." Bret stops filming.

"Welcome your newest *U*ncle!" Idowu says.

Every man present, stands and cheers.

Two men in orange speedos pick Margaret up and carry her away.

I reach up and press my right earring.

THE KING'S FEAST

*U*ncle Maduka pats Peter's back after he's zipped his pants back up. Peter nods and Bret takes Peter's neon blue bracelet and replaces it with a purple one. The two of them walk away laughing. Those in orange rise to their knees after Margaret's body is gone.

I stand still while a man with dark hair passes Fitzroy. I notice the Chinese flag. It's Xinyi Min Yuen, the *U*ncle from China.

I know five of the fifteen *U*ncles. How many others will I see today?

"Greetings," he speaks into the microphone. The crowd greets him with cheers. "It is coronation day!" The *Johns* cheer louder. "We welcome *U*ncle Fitzroy."

Fitzroy steps forward.

"Come *U*ncle," Yuen waves a hurried hand. A few

of the *J*ohns in the audience snicker. "Have you the fee?" he asks when Fitzroy reaches him.

"Yes," Fitzroy's voice is calm.

"You're prepared to pay the cost and the price of admission to become *K*ing?" Yuen says vehemently.

"I am," Fitzroy says, still calm.

"Then pay it," Uncle Yuen says through clenched teeth.

I swallow hard. What will happen to me now? Will I be bred or killed in front of all these people?

Fitzroy nods once and walks into the circle. A man wearing a white speedo passes me. His eyes are as glassy as Margaret's had been. Someone takes a step to stand beside me. I look over and Felix stares at me. Everyone else watches as the man takes his place in front of Fitzroy.

Felix stands close to me but does not touch me. I take a deep breath. I know without a doubt that if anyone tries to kill me there will at least be a fight. I don't know how I know; I just do.

"Bret," Yuen says.

Bret again removes the briefcase and counts the money. He whispers in Yuen's ear.

"The cost to be *K*ing, one million dollars, has been paid. Now," he waves a hand to Fitzroy, "the price of admission."

Fitzroy puts his hand out. Bret places a knife in

Fitzroy's hand. The blade is long and curved. The hilt is jeweled and golden. Fitzroy circles the man in white as he sits in supplication on his knees inside the circle. Bret begins filming.

Fitzroy grips the man's hair in one hand. "The virgin was sacrificed, and now too shall be the blood." He pulls the knife across the man's throat. Blood sprays out in an arc and splatters against the patio. I do not move.

This ritual is a way to keep secrets. Everyone here must've had some sort of video of themselves doing something horrendous. The way Peter and Fitzroy have allowed themselves to be videoed killing people.

I've known about the money. How could I not? I've recently learned about the killings and the cannibals. I'd never have guessed that to be promoted sacrifices were also made.

Fitzroy pulls the blade to his mouth and licks the blood from the blade.

"The price has been paid," Uncle Yuen is as loud as Idowu had been before. "The cost has been collected." Bret stops filming again after Yuen has spoken. "Welcome your newest *K*ing!" Yuen bends down on one knee.

Every other man present follows suit. Including Felix at my side. All those in orange lay their bodies flat against the ground.

Bret stands, walks over, takes Fitzroy's purple bracelet and switches it out for a red one that looks a lot like mine but wider. He secures it with a screw, too.

"Prepare the feast!" Fitzroy's voice roars.

All those in orange get up and leave without a single glance back. The man who'd been sacrificed is not touched. Blood seeps out of his body.

I look away.

Fitzroy comes over beside me. "Felix." He holds out his hand.

Felix drops something into Fitzroy's waiting hand.

Fitzroy looks at me. "Take that off," he waves a hand to my bathing suit.

I do as I am bid. I strip while the area empties. Everyone heads somewhere, but I have no idea where. No one looks at me.

"Put this on." Fitzroy holds out a red bikini top to me.

I comply. "Yes…" I stop myself before I can say *U*ncle. Fitzroy is no longer an *U*ncle, "my *K*ing," I say as I put the top on.

"And this." Fitzroy holds a piece of golden mesh.

I take the weird fabric. I've never seen anything like it. It's a bikini bottom made only of golden mesh. The cloth is hard, but pliable.

"It's made of pure 24 Karat gold." Fitzroy shoos Felix away.

Felix takes several steps back but does not leave the patio. He looks at me. The nod he gives me is so miniscule I hardly believe I've seen it. I take it to mean that I'm still okay. I am safe. Though, I don't feel safe.

I put the mesh bottoms on. Fitzroy puts his hand up. His arm bends at the elbow, his hand is near the same height as his shoulder. This must be some other part of the ritual.

I put my hand on his and he leads me to the elevators. We get on, there's a robe hanging on the back wall. Felix's eyes close as the doors hide him from my view. The elevator descends—plunging my heart into my throat. Fitzroy pulls a little blue pill from his pocket and swallows it, then he changes into the red robe.

B2 lights up on the screen as the doors open. The room is dark apart from a few lights. The lights are held in place from cords. Each bulb is above a chair. Each chair sits at a long oval table. I count. There are fifteen chairs, and one very large throne at the head of the table.

Fitzroy had spoken of a feast, but there is no food.

The table itself is different than anything I've ever seen before. It looks mechanical. There are mounds atop it. I can't see what they are, but each mound is covered by black velvet. It isn't the same height as a normal table either. It's odd to say the least.

Fitzroy leads me around the room. Murmuring

comes through the curtained walls. The curtains wave from movement on the opposite side. My heart rate spikes as he leads me to the throne.

"You'll sit here." Fitzroy places his hands on my waist. He lifts me and sets me on one of the mounds. He presses a button after I'm in place. The mound makes a whirring sound and separates my legs, cuffing me in place at the ankles. Fitzroy pushes my chest back so that I am looking at the ceiling. He removes my shoes then sits on his throne. Another whirring sound plays. I look down. The throne pulled itself closer to the table.

Fitzroy's head is now inches from my crotch. He breathes in deep. "Ah, my Alyx," he says.

My chest rises and falls following my quick breaths.

"Don't be nervous," Fitzroy whispers. "Only the King can feast on his Queen."

Holy fucking hell. This is the feast. I am on the menu. The curtains around the room rise. Some who had been out by the pool now wear black robes. Fifteen in fact. It's the Uncles. They each take a seat at the table.

Behind Fitzroy a person steps forward. A Dolly wearing a red bikini top, no bottoms and two bracelets —blue and green. This girl is not only new but is also for sale. She would have a new handler soon, too. Fitzroy puts up a hand to stop her.

There is a rail holding men back away from the table. Heads bob up and down, craning to see. They aren't allowed to step any closer.

"Send in each *Uncle's* chosen server," sounds over a loudspeaker.

Several men, each wearing a peach bracelet come into the room. They all wear black shirts, and shorts. One stands between each seat at the table. They each place a small silver and red box on the table between the mounds. They look like tissue boxes, as some kind of white cloth rises out of them.

Every light in the room goes off apart from the one above Fitzroy's head.

"Now the *K*ings Feast begins," a voice says over the speaker again.

Fitzroy's head plunges into my crotch. He sniffs me through the mesh. He reaches up, sliding the mesh to the side and puts a finger inside me. My breathing picks up more than it already had. He smiles at me. I don't have the ability to smile back. I have no idea what is about to happen.

I'm frozen.

In terror.

Fitzroy removes his finger and then licks it. He leans over me and tastes me for a moment before he roars with delight. Fitzroy stands from his chair and enters me. He thrust his hips forward twice before pulling out and sitting back down. He pushes the mesh back into place and leans back in his chair.

The table clanks and my body is moved to Fitzroy's left. I am now in front of one of the standing men who wears a peach bracelet. I look to Fitzroy. He shakes his head no. The man isn't allowed to touch me.

The girl who'd been standing next to Fitzroy is helped onto another mound. The mound separates her legs and straps her down. The man who stands in front of her pulls one of the white cloths from a container. It drips as he lifts it. He bends over her and meticulously cleans her vagina. He holds her open with two fingers of one hand while he wipes her clean with the cloth.

As soon as he finishes the table shifts. The girl is now in front of Fitzroy, and I am in front of the *U*ncle to Fitzroy's left. The light above this *U*ncle lights up.

Fitzroy leans in close to the table, he sniffs the woman, he fondles her, then he tastes her.

The man in front of me leans forward while Fitzroy's head is lost between the woman's legs. He inhales deep and licks his lips. He does not touch me.

When Fitzroy's head lifts from between her legs, he rises from his chair again. He inserts himself inside her. His eyes roll back into his head while he gyrates. When he finishes his second thrust another woman steps forward. The process repeats.

The *U*ncle before me sniffs and moans as he takes

in my scent. The man beside him is eager to grab a cloth and wipe the next girl. The table moves and I watch as he cleans the woman, sniffs the cloth, then places the used cloth in his pocket.

The table shifts, the women—aside from me—are cleaned, and the table moves again. A new light comes on each time a new *U*ncle's turn comes up.

Allowing Fitzroy, a taste of every new Dolly—and every *U*ncle, a whiff of my scent.

The *U*ncle who the first girl was now in front of fondles her. He tastes her, too. The process also allows every *U*ncle to taste the new Dollies. Just not me. This *U*ncle also stands and inserts himself inside her for two gyrations.

The ritual continues on. Each man inhales my scent, no one touches me. As the table approaches the eighth *U*ncle my breathing picks up again. It's Peter.

He smiles wide as the table clanks to a stop. "My *K*ing," Peter says, breaking the silence in the room.

I can't see Fitzroy, but chair legs scrape the floor. "May I?" Peter asks.

"No," Fitzroy says.

Peter looks up at me and shrugs. The man to Peter's right dives into the woman in front of him. Peter whispers to me, "I've been waiting for this, for a very, very long time." Peter lifts his hand and strokes it atop the golden mesh. He slides it to the side and moans as his fingers sink into me. His gaze is greedy as it rakes over me.

I'm mortified. This is the first time I've ever been touched in a way I didn't accept beforehand. Even Sempers. I'd accepted that I would be touched by him. I'd be paid for it. It would further my existence somehow, so I had allowed it. When I got paid, it was *my* choice to be touched.

Wasn't it?

But not this... Not Peter.

He pulls his fingers from inside me and puts his head between my legs. I pull back trying to get away from him. The seat somehow prevents me from moving. I look over and there are bars above my shoulders, holding me in place. I don't know when they arrived, but they lock me in place.

"No," I say as Peter continues licking me.

Fitzroy comes into view. His anger is fierce. I've never uttered 'no' in front of him before.

Fitzroy puts a hand on Peter's shoulder and pulls him back.

Peter looks up at Fitzroy, jerks his shoulder out of his grasp and dives back into my crotch. Licking and sucking on me. He puts fingers inside me while he continues.

"Enough," Fitzroy yells, but Peter doesn't stop. Fitzroy yanks Peter back, sending his chair flying.

Peter jumps up. "You said I'd have my moment with her before we left the city. You promised that I'd get to have her. Now is my time," he pushes past Fitzroy and comes back over to the table.

"Don't fucking do it," Fitzroy says with fire in his eyes.

Peter looks at me, licks his lips, then slides his robe to the side. His hardness ready. He gets close to the table and plunges himself inside me. Letting out a low growl of satisfaction.

Fitzroy comes up behind him and puts his arm around Peter's neck. He squeezes but Peter doesn't give up his assault of me.

It takes three men to pull Peter out of me. They throw him to the floor.

Fitzroy screams his anger. "Get him out of here!" He yells. The men grab Peter and drag him from the room.

Peter yells. "I've tasted the Queen, and it was glorious! Her warmth encompassed my manhood and there is nothing better! I will have more!"

"Like fuck you will!" Fitzroy roars. He comes over to me. "My Queen," he tilts his head downward. "I apologize for that cretin. He will not touch you again, ever," he says. "No one is to touch the Queen!"

Fitzroy lays his head on my chest. "You are *only* my Queen." He clicks a button, and my mound begins to lower and straighten out. I'm being laid down on the table. "No one else gets the scent, apart from this," Fitzroy grabs one of the cloths and wipes me clean. He hands the cloth to the Uncle in the chair to his left. The one who hadn't had the opportunity to smell my scent. "This is how the rest of you will taste of the Queen."

My body is pulled by a mechanism into the center of the table. The mounds revolve around me, Fitzroy takes his place at the head of the table and continues tasting the Dollies. Each Uncle is passed the cloth with my scent on it. Each one takes long drags of sniffs. Some lick their lips and stare at me, while others attempt to touch the cloth to their tongues without being caught by the King.

The men behind the tables still crane necks to see each woman. They sniff trying to catch a smell. The Uncles at the table each have a taste of the Dollies. There are no second tastes. When a girl has been around the table she gets up and is replaced by a new girl, until every new girl on the island has been tasted by the King.

After the line of Dollies disappears Fitzroy stands and climbs onto the table. He walks over to me. I am still held in place. He presses something with the tip of his foot and the bars that hold my shoulders and ankles let go and disappear into the table.

Fitzroy smiles at me. "It is time to complete the

coronation," he says. The table beneath me flattens out. Fitzroy puts a hand out for me to take. I take the offered hand and he lifts me up. "Strip," he says.

I nod once and take off the red top and golden mesh bottoms. Fitzroy sets the items in a neat little pile, and then he too undresses.

"This," he looks to the other *U*ncles as he speaks, "is how a very good girl behaves," his gaze goes around the room. "There is no other way for a good girl to behave. If yours aren't this well behaved, end them and get new ones." He laughs.

"Clean me." He points to the cloths.

I grab one. It's thick and wet. It smells of coconut. I clean his penis, wiping it and grab another cloth. Fitzroy pulls me to my feet, and I wipe his mouth off, too.

Fitzroy puts his hand on the back of my neck and pulls my lips up to meet his own. I do as I am commanded. I lean up onto my tiptoes and kiss him. I drop the cloth. He pulls me closer, and I moan as he kisses me. His hands slide between my legs and I allow him access to my warmth. His lips leave mine and he begins kissing and sucking on my nipples.

He lays me down onto the table. He kisses every inch of my skin, even flipping me over to kiss my backside. He lingers on my ass, tracing his tongue around my backdoor. He flips me back over and plunges his fingers inside me. I arch my back and moan with the appropriate fervor.

I won't die today.

"Please my *K*ing, please." I lick my lips and reach my hand out wanting in the direction of his member.

A smile plays in his eyes. He lifts his head. His mouth glistens from tasting me. I rise forward and lick my wetness from his face. *U*ncles and men in the crowd gasp. I'm tender as I push at *K*ing's chest, forcing his back onto the table. Fitzroy goes willingly.

I wrap my mouth around his cock as his hands grip into my hair. Fitzroy lets out a growl. I lick and suck hard, pulling my cheeks in tight as I go up his shaft, letting go with a pop sound. Fitzroy's moans are loud in the room.

I must put on a good show.

Several *U*ncles begin fondling themselves.

I mount Fitzroy, letting drool slide out of my mouth as I lower myself onto him. I moan as I go down, feigning that it is difficult to allow all of him inside me. Fitzroy's hands go to my waist, then one hand slides forward, he uses his thumb to rub my clitoris while I ride him.

My hands are in my hair while I move on top of him. I moan and yell out my joy at having him inside me.

Fitzroy's gaze moves around the room. He smiles as

he notices that every man— every single one of them—
is jerking off.

I grab his hand that had been rubbing me. Fitzroy
smiles wryly at me as I suck on his thumb.

I am a good actress.

Thank fucking god!

"Bring them in," Fitzroy manages between heavy
panting breaths.

Vixens and Dollies flood into the room. Every
*U*ncle grabs whichever one suits them. Some grabbing
and fighting for a new Dolly they'd tasted; wanting to
have them first. Bodyguards break up the fights placing
Vixens and Dollies where they want if the fights don't
ease.

*U*ncles, *F*athers, *B*rothers, *G*randpas, and *C*ousins
all have someone. Male or Female, they've chosen their
Dollies and Vixens according to their desires. They all
fuck one another while the *K*ing takes his Queen.

Everyone fucks until they come. The *K*ing rolls so
that he is on top of me now. My legs go around him the
way he likes. The *K*ing has to be the last to finish, to
show his power over everyone else. The satisfied look in
his eyes tells me that he loves this moment more than
anything else he's ever done.

Fitzroy gyrates and pounds into me. I give the best
show I can. I suck on his fingers. I rub myself while he
drives himself inside me, over and over again. I scream

and moan my pleasure. "*K*ing oh, *K*ing, fuck me HARD!" I scream.

Fitzroy growls with delight as he comes inside me. He lays down on top of me. Staying inside me while others come to observe his member inside me. One man holds a hand up silencing everyone else in the room.

He taps the table twice.

Fitzroy pulls out of me slow. The man who wears a black robe—I've never seen him before— watches close until Fitzroy and I are no longer attached.

"The *K*ing's fluids have been delivered." The man taps the table again. "Our new *K*ing!" The man places an actual fucking crown on Fitzroy's head. The crown is gold with bright red rubies encircling it.

The crowd roars as the *K*ing is crowned and the coronation ceremony completes.

"Now," Fitzroy yells as the crowd quiets, "Let's go find Peter and teach him a lesson."

Fitzroy and the crowd gather their clothes, some using the wet wipes on the table to clean themselves. They all dress, or zip up, whatever they need to. Fitzroy leans over the table. I lay still.

"Do you want to see *U*ncle Peter be punished?"

"No. I trust you'll do what is necessary, my *K*ing," I say.

Fitzroy leans in and kisses me. "Go to my new

room. Fifth floor. There's only one room. Wait for me there." He lays the red bikini and golden bottoms on my bare stomach.

I nod.

"She is a good girl, isn't she," the man who'd crowned Fitzroy says.

Fitzroy smiles bright before a slight sneer plays in the corner of his mouth. "Indeed, she is."

I hold my breath as the room empties. Everyone amped up for whatever punishment Fitzroy is going to put down on Peter.

I dress taking in the much-needed air.

At least *I* am still alive.

VIXENS AND DOLLIES

I wait in the throne room—or Feast Room—whatever the fuck it's called, until the sounds from all the men leaving dies down. I don't want to get pulled through the crowd and end up seeing Peter again. I fight back the tears that are trying to break free. I grab one of the wipes and clean myself. Getting as much of *h*im out of me as I can.

I don't know where the girls who'd been part of the feast are now, but I know which way they'd left the room as they were escorted from the table. I want to know more. I walk to the far left end of the room and go behind the curtain. They'd all disappeared this way.

The hall is lined with purple velvet walls and carpeting. It's soft beneath my feet. The lights are dim, but bright enough that I can see down the corridor. Muted voices and steam wafts from a bright room at the end of the passageway.

The voices grow louder as I approach. I peek in before making my presence known. Vixens and Dollies —male and female alike—fill the room. There are showers along one wall. The room smells of lavender and rose. It seems that the Vixens assist the Dollies.

Some of the Dolly's heads loll to the side—they're still drugged.

"Stop being a peeping tom and come in already," a woman's voice says from inside the opening.

I turn my head. The woman has long red hair. Curls flow to her waist. She's slender and can't be over eighteen. She's probably closer to sixteen. "Sorry," I say as I come into the room.

"Don't be. Feasts are hard on everyone." She shrugs. "I'd offer to shake your hand, but," she motions a hand up and down my body, "you're the *Queen*, no one's allowed to touch you." I notice her green bracelet.

"Can I ask you a question?" I tuck my hair behind my ear.

She nods her head.

"Your green bracelet, I know it means you're for sale, but what does that mean? Does it mean you'll be sent to a new handler?"

"How long have you been a Vixen?" The girl's brow raises.

"About two years." I answer honestly. I'd been given my title at the party after Sasha got hurt.

"And you don't *know* what the green bracelets mean?" She cocks her head to the side as she looks me up and down.

"Not really. I know that I don't see the girls who wear them afterwards. They're no longer in the roster."

"That's true." She leans back against the door casing and puts one foot against the wall. "I've been sold four times already. It's not that big a deal. Get to go to new places. Meet new people." She looks down at her fingers. She twiddles her thumbs and sighs.

"I'm sorry, I didn't mean to upset you."

"You didn't, my Queen." She stands up straight, her eyes wide. Like a kid who has done something wrong and is about to get caught.

"You're okay. I'm not a real queen." I look down at my body. "Just a girl like you that does what I have to."

She stares for a moment, trying to see if I'm telling the truth or not. When she decides I must be she resumes her position against the wall and props her foot back up. "I'm Fallon, by the way." She smiles at me. "With a Ph, not an F," she clarifies then laughs.

"Hello, Phallon. I'm Alyx." I put out my hand. When she stares at it, I say. "Oh, right, sorry." I stuff my hands behind my back and interlock my fingers together.

"I appreciate that, but you're my Queen, and I cannot call you any different."

"I understand." I smile.

"I'm not sure you do." She looks down at her thumbs again. "I bet you're one of those career girls. You get paid, don't you?"

"Do you not get paid?" After the words are out of my mouth I remember; no one gets paid for work at The Island. "I mean, when you're not here."

"Why would I get compensated?"

"Aren't you a Vixen?" I point to her ankle bracelet.

"I am, but I don't have a wage. How much do you get?" Her brow shoots up.

"Depends on the client. Their level in the hierarchy and stuff like that."

Phallon's head bobs up and down. "How long have you been doing this?"

"I started when I was fourteen." I'm surprised again by my honest answer.

"Were you kidnapped, too?"

Too? The question pops in my head but not out of my mouth. I stare, my brain won't ask the question for me.

"So that's a no." She leans away from the wall and shuffles her hair to the opposite side. "I was," she offers the information. "I was four. I don't remember much. A green lawn. Some toys. My mom on the front porch drinking some tea. The phone rang in the house. She got up to answer it."

My chest rises and falls as I listen, as I hang on her every word.

"A woman walked past with a puppy. 'Want to see it?' she asked sweetly. I was four, ya know?" Phallon's lips press together, and her brow tightens. "I didn't know any better. The woman looked harmless. Even now when I think about what she looked like. She was so pretty. Wearing nice clothes. She had a puppy for fucks sake. How could she be dangerous? How could any child think danger?" Phallon's head shakes side to side. I reach out and rub her shoulder. She looks up at me. "Thanks," she says. "The woman handed me the puppy. I held it as it licked my face. 'I have more, up there, see the van?' she asked me. I walked away from my home, willingly." Phallon blows out a breath.

"I'm sorry." I drop my hand. "I had no idea." Why don't I know that there are girls who've been kidnapped? *How do I not know this?*

"Are you sure you work in this business?" She asks. Phallon isn't trying to be mean; she doesn't understand my lack of knowledge.

"Yeah. But maybe that's the difference," I say. "Maybe I work, while you're..." I can't find the right word.

"Used," Phallon offers the term.

"I wish there were a better expression for that. But yeah, I guess *used* works."

"It's okay. The younger you are when you start, the easier it is to not die," Phallon pushes away from the wall and steadies a male Dolly who passes by headed for the showers.

"How do you mean?" I ask as another girl comes over to help him get showered.

"When you learn what's expected of you and you do what's expected of you, you live a lot longer. Fucking Margaret had only been here a few hours." She swallows hard. "They took her from fucking Alaska, can you believe it?"

My brows shoot up. They'd kidnapped a girl, to kill her. My stomach roils.

"Toilets are over there," Phallon points. "If you're going to be sick, be sick there," she says.

I put a hand to my stomach and take several deep breaths. I've been lucky, my whole life, and I haven't even known it.

I'd been pulled into the spider's web in subtle ways.

The first time I met Fitzroy he'd feigned a biking accident. I'd helped by holding a heating pad to his back. Later that same day, I'd rubbed his feet while we sat by the pool. Ana and a few other girls swam, while I sat and talked with uncle Fitzroy. He was funny, we laughed a lot. That was before I knew he was an *U*ncle, not a blood relative uncle.

Each time after that, he'd invited me to touch him in some way. Making it easier and easier for me to be comfortable. Then... the first time I was alone with no one else there. He'd gotten me to come over, for—I rubbed a hand through my hair as I tried to remember — he'd had me come over to help him set up his new Blu-ray player.

He put on a movie, 'Watch this with me,' he'd said as he smiled. He had a theater in his house. Popcorn, candy, drinks, everything was there. He grabbed us some snacks then started a movie I'd never seen before —Bram Stoker's Dracula. Fitzroy sat down next to me. He flirted with me, rubbing a hand up and down my leg while we watched. He held my hand on the scary parts.

The movie was hot and sexy, even though it came out before I was born. I liked it. I liked his attention, too. I was nervous, but I didn't mind. I'd already touched him in so many other ways. Hugs, kisses on the cheek as we'd leave. All the other girls kissed his cheek, too. I didn't want to be out of place. He'd never hurt any of them, nor me. So, when he told me he had a crush on me, I was flattered. There were so many other girls, including Ana, who were so much cuter than I was, but this *man*… liked *me*.

He pushed my hair behind my ear as I blushed. 'Alyx, may I kiss you?' he asked as he got close to me.

My breathing picked up, but I bobbed my head, giving him the yes he asked for. He moved slowly, putting his hand that had moved my hair to my neck. He swept his nose against mine and then kissed me with sweet little kisses.

'Thank you,' he'd said after.

The kiss hadn't lasted for more than thirty seconds. But that was it, that was the beginning. Every time I went over after that, he'd make sure no other girls were there. It would be just him and I. There'd be movies, and kisses. Hot tubs and kisses. Swimming and kisses. He waited until I was comfortable kissing him.

Until *I* wanted more.

After that he'd suggested the touching.

'I'll touch you; you don't have to touch me.' He'd given me a dazzling smile. 'I… I want to be closer to you. I know I shouldn't,' he'd swept my hair back, 'but I can't resist you. You're too perfect,' he'd say.

So, I let him. He fingered me for the first time, on a beach, under the stars. Warm water lapping at our feet. Later that same night, while fingering me again—up in the tower where Ana had taken me on my first trip there— he'd convinced me to use my hand on him. He licked my hand and then put it down his shorts. 'Touch me, you don't even have to move your hand. I want to feel you, wet and warm, holding me,' he'd said as he fondled me.

I agreed. My hand was already in his shorts. When he moaned after I'd accidentally moved my hand shifting positions, I was made to believe that I needed to move my hand, to please him. That was the first time he went down on me, too.

I'd pleased him and he wanted me to have something from him. 'I never do this to women,' he said. 'But Alyx,' his breath was hot on my neck 'I want to taste you, *please*. You're so sweet, I know it,' he begged me.

I allowed him to do it.

I waited a week before seeing him again after that. I got lucky that he'd gotten called out of town. I was a wreck. If my parents found out a boy had touched me, they'd be furious. If they found out it was someone older, they'd be out for blood. Not only did they want me to wait until I was married—they'd both waited, at least that's what they claimed—but they'd send Fitzroy to jail for something like that.

I couldn't do that to Fitzroy, he liked me, and I liked him.

During that week, I'd found out. No, I'd figured out, my parents had lied. I'd been the result of a romp between the sheets, *before* they got married. When they found out I was on the way, they got married *after*.

When Fitzroy returned, I was pissed at my parents. They didn't need to know about my life if they'd never been honest with me about theirs. I went over to his house as soon as I knew he was home—when the lights went on in the tower that could be viewed from my back porch.

Fitzroy's house was four streets from ours, but close enough. I hopped on my bike and rode over. He never locked the front door anyway.

When I got there, Estelle was there, too. Floating around the pool in her skimpy blue bikini. Fitzroy laughing while sitting on the side. I'd been furious when he jumped into the pool and grabbed her.

Jealousy got the best of me as he lifted her above his head and then slowly lowered her body, he kissed her when her lips were in reach. I tripped over a chair as I tried to leave without being seen. I was so embarrassed. Why had I ever believed someone like him, older, mature, wealthy, could ever choose me over someone like Estelle.

'Alyx,' he yelled my name.

I got up and ran toward the front of the house.

Fitzroy caught me.

'Alyx, dear, what are you doing? Why are you running away?'

'Why?' I pulled out of his grip. 'Obviously, I'm not your type. I'm stupid,' I said then slapped my forehead. 'I'll get out of your way, so you can do… whatever.' I pointed toward the patio.

'Alyx, I …' he trailed off as he looked down. He met my eyes again. 'I'm a man, I have certain *needs*,' he said.

'Do you mean, like touching you?' I asked as my cheeks blushed.

'Yes, but touching isn't always enough, you know?' He pulled himself closer to me. Asking as he did so. Looking to me making sure every step was okay. I nodded and he wrapped me up in his arms. 'I'd much rather have you,' he said. 'But while I wait for you to be *ready*, I have to… you know, get taken care of somehow. Estelle is pretty enough I guess.' He dismissed her beauty. 'You're much prettier,' he said, and he nuzzled his head against the top of mine as he bent over.

'Well, what would I have to do, to you know, make sure you're okay, too?' I'd asked. I didn't want him to be with anyone else. I wanted him for myself. I thought of him as mine.

'Should we go up to the tower? I can show you if you want.' He offered. Making sure the decision was mine.

'What about Estelle?' I turned my head to look outside.

'She'll never know. I'll send her away. But first, I'd like to see you, I've been gone all week." He swept me up into his arms.

I giggled as he carried me through the house. When he reached the door to the tower he stopped. He looked into my eyes then kissed me fiercely. My arms wrapped up around his neck and I leaned into his kiss. He pressed my body against the door as he held me. He pulled back. 'Sorry, got a little carried away,' he said as his breathing slowed. 'Are you sure? Do you want to... you know?' He looked down.

'No one can be a virgin forever,' I said. 'At least I'll get to have you as my first.' I kissed him. I allowed myself to want him. I allowed myself to believe his words. He'd never given me a reason to doubt him.

'Open the door?'

I reached over and opened the door. He walked through it, still carrying me and kicked the door closed with his foot. He set me down and then chased me up the spiral staircase. We laughed and giggled all the way up the stairs. There was a bottle of champagne waiting there. I looked at him with surprise and delight.

'I hoped you'd come over when I turned the lights on. Estelle showed up a few minutes before you did.'

'You set this up for... *me*?' I was flattered at the thought.

He popped the cork and poured two glasses. Handing me one he said, 'Is that alright?'

I nodded my head and drank the alcohol. It burned as it went down my throat. He poured me a second glass. 'Helps with the nerves,' he said. I drank the second and then he laid down on the floor. 'Come over here,' he patted the carpet.

It was the exact same spot where he'd gone down on me the week before. The memory of his tongue sent shivers through me. I wanted him. I pushed him over, making him lay on his back and I sat on top of him. I leaned down and kissed him the way I'd seen women do in the movies we'd watched together. His arms wrapped around me. 'I need to hear you say it,' he said as he pulled away. His hands ran up and down my back.

'Say what?' I'd asked him.

'That you want me... inside you,' he said into my ear.

I stood and undressed. His eyes never left my body while I did so. I poured myself one more glass and drank it down, all while his gaze assessed me. I went back over. I sat atop him. I could feel as he hardened under his swim trunks. 'I want you,' I said as I laid my bare chest against his. 'Inside me,' I kissed him.

Fitzroy's arms wrapped around me and before I even knew what happened he was on top of me and I was under him. He kissed me between my breasts and put his fingers inside me. He didn't take his swim trunks off, just pulled them down, then he entered me for the first time.

It hurt, but it was bearable. I'd wanted him to do this after all, I could handle what pain came with this first. Because Fitzroy wanted *me*.

His moans of pleasure made me smile. Younger me moaned along with him.

Phallon snaps fingers in front of my face. "My *Queen*, you good?" she says.

"Sorry," I say. "I'm…"

"Remembering the first time it was *your* idea?"

"How could you know that?" I ask as she'd somehow managed to know exactly what had happened.

"I've seen it happen enough times," she answers. "Was it your idea?" Recognition lights her face.

"I'd thought it was, that's for sure," and I had. I'd thought that all of that was my idea. That I'd allowed it. That I'd wanted it. But… I'd been manipulated and conned—a fly lured into his web with honey. *I had been groomed.* I was nothing but a tool for his desires. His twisted self that wanted to have a fourteen-year-old girl be his.

How had I never seen this before now?

"You didn't know any better. You were a kid." Phallon helps another Dolly to their shower.

"How do you keep answering my thoughts?" I follow her.

"I've been around this stuff for a long time. I have this job, helping others because I'm good at reading and calming people." She turns the water on for the Dolly to get clean.

"I guess," I say. There is a bench in the center of the room. I need to sit down. I make my way over and as I sit my mind becomes clear—for the first time ever. I may have chosen to allow Sempers, Blake, Jennson, and so many others to touch me, because I needed to have money. I needed to take care of my brother. But I only needed those things because someone had tricked a child into sex and when that sex was about to run out, they killed my parents in order to keep the sex coming.

That won't fucking do, at all.

NEW FRIENDS

I stand from the tufted bench and notice my reflection in a mirror. "Shit," I say. "I need to get to the *King's* room. I'm expected." I know I'll go along for now. I need to make it back to New York from wherever the fuck I am. However, once I'm back, I'll be taking that money I stashed with Trent, and we'll be fucking history. If I don't take what's theirs, maybe that will keep them from following after me.

"I'll have someone escort you." Phallon comes over to me. "I'd take you myself, but I have more to help before the sale starts."

"What sale?" I ask as Phallon snaps her fingers in the air.

Phallon shows me her bracelet. "If I do a good enough job, I'll get to stay here for another few months.

They might remove my bracelet and let me stay forever if I do well. But the sale will begin Sunday at 2:00 PM. Everyone with a green bracelet must be cleaned and polished up by then. And of course," she says while she hands someone a towel, "I'll have to re-clean them if any *Johns* get their hands on them between now and then.

"Of course," she continues as she lifts one of the girl's arms. "You missed a spot shaving, redo," she says and turns back to me. "Usually most of the *Johns* are satisfied after the feast has finished. A few will order in for blow jobs tonight though," she shrugs a shoulder "blow jobs don't always require more polishing though. Men like to fall asleep with their cocks in someone else's mouth. If they could reach their own cocks then women would rule the world and men would all be in a room somewhere with their own cocks in their mouths, starving themselves to death." She laughs.

"Vixen Phallon," a female voice says from behind me. "I can escort the Queen, I'm all clean and ready for transport."

I turn my head to see her. Her hair is dark, and her brown skin is slick with lotion. She's naked apart from her green bracelet and white ankle bracelet. She's thin and curvy all at the same time.

Phallon stands and looks her over. Phallon holds

one of the girl's hands while the girl twirls. Phallon making sure nothing is out of place. "Looks good. Bring some more towels on your way back though, could you, Bec? We're going to need more."

I twist my head to the side, but the girl's back faces me. The girl who Phallon had called Bec walks over and grabs one of the many red robes that hangs on the wall.

"Red robes are used any time a new *K*ing is crowned. *K*ing gets first dibs on anyone. Red can't be removed until the *K*ing says," Phallon huffs and grabs another one. She holds it out for me to put it on.

I allow her to help me. She makes sure her fingers never touch any area of my skin. I look around the room, looking for cameras. Everyone here is so well behaved. They're following rules that I didn't know existed. I don't see any cameras, but of course, these workers probably see things like what happened to Margaret and that man a lot. It's easy to keep them in line with the constant threat of death.

Look at me even. The things I'll do to stay alive. Also, by the glossy looks, most of these people are still drugged.

Bec walks back over to us. Her dark skin looks fresh. The red suits her. I study her face as she looks at me. My brows raise as the recognition sets in. "Becca?" I ask. "Becca Thwaite?"

Her head is slow as it moves side to side. Her gaze locked on me but with no understanding at all. "Take me to the *King*'s room."

She nods once and leads the way. I follow after her.

I watch her close as we head to the fifth floor. She stops at the elevator and points to my wrist. I scan the bracelet and we both get on. She presses the button for the fifth floor. I watch her as the elevator ascends.

The doors open and we walk down a long wide hall. There are oil paintings along the red velvet walls. Statues between each window. The sun is setting. I look out and notice that down by the pool someone is taking a beating. I grimace as the person is shoved into the water. They float face down for a few moments before turning over. I can't hear anything; but people pat backs and high five. Happy with themselves.

The punishment of Peter is over. He's still alive, floating in the pool.

Bec opens a door with some force. The doors are over twelve feet high; they must've been heavy. "This way, my *Queen*," she says as I come in. She shuts the heavy doors behind us.

When the doors shut the sound echoes in the room. There's a large bed in the center of the room. Red velvet hanging around it like in the *Uncle*'s room on the fourth floor. This bed is larger than the other one though. Everything is either red or gold.

"How do you know my name?" Bec rushes over to me and puts her hands on my arms. "Did someone send you for me?" she begs.

"Holy shit! You are Becca?" I hug her.

"Yes, how do you know me? I don't recognize you." She pulls away.

"I know your dad."

"How?" Her eyes blaze and her jaw tightens.

"No, not like that?" I shake my head. "He's not a client! No, no, Corwin is a friend. I didn't know… He thinks you're dead. Everyone does."

"That fucking fire! I knew it. When Estelle pulled me out of school, smoke billowed out of the science lab's windows. I knew something was off!"

"How are you here?" I beg the question. "Are you sure it's okay to touch me?"

"There are no cameras on this floor at all! That's why only the King is allowed here." Becca takes a deep breath. "Estelle asked me to go on one last shopping trip with her. God damn it, I should've known better. Fuck, I wanted to go to college." Her body trembles. "So, dad's not looking for me?" Tears fill her eyes.

"Actually, I think he is. See, I go to dinner with him once a week…"

"I thought you said he wasn't a client."

"He's not, but he went to school with…"

"Estelle, I know." Becca rubs her forehead.

"Well, Estelle is my handler."

"Oh," Becca says.

"She sent me with him for networking, is what she told him."

"But she wanted to see if he suspected anything. That fucking cunt. Does my dad know you're here?" She asks me.

"No," I huff. "I don't even know where here is."

"I've been trying to figure it out for a while. I haven't come close to finding anything. I've even checked shipments when they arrive. Food comes in once a week, but there's nothing on any labels that show the location. It's impossible to figure out where we are."

It dawns on me. The trackers. I push her hair back. She has a pair on, too. "Here." I take out my right earring. "Trade me."

Becca is quick, she already has it figured out before I can open my palm to give her the earring. She gives me one of hers and we each put the new earring in our ears.

"Listen, the next time you're near a phone,"

"That might be a minute. Phones aren't allowed on

The Island, but," she holds up her wrist. "I'm wearing green so Sunday afternoon, I'll be gone."

"Okay, well, there's an agent. She gave me a phone number to call. It's 5212 and then press the star key. Apparently, the number won't show up as dialed but you'll be connected to the FBI, and they'll be able to help you."

"How will it not show up as dialed?"

"I don't know, but she assured me that if you call the number 5212 and press star that she'll have access to your location and the number won't show up in the recent calls or even on the phone bill."

Becca nods. "Are you going to be, okay?"

I hug her. "I know I don't know you, but god damn, I love you." I smile. "I'll be fine."

"You certainly know how to handle Fitzroy." Her brow shoots up.

"I didn't even realize I did until the past few days."

"How did you convince him to let you be his Queen? I thought Estelle would be his Queen."

"I didn't even know what a Queen was. I still don't. All I know is it means I'm to birth his children."

"Estelle is going to be pissed when she finds out. I know she's been waiting for the promotion for a long time."

"Promotion?" I ask. "I thought this meant that I

would have kids to further his line or whatever sick shit."

"Fitzroy has one daughter here, he wants more. But if you're his Queen, you're the new Estelle. He's going to train you how to do what she does. But you're still going to have to do what you already do for him and bear his children, too."

"Do you know where Everleigh is?"

"So, you know Ana, too! Is she here?" Becca looks at me expectantly.

"No, she's not here." I can't tell her that Ana's dead. I just can't do it.

"Everleigh is on B3 until Monday, then the kids will be let out. The kids aren't allowed free roam during events. Unless someone has some seriously deep pockets. Five million will get you a kid during an event but nothing less than that."

My mouth opens in shock and horror. "They really do that? Use the kids, the same way they use… *us*?" Had I known that before? Hadn't Ana suggested it? Why hadn't the information truly sunk into my brain?

"When you aren't one of them, it's hard to believe the things that they do. Because you don't think that way. Even when you have sex for a living, if you aren't a pedophile or a hebephile, you don't think that way."

"A what? Hebe…?"

"It's someone who is attracted to young adolescents.

Hebephilia's claim it's due to the 'reproductive qualities' younger people have, but it's as abhorrent and illegal as pedophilia."

My head whirls. "Fitzroy is a hebephile, then?"

"He's a bit of both." Becca sneers.

The bedroom door opens. We both look up. I take a step away from Becca. "Thank you so much for escorting me back. Please see that the towels are sent to the washing room. I want everyone to be clean for their *K*ing! Do you understand?" I yell.

Becca smiles then bows. "Yes, my *Q*ueen!" She hurries out of the room.

I blow out a breath as she closes the door behind herself. The breath is in part because I'm so happy I think quick in stressful situations—*sometimes*. I want to hug my dad for that. It's also in part because it helps me appear frustrated with the *staff.*

"Always taking such good care of me." Fitzroy wraps his arms around me, under my robe.

"Of course, my *K*ing." I wrap my arms around him, too. "I need to shower, so that I can be clean for you." I nuzzle into his chest.

"Allow me to wash my *Q*ueen," he says, pulling away. He lets his hand run down my arm until it reaches mine. He interlocks our fingers and pulls me toward the far end of the room.

He opens a set of doors into a large bathroom. The

floors are marble. There are two sinks, a shower meant for at least twelve people, and a large tub. The tub is set into the floor. It's the size of a large hot tub. It's filled with water, steam rising from it. There is a bottle of champagne and stemware there, too.

Atop one of the counters sets a large tray of sliced pineapples. "I knew it was your favorite." Fitzroy grabs a piece. He sucks on it then eats it. He plucks another piece and puts it in my mouth.

"Mmm." I eat the fruit.

*K*ing pulls me over to the tub and slides my robe from my shoulders. His sticky fingers sliding down my left arm. His breathing picks up.

"How is it?" I ask. I almost take a step back. I spoke first—a no, no. But then, I am *Q*ueen after all. Maybe I'll be allowed to speak first now.

"How is what?" He asks as he undoes the strings on my top.

"Being *K*ing," I smile as he cups my breasts in his hands.

He nibbles at my tits. "It's fucking glorious!" He bites my nipple.

I flinch back at the pain as it flashes through my chest. I giggle. Hopefully glossing over the pullback.

Fitzroy slides my bottoms down off my hips. Letting them drop to the floor with a small clang as the gold hits the marble.

"Good fucking god." He licks his lips. "All I want to do is touch you," a shiver rolls down his spine.

"Then touch me," I say as I slide a hand between my legs. "I'm… warm." I close my eyes and roll my head to the side as I feel myself. "And," I take my finger out of myself, and I put my finger in his mouth, "I taste wonderful."

That should insure my life for a while.

Fitzroy's hardness presses against me as he sucks on my finger. "Get in." He tilts his head toward the tub.

I sink into the warm water. He walks over to a cabinet and pulls a red cloth from it. King drops his pants and gets into the water with me. "I'm going to make sure that every square inch of your body is clean." He pumps some soap onto the rag.

"I am honored, my King." I lean back and put my foot out for him to wash.

"I can see that I chose my Queen wisely." He washes my foot.

King—I need to think of him this way, so that I don't falter—King washes my leg, not missing a single area. When my right leg has been scrubbed, he moves to my left. He pulls me into his lap, spreading my legs to either side of him.

King's member throbs against me as I sit there, but he does not enter me. He washes my back, then gets more soap. He washes my navel, and my breasts, slow as he circles my nipples. He washes my neck, and my ears. He moves in even closer while he washes my ass. He lingers with the cloth while washing my asshole. I press my breasts to his chest while he does it.

Leaning me back *K*ing washes my hair.

"Now," he rinses me off, "I shall clean your beautiful flower."

He lifts me up so that I sit on the edge of the tub. Which means that I sit on the floor. The marble must've been heated because it's not cold. He buries his head between my breasts, kissing me. He leans me so that my back touches the floor. I lay down and he sets each of my feet on the edge of the tub as well.

He grabs another cloth and dips it in the water a few times; then he cleans the jewel between my legs with methodical care. The reason he keeps me around is because he likes this jewel more than he likes the others that he owns.

He does own me, too. All this time whenever someone being sold is mentioned, I've thought of them as transferred to another handler. I see now that actual money is being exchanged. It's probably even how Fitzroy... no *K*ing, afforded to become *K*ing. One million dollars isn't an easy thing to come by. Though, *K*ing does own a lot of properties as well as a lot of Vixens and Dollies. The cost is a drop in the bucket of what he has.

I look around the room while he cleans me. The knobs on the cabinets are made of gold with little diamonds in the center. I suppose those are real, too. There are tiny jewels outlining the mirrors, many different colors. The towel rods look to be made of opals, but those were soft jewels, so those might be fake.

Fitz... King gets out of the water, "Don't move," he says.

I nod and watch him.

He walks over and grabs the plate of pineapples. Getting back in the water he sets the tray down next to me. He puts one in my mouth and takes another from the plate. He rubs the fruit between my legs, then eats it.

Burying his face between my legs, he tastes me. His hands find their way to my hips, and he holds them tight while his tongue goes in and out of me. I feel like a damn ice cream cone the way his head bobs up and down. He pulls me down into the water and sits me back in his lap. "Now, I want you to ride me." I feel the muscles in his hips tighten. "But," he licks the side of my neck while his hands run over my breast, "before I come, I want us to move to the bed. Understood?" He looks into my eyes.

I stare back. "Anything for my King." I move my hips so that I can pull his member without using my hands. He gasps out a hot breath against my chest and his hardness goes inside me.

I can do this. I can ride him, fuck him, use him. The same way he's been using me all these years.I can use him until I'm back home and then, when Trent is safe, I'll speak to Agent Shwetz and tell her everything.

Sometimes for the fly to survive it must kill the spider by trapping it in a web of larger bugs.

A KING'S BED

The bed is the softest bed I've ever laid in. *K*ing rolls us over so that I can ride him. His hands play with my breasts. I work my hips so that he can finish. He rolls us back over again and gyrates inside me, grabbing my legs and holding them straight up in the air. He comes inside me… again.

He holds my legs up, not allowing his baby making juices to leave my body. He shoves a pillow under my butt. "Don't move." He climbs off of me.

"Yes, my *K*ing." I lay perfectly still, my legs in the air.

I need to get my bag. I have no idea where it is, but my clothes keep showing up, so it has to be close by. The next time I'm alone I'll take another pill.

*K*ing pulls a phone from the bedside table. The receiver blends into the wood. "Send up food and drink, now." He puts the phone back down. "After we eat, we will sleep."

"Yes, my *K*ing." I offer a sweet smile.

"Alyx?" He leans over me.

I stroke his hair. "Yes," I say, allowing my lip to quiver.

He places a hand on my belly. "I want you to have my children. All of them." He looks at me so intensely. It feels as though he truly means this.

"I imagine you already have tons of children. With your beautiful eyes." I sweep a soft finger across his eyelid. I have to keep myself in the moment. He can't see me thinking about anything other than him.

"I have no children," he shakes his head, but his jaw tightens.

I don't need him getting angry, so I ignore the lie he just told me. "I shall bear as many as you'd like." I put my hand over my vagina. "I'll hold on to all of you until you have what you want."

"Fuck!" His smile spreads across his face. "You surprise me every time I'm with you." He kisses me.

"You are…" I hold on to the word searching his eyes, "different here," I say. "You show me so much… *affection*." I put my hand on his neck and kiss him once.

"I can finally do whatever the *fuck* I want." He laughs. "I'm a *K*ing now. I make the rules, all of them."

"You made all the rules before, too." I laugh. "I like it when you make the rules." I make sure to throw in some more praise. He needs to believe that I want to be here, so that he won't be watching for me to leave. My escape will be quiet.

"I remember the first time I caught a glimpse of you; you know?"

"Oh really," I say. "How? I've known you forever." I use a playful teenage-girl-like tone.

"You were coming out of school. In your little blue and white skirt." He bites his lip. "I got hard watching you walk." His head moves slowly side to side as he relives the memory. His eyes close. "I imagined how you smelled. How you tasted, how it would feel to be inside you. Soft and warm and tight. I wanted you from the moment I caught sight of you." He strokes a finger down my chest as he lays his head on the pillow next to mine.

"Was I as good as you imagined?" I ask.

"Better," he rubs his hand over my right breast, "so fucking much better."

The doors to the room open.

I don't try to cover myself, that would be pointless. Instead, I reach over and pull his mouth to meet mine. If I am his Queen, everyone has to see me behaving as such.

His eager lips meet mine. His hands trace around my chest as he kisses me.

"Oh, my fucking Queen!" *K*ing yells out. Something clangs and drops; his loudness must've startled someone. He stares into my eyes. "I don't even care that someone made a mess, that's how happy I am right now. Clean it up," he says over his shoulder, "then get the fuck out so I can have my Queen again." His brow raises and he smiles.

The mess is cleaned, and we are alone once again. "Can I ask a question about the business?" I stroke his back.

"You can ask me anything." *K*ing gets up and grabs a plate from the cart. He sits back on the bed and leans against the headboard.

I lay still, making sure not to slide off the pillow he has me propped on. "Why do you pay me, and not some of the others?"

"Are you complaining about that?" He snickers.

"Of course not. I'm curious. Like, what do you pay Ruby? She does all sorts of things for you here, right?"

*K*ing nods his head as he takes a bite of the BLT sandwich. He swallows before he answers. "Ruby acts as a tour guide for any new Dollies, or anyone who hasn't visited here before."

"But when she's not here, she has clients, too."

*K*ing takes another bite. "Yeah," he says around his

food, "but, that's few and far between. Her skills are better used here. No one here gets paid because everything is provided for them. There's no need to pay them."

"That still doesn't answer why I get paid and other girls don't. Am I that much better?" I bat my eyes playfully.

"Honestly, Alyx, girls who come from a wealthier background, like you, well, they handle money better. They handle clients better. It's easier to get a higher price, because you're a higher caliber girl."

I need to seem upset by this. I need him not to look at me like everyone else. "I'm just another girl then?" I look away, rolling my head to the opposite side.

"No, by no means are you just another girl." He chuckles. "You are special in many ways."

"What ways?" I turn back toward him, my eyes wide, a smile on my face.

"Normally I'd say because you never ask questions, but tonight, well," he waves his free hand toward me and takes another bite of food.

"I'm sorry, my King. Shall I stop?" He scrunches up his nose. "I guess I have more questions now that I'm your Queen. Does this mean I'll have new responsibilities?"

"For the next few weeks your responsibilities are to please me." He smiles, the right side of his lip curling up as he does. "After that, we'll see what needs to happen. If you're pregnant by then, then you'll stay here. If you're not, we'll return to the city. I'll be your sole client. Estelle will show you the ropes while you stay at the manor. You'll train the new Dollies on how to behave."

"I won't get paid anymore either will I?"

"Why?" he swallows the last bite of his sandwich. "Do you need more money, Alyx? What do you need money for?"

"To buy pretty things," I rub my hand down his leg. "To make sure my body is perfectly manicured for you. Every single inch," I say as I slide my hand to my nether region. I trace my finger around my clit and bite my lower lip.

King rises from the bed but watches as I play with myself. He takes a drink from the cart, watching me while he swallows. "Well, let's say this," his member stands to attention, "you're getting a raise when we get back." His brow shoots up and then he comes over to the bed.

"My King," I moan, "you honor me. You protect me." I grab my breast as he comes over to the bed, playing with my nipple with one hand and my warmth with the other. "Can you devour me, too?"

King nods. "Yes, my Queen, I can." He crawls up

from the end of the bed. He slowly pulls my fingers out of me, licks them, then enters me.

"*K*ing, *K*ing," I moan. I put my hands in his hair, tugging at it. "I only want you," I say. Who knows, maybe telling him this will take me off the market for good.

It's worth a shot.

He fucks me until he can't anymore.

For the first time since I've known him, he gets under the covers, and pats the bed telling me to join him. "Goodnight my Alyx, my *Q*ueen." He nuzzles into me, snuggling me... until he falls asleep. He stays by my side, the entire night. Every now and again his hands move up and down my naked body. Like he's checking to make sure I haven't disappeared.

I follow suit, making sure he thinks I feel the same.

This might be easier than I thought.

SUNDAY BRUNCH

My *K*ing wakes me at ten, carrying me to the shower. "You are my snack before we have brunch." He acts so strange. If I hadn't known better, I'd think he actually like, *liked-liked* me.

I've seen him be sweet before. I was fourteen then, but still, this is different *somehow*. He doesn't seem to have a care in the world. Even though yesterday he was filmed killing someone. If I'd ever been filmed killing someone, I think I'd be worried. But *K*ing has not a worry.

"I thought snacks before meals were bad. Ruining appetites and such," I wink as he sets me in the shower.

"Oh, no. You my Queen, get my motor running full speed. But," he presses a button on the shower wall, "my motor requires much more today."

Five nude girls come into the bathroom, followed

by two nude men. The men wear neon blue bracelets—they are *F*athers. The girls seem to be from different continents. I knew his sweetness wouldn't last forever, but I'm surprised it only took one night for him to try and put me down. He wants me to be jealous. I'll give him that, but I'll have to fake it, because I don't care.

He just can't know that.

"I'm having a very worldly snack," *K*ing says as he watches me look the girls over.

The shower steams hot from the many overhead fixtures. Water pours from all twelve of them.

*K*ing looks to the *F*athers. "You may feast your eyes on my *Q*ueen, but you may not touch her. If Peter had still been a *F*ather, he'd have died yesterday. Do you understand?"

*F*ather one's skin is dark—I have no way of knowing his name—he is on the shorter side, around five-eight. He is well endowed, and ready to party from the way his member stands.

*F*ather two's skin is fair, but his hair is dark. He is almost as tall as *K*ing. Not as endowed as the others in the shower. Though, I've learned long ago that endowment has nothing to do with pleasure. Pleasure can be had in many, many ways.

The girls—I hope—are eighteen or older. I can't know for sure. I look seventeen but I'm older than that, too, so who knows. Their skin tones are all different. If we were to stand next to each other I'd be third in the line, if we were arranged from lightest to darkest. Three wear Vixen bracelets on their ankles, the other two wear green bracelets on their wrists.

Each girl gets to their knees, making a circle around the *K*ing. I notice *K*ing peek at me. This is indeed some sort of test.

I'm not about to fail.

I move through the small crowd of girls and stand in front of my *K*ing. I put my hand on his neck and pull him into a kiss. "You're mine first," I say as I go down to my knees and suck on him.

"Do you see," *K*ing says to the other *F*athers while I have him in my mouth, "this is why she was chosen. First rate at fucking everything!" He laughs and puts a hand in my hair. The other girls begin putting their hands on him, and each other. They aren't new to this either.

The *F*athers stay put, watching.

*K*ing pulls out of my mouth and inserts himself into another girl's. I get to my feet and make him kiss me again. I have to show him I am his Queen, and he is *my K*ing. One of the girls slides her hand up my leg. "My *K*ing." I look down at her hand then back to him. "Does this please you?"

He looks down, "No one touches the Queen!" He

pushes her away. He looks to *F*ather one. "Take this one."

The man hurries over and pulls the girl back to her knees so that she can suck him off.

*K*ing pushes the girl who has his own cock in her mouth so that she too can service *F*ather one. He grabs someone's red hair and then she has his member in her mouth.

*K*ing is sucked by each girl present. He watches me, watching him be pleasured. I sit down on the long bench and play with myself. I know he wants a show.

*K*ing pushes two girls to *F*ather two. He does with him the same as the others. Cocks needed to be sucked today.

"Alyx," *K*ing says in a gasping breath.

He's about to come. I stand and go over. He turns me around, pulls the girl off his cock, bends me over, then shoves it inside me. All his juices are meant for me. No matter who brought him close, I'm the receiver.

I'm not sure how many blue pills *K*ing has taken, but I'm certain he's been taking them every eight hours since he got here.

When he pulls out of me, he lays me on the bench and puts my legs up. "Stay," he says.

I nod and lay there. *K*ing pulls another girl off *F*ather one's cock and makes her lick him clean. *F*ather one makes a move to grab her, but the look *K*ing gives him stops him in his tracks. The man grabs another of the girls and pushes her against the shower wall, fucking her from behind.

Father two, sits on another bench, pulls a girl into his lap and has her ride him. He reaches and grabs one girl by her hair, making her stand atop the bench, then buries his face in her crotch, the other girl has to lean back so far, I'm surprised she's able to still fuck him without sliding off in all the water.

That girl has some talent.

The other two girls take turns touching the King, while he touches and tastes them. His eyes stay on me for the most part though. I bite my lower lip to show him I want him.

My stomach rumbles, reminding me that I'm hungry in another way.

King laughs, pushes the girls off of him and comes over to me. "Does my Queen need to eat?"

"All this work to fulfill your wishes has me famished." I lay there with my feet up against the wall.

"Get the fuck out!" He yells.

The girls who aren't being fucked are quick to leave. The others must squirm to get away. They know to obey King above all else.

The Fathers are perturbed but don't argue. Father one turns. "My King has a lovely Queen. May she bear you many offspring." He bows before leaving.

"And you," King says to number two. "What do you think of my Queen?"

"I'd love a go at her." He chuckles. "Maybe one day." He licks his lips. "She looks amazing."

King takes a step toward him.

"No, King, a compliment. I know my place." He puts his hands up.

"Leave," King says.

They leave slipping on the marble as they hurry away.

"I'd like you in your one piece today, Alyx." King helps me up.

"Of course," I say.

"Wash me?" His gaze is sweet and wanting again.

I nod and wash his body. He washes mine.

We dry off. Dress and leave the fifth-floor heading for the first floor and food.

FINDING RUBY

I can't let *K*ing's sweetness distract me. It's as off-putting as it is a relief. It makes me want his attention when he's nice. Though, as soon as those desires build up in my head, Sempers flashes in my vision. *K*ing sent me there, knowing what he was.

That isn't kindness or love.

Had that been the plan. Had *K*ing wanted Sempers to do a job he couldn't? Maybe *K*ing valued me to a degree. When I survived Sempers, I somehow became even more valuable. Which must be why he's chosen me as his *Q*ueen.

"*Q*ueen," *K*ing says as we step off the elevator, "Jennson,"—he points to Jennson who stands waiting as we exit— "and I have some business to discuss. Why don't you find Ruby and get something to eat? I'll send for you when our business has finished."

I nod once and walk away from them. When I'd been in Jennson's office last Monday, he'd mentioned something about a busload of kids. After meeting Phallon and learning about Margaret, is the busload of kids' just product being sold? There is one way for me to find out.

"Will everything be ready by Tuesday?" King asks.

"Like I said yesterday. We've got to up our exports. You being a King now, it all falls to your discretion," Jennson says.

"Move them all on Tuesday, like you planned. I want to start my reign strong."

The two men laugh, and I leave to find Ruby.

Ruby isn't hard to find. She's used to The Island and its guests. She knows how to blend better than I do. Sometimes you blend by standing out of the crowd. Her laughter echoes down the marble hallway. When I come into the room with the buffet Ruby is dancing on a table, topless. Several peach bracelet Cousins vying for her to come with them.

Ruby ignores them while winking and waving to those she can't refuse. She spots me and throws me a wink, too. "My Queen," she says, jumping from the table. "May I assist you in finding your breakfast?" She grabs a plate and smiles at me.

For good show, I turn my nose up while rolling my eyes. "That will be fine. Fruit only," I order.

I feel like an asshole, but all the men seem pleased at my behavior.

"My *Queen*," Ruby says with a smile.

After working in our positions, we've learned to read each other so well. I've been learning it is out of necessity of life. Though not until recently. Why hadn't I?

Was it selfishness? I can't see how that could be it. Though, staying alive is a good reason to be selfish. I have to stay alive, not because I don't have a desire to die, but because what will Trent do without me? If I start thinking about that I'll spiral.

I follow Ruby to the elevator while she carries my plate of food.

"I know the perfect place for you to eat my *Queen*," Ruby says.

I nod and wave my bracelet for the doors to open. We step on to the elevator and the doors close.

"All those fuckers are insane," Ruby barks and hands me the plate.

I take it from her and eat a strawberry. "Completely," I agree.

"It'll be less crowded in the kitchen, at least as far as the number of *J*ohns, if you don't mind people running past you with hot food."

"Fine by me. No one's allowed to look at me anyway." The elevator doors open into the B2 level. "Can I ask you a question though?"

"Sure," Ruby says while she takes a grape from the plate and exits the elevator.

"Did you know what Sasha, and Ana were up to?" I follow her down the hall.

Ruby stops and turns toward me. "Follow me," she says. She inclines her head toward the ceiling. I understand what she means when the little green light blinks. There are cameras on this floor.

Ruby pulls me into a bathroom and turns on a fan. It rattles and sputters to life. She leans in and whispers in my ear. "We broke the fan in here because it hides our voices. But yeah, I know what Sasha and Ana were doing. They were working with Dorian, trying to get everyone off this mother fucking island."

"Are you sure?" I whisper back.

Ruby nods. "I know you've met Shwetz. I have, too. She met me outside L'appart that night. There wasn't enough room in the car, so Felix waited with me while Collin took everyone where they needed to go. He ran inside to use the facilities and then there she was."

"Why didn't you go with her then?"

"I didn't want anything to happen to Felix. He's Ana's brother. Ana was my sister, like you're my sister. I couldn't leave. What would they do to Felix?"

Ruby's right. What would they do to Felix if he misplaced their product? If they killed Sasha for taking money, they'd do worse to Felix for losing what makes them that money. "Hey, do you have that number?"

"The one that ends with the star key?"

I nod.

"Yeah, I've got it, but there aren't any phones here. So lotta good that'll do."

"Do you know where my bags are?"

"Yeah. They're still in the room Fitz had when he was still an *U*ncle," Ruby chews on her fingernail. "Why?"

"There's a disposable in my makeup bag. Get it. Keep it. Do what you will with it."

"How did you get it here?"

"I came with *K*ing," Even with Ruby I can't afford to call him anything else. "He brought me on the helicopter. No one checked my bags as far as I know."

"You keep going down this hall, last door on the left will take you to the kitchen docks. Wait for me there, okay?"

"What are you going to do?"

"I'm going to go find that phone and stash it before anyone else can find it. You'll need makeup tonight for the sale. Someone might find it if I don't go now." Ruby opens the door and I do as she asked.

I'm good at doing what I'm told. At least with Ruby it's beneficial for both of us.

The kitchen is buzzing with workers. I do notice however that all of them are like me, either Vixens or Dollies. However, no one has on a green bracelet. These workers are useful in more than one way; therefore, they aren't for sale.

I shimmy past a teenaged boy as he carries a heavy tray of plates. He smiles at me and tries to open up the space between us. I smile back and go outside to the dock. The smell of the ocean always seems to make me remember home. I love and hate it.

Remembering home makes me think of mom and dad. Thinking of them makes me remember that I'm responsible for their deaths. Not that I actually killed them, I know better than that, but had I not done stupid things when I was a kid, they'd still be alive.

A boat pulls up to the dock. Tall wood boxes stacked high. A bell rings from behind me. I turn and that boy from earlier rings the bell, a sign above says 'delivery.' Three others join him, and they go over to the boat.

I go to the end of the dock so as to be out of the way. I don't want someone to accidentally hurt me and cause their deaths, too. *K*ing will kill anyone who touches me, even if it is an accident. I don't need more deaths on my hands.

I watch them work as I finish eating and then toss my plate in a trash can. Each of them has no way off this Island. The people on the boat also wear bracelets. Sapphire blue, they're *B*rothers. One of them begins walking towards me. I brush my hair away from my face, so that he can see the bracelet on my wrist. He stops, turns his gaze downcast, then walks back to the boat.

Laughter trills from further down the dock. When I turn, I notice that the dock goes around a small corner. I follow the sound—it is masked by noise of the delivery as well as the ocean, but I'm certain it came from this way.

When I round the corner I see Becca, she's leaning over someone, a finger in front of her lips, shushing them. Becca stands and there is a little girl in front of her. The little girl waves—a bracelet dangles from her wrist, but I can't see the color. I wave back and Becca turns.

Becca puts a hand over her heart. "Jesus, Queen, you scared me." She positions herself between me and the child, putting a protective hand on the child's back.

"Who is this?" I say as the little girl peeks out from behind her.

Becca shakes her head, telling me no. My brow pinches together.

The girl comes out from behind Becca. "I'm Everleigh, but my momma calls me Ever," she smiles.

I smile and bend down. I know this is Ana's daughter, they have the same eyes and nose. I can see Fitzroy in the curve of her lips, too. "Are you doing well?" I look her over. She looks unscathed, but not all scars are carried on the outside. Her bracelet is red like mine. Becca and I share a glance; at least it isn't green.

"I am, thank you," she smiles at me. "Have you seen my momma?"

I want to cry, but that won't help anyone's scars. "I haven't, I'm sorry."

"It's okay. Momma said she'd be back. She will be soon." The girl runs to the edge of the dock and peers into the water.

"Becca, are you crazy?" I lean in and whisper. "You said the kids couldn't come out until Monday."

"I won't be here Monday. I don't have any other time." She stares over at Everleigh. "I promised Ana that I'd take care of her. I can't break that promise." A tear escapes her. "I'll do all I can while I can."

I look out over the water. The vastness of the ocean always amazes me, but looking at it from this place, an emptiness settles in my stomach. All these men and women, boys and girls, the people who've been forced to come here in one way or another. They have nothing else. I have the hope of going home because I'm a Queen.

What do they have?

"Where do you think they'll take you?" I ask. Becca has been here a while, maybe she knows more.

"I think the Russian *Uncle* is looking to up his product." She rubs her arm in a nervous manner. "That's what I've been hearing anyway. He's paid a fortune to get first pick."

"How much?" I look over and Everleigh lays flat on her belly letting the water come up and touch her fingers as the waves roll toward the shore.

"I know it's six figures, but I don't know the exact amount. Idowu goes second. I know he's requested at least twenty. Other than that, I have no idea." Becca shrugs and looks toward Everleigh. "How will I keep her safe when I'm not here?"

Footsteps behind us make both of us turn.

"Good, you're both here." Ruby comes over to us. "Listen, I'm not sure how long it will take, but they'll be here soon, I hope."

I arch a brow.

Becca looks at Ruby. "Who will be here?"

Ruby looks around and holds up the phone, then she tosses it in the water.

Becca dives for it but misses it. "Why would you do that?" she asks as she raises up.

"Don't worry, they already got the signal." Ruby smiles.

"Holy hell, Ruby! Did you already call?" My eyes widen.

Ruby's smile answers me. She called the FBI. They'll be here, and soon. When is the question. "Did they say how long?" I ask. "Do you think they'll arrive before the sale?"

Becca runs over and grabs Everleigh up in her arms. She looks to Ruby waiting for the answer.

"All I know is she says they have the location, and they are coming. She promised."

"Shwetz?"

Ruby nods.

My heart beats fast in my chest. This will be it. But what of the ones Jennson and Fitzroy spoke of earlier? How will they be saved? No one else knew about them, not even Felix.

"Becca," Ruby says. "You should take Everleigh inside. Who knows if they'll come in hot or not."

"I can't leave her," Becca says. "I'll take her over to the beach for a swim." Becca inclines her head toward the shore.

There's nothing but rocks. "There is no beach there," I say confused.

"There's a hidden beach. Vixens and Dollies are the only ones allowed."

"Only Vixens and Dollies know about it," Ruby corrects. "Otherwise, all the *Johns* would be there, too. Looking to get some."

Becca sets Everleigh down. "Let's swim over to the secret beach, okay love?" she says.

Everleigh smiles. "It's my favorite," she giggles. "I'm a good swimmer."

Becca dives into the water, when she surfaces, she puts her arms out for Everleigh to join her. The child jumps into the water and into the safety of Becca's arms. They swim away.

"Do you think they'll be okay?" I ask Ruby.

"No one, not even Fitz knows about that beach. We make sure that only a few of us go at a time. We ring the bell three times if anyone is needed. They know to come back. It's the only place we have for any peace." Ruby's head bounces side to side.

"Why didn't you ever tell me about any of this? Why didn't you all ask me to help? Maybe, maybe they wouldn't be gone if I'd helped?" I look down at my feet. Or maybe they'd have died sooner if I had. I'm not very good at helping. I've magically managed to keep my brother safe and that is because of Corwin.

"You weren't ready to see any of it, Alyx." Ruby

strokes a hand down my arm. "You'd have told on us," her brow goes up.

Would I have told on them? I tried to go back to before... before Sasha died and I was covered in her blood. I was content, no matter how much denial I swam in every day, I was *okay* with my job. I'd chosen to do it so I could survive, but I'm not sure that's enough anymore.

"Don't take offense," Ruby says.

"I don't. I'm trying to remember a time when everything wasn't so complicated."

"You'll need to think back to before you ever knew Fitzroy. Because let's face it, it's been complicated since then."

"How did you get into this? Were you kidnapped, too?"

Ruby looks out over the water. "No," she takes in a deep breath. "I ran away from home. Not because I had a bad life. My parents were wonderful. They took my phone because they found out I sent nudes to a few of the boys at school." Ruby laughs. "I was old enough to make my own damn decisions. Fuck, if I'd have known better, I'd have listened. I ran away from a damn four-story house, with all the amenities." She rolls her eyes but smiles. "It was a good home. I was a stupid kid."

"I understand that."

"We always think we know better and that they're

telling us what to do. That they want us to bend to their will. I see now that that's not at all what happened. They knew more than I did. They had more experience. They weren't trying to lord over me; they wanted me to learn how to be safe and how to make the right choices. They may not have known how to train me, to get me to understand, but they wanted good things for me. I wish I would have grasped that, then maybe I wouldn't have kept secrets."

"The secrets that we keep, right?" I shake my head. "At least you know now. As little comfort as that brings." I look out over the water again. I take in a deep breath, letting the salty smell fill my lungs. "Are your parents still alive?"

"Yeah. My brother, too. All of them are still happy living in Boston."

"How do you know?"

"Fitzroy shows me pictures."

"Why?" I turn and face her, my brow scrunches together.

"Because he wants me to know that if I try to leave, he knows where they are. He will use them to keep me doing what I'm supposed to do."

"He's threatening to hurt your family? I'm so sorry, Ruby." I hug her.

"He already killed yours." She hugs me back. "I don't want him to kill mine, too. Who knows, maybe

I'll get lucky and get to see them at least once before I get too used up and they kill me, too."

The bell rings out five times.

Ruby let's go of me. No one can see us touching. "The boat's fixing to leave," Ruby says.

I take three steps away from her and the bow of the boat comes into view. The driver waves to Ruby. Ruby waves back.

A loud shrill alarm rings out. Like a tornado warning. I clamp my hands over my ears. The speaker is above our heads.

"Fuck," Ruby yells out. "Come on, we've got to get inside. That's the headcount alarm!"

"What about Becca?" I ask.

Ruby looks past me, as I turn, too. Spying for any sight of Becca and Everleigh. Ruby tugs at her hair. "They'll have to go in a different way. This way takes too long. Come on," she waves a hand for me to follow her.

We run down the dock. The doors are open. There are lights flashing in the kitchen, but it's empty. Ruby runs toward the hallway; I follow after her. "Where are we going?" We hurry down the empty corridor.

"First floor. Everyone will line the hall for the head count."

"Where do I go?"

"I'd say by the elevator to wait for *K*ing, since you're Queen."

The alarms stop and a voice comes over the speaker.

"*U*ncles, please report to the roof. I repeat, all *U*ncles, to the roof now. Code seven."

"What the fuck is a code seven?" I ask Ruby as we take the stairs two at a time to get to the first floor.

"I don't have a clue," she says.

We come up to the first floor, Dollies and Vixens line the walls. Their heads are down. *F*athers and *B*rothers have clipboards and are each checking off spots on their papers as they count. The floor is littered with discarded bracelets. "On your knees," a *F*ather says to Ruby as he grabs her wrist and forces her to the floor.

"I'm escorting the Queen," Ruby says.

The *F*ather backhands her. "The *Q*ueen is capable of taking care of herself, she doesn't need a whore like you for help." He smacks her again.

"Don't fucking touch her!" I glare. "Ruby, stand!" I order.

Ruby gets up.

"Check her off your fucking list." I notice Quentin. "And him, too," I point to Quentin. "He's coming with me."

The *F*ather doesn't meet my gaze. He nods and

makes two marks on his clipboard. I have more power than I realized and it's about time I use it.

I look around for Phallon, Everleigh, and Becca. I look around for any familiar faces. I don't know what I need to do, but I want to keep them safe.

As we pass each Vixen and Dolly who stands against the wall my heart aches. I want to claim all of them. I want to take them all away from here. Their lives are at risk, every single second. If I knew when the FBI would arrive.

If I knew without a doubt that Shwetz was an FBI agent and not someone who works for Fitzroy I might feel better about it all, but right now, I feel a knot in my stomach. If it is Fitzroy, my *King*, would he think I called the number, will I die for it?

"What the fuck is that?" A *B*rother stares out the window towards the pool.

Everyone turns. There is a black line, coming across the water. Water spurting up behind it. I walk closer to the windows and squint. It's boats. Lots of boats, headed full speed, towards The Island.

Ruby gasps. She realizes it, too.

Agent Shwetz had stuck to her word. They are coming.

"Queen report to the roof, immediately!" sounds over the loudspeakers.

"Stay," Ruby says. "They'll be here any minute."

"I have to find Felix," I say, realizing I haven't seen him today.

I run over to the elevator and wave my bracelet. The doors open and I step on. Ruby and Quintin stay outside the doors. "They'll help you," I whisper. "Stay together, please." The doors close, I press the option for the roof.

COMPROMISED

The roof is alive with chatter. I don't know where the rest of the *U*ncles are, as there are only five on the roof. But I imagine they are headed here, too. *U*ncles crane their necks looking toward the approaching black line. Whether they know it's boats or not is beyond me, but they are all worried. I don't see Felix or *K*ing anywhere.

"Where is my *K*ing?" I yell out.

"He's below, my Queen," one of the *U*ncles answers me with a bow of his head. Even though he worries he doesn't falter from his role as *U*ncle and mine as Queen. He shows me the respect that he thinks is due, somehow still fearing what *K*ing will do if he finds out.

"Where?" I order, making him look at me again.

"B3, getting the children," he says.

"Why?" I say through my teeth.

"We've been compromised," he says, pointing a hand toward the boats.

"How do you know this?" I ask.

"Another of the Kings called. They told us of the threat as soon as they were informed." He looks out over the water. "They are five miles out, they'll be here soon."

"What are you waiting for? Why aren't you leaving?"

"We have to wait on the helicopter." He points in the opposite direction that the boats are coming from.

I look up as a huge helicopter flies toward the Island.

"We can't leave without King, we won't!" he assures me.

"I'll get him myself!" I want to find Everleigh and Felix, but Uncle doesn't need to know that. I run back to the elevator and get inside.

Someone at the FBI must be working for Fitzroy. Either that or someone at the FBI told someone who is. I press B3.

When the doors open the room is filled with children—several of whom have on green bracelets. A few Vixens are consoling them as they cry. The alarms must've scared them.

King and Felix come into the room looking

through the children. "Where the fuck is she?" Felix says to *K*ing.

"She has to be here, she wasn't in any other room." *K*ing grabs each little girl with dark hair. He looks her over then releases her when he doesn't find Everleigh. "Rissy where is Everleigh?" he yells to another adult in the room.

"I'm not sure sir, she was here earlier," Rissy replies as she too looks through the children.

"They're close," I say.

Felix and *K*ing both look toward me. Rissy wipes tears from her face. I can't tell if she's happy or scared.

"I told you to go to the roof!" *K*ing says. "You were supposed to wait for me there. They won't get my *Q*ueen." He comes over and kisses my forehead.

"*K*ing, who are you looking for?" I ask.

"Everleigh, she's mine. She must come with us." He pulls a cell phone from his pocket and shows me a photo. "Look for this girl," he hands me the phone.

I nod my head and look around. Feigning that I too am looking for the child. Though I know that she isn't here. If I can keep him here long enough, maybe they'll get him, too.

As I look at each of the children, Jennson pops into my head. Jennson is moving more children on Tuesday at *K*ings behest. These children aren't those ones. If they were, he'd have said they needed to get these ones off The Island.

The only way to save the ones in the city will be to leave and tell Shwetz more when we are in New York. "We must leave," I say to King. "They'll be here any second."

King tears his gaze away from the children. I put my hand out. He takes my offered hand and we run to the elevator. I wave my bracelet in front of the digital panel and the doors open up.

"Felix," King screams. "We must go."

"No, I'll find her!" Felix yells.

"Felix," I holler. "We will get her later!" I hope the look in my eyes lets him know that I already know where she is and that she is much safer there than here. I nod my head. "Come on!"

Felix runs over to us, and we get onto the elevator.

King pushes the button for the roof. As the elevator ascends the B2 clicks but then the elevator stops. The lights go out.

"Fuck!" King says. "They've cut the power!"

"I'll get you out of here," Felix says. He presses the stop button then goes to his knees. He pulls at the bottom of the elevator doors until they open. Light fills the small space.

"Good, the flood lights came on," King says.

Felix pulls himself out of the elevator and reaches back in for my hand. "May I help her *K*ing?" he asks.

"Yes! Fuck, hurry up! We have to get out of here!" *K*ing lifts me and Felix pulls me through the space.

I worry for a second that the elevator will collapse and chop me in half. But by the time the thought has passed through my head I'm out and standing in a hall-way. *K*ing coming up behind me.

"This way," *K*ing says. "We're on the floor with the kitchens, we'll need to take the stairs." He runs down the hall.

Felix and I follow.

*K*ing slows down when we hear movement ahead of us. He inclines his head to the right, and we follow.

We pass the doors to the kitchen; several boats are docked. Groups of agents are gathering. Those in charge yelling orders as others check their weapons.

"My *K*ing," I whisper, pulling him back. "There's a secret beach, some of the Dollies talked about it. Send Felix there to look for your child," I say. Maybe I can save Felix and he can be with Everleigh.

"What? Where?" *K*ing says, coming to stand next to me.

"Out those doors, and to the right, that's all I know."

Felix's eyes flash over to me. The look says he doesn't want to leave me or Everleigh.

"Perhaps someone took her out there before the alarms went off, where else could she be?" I say. "You need to get to the roof, but Felix, he can go look and meet us there."

"Helicopter!" Is yelled out from down the hall.

"Fuck!" *K*ing says. "I can't lose Felix. I'll get Everleigh a different way. Come on!" He grabs my hand and pulls me past the kitchen.

Felix follows us.

We go up the stairs. *F*athers, *B*rothers, and everyone else in the hierarchy are running around. The Vixens and Dollies run, too. I know they are scared because prostitution is illegal. We have all been told at one point or another that we'll rot in jail if we're busted. That our families will die if we're discovered. We cannot be caught. Everything is loud and no one knows what to do.

*K*ing puts up a hand to keep Felix and I from talking. We nod. "Follow me, there's a secret stairway. It goes to the roof. We'll go one at a time, so no one sees us, understand?"

We nod again and *K*ing takes off. He hurries past the opening and down to another hall. He waves for Felix to come over. Felix does as he is commanded and then it's my turn.

A hand grabs my arm. I look down the stairs and it's Shwetz. "You're not going anywhere," she says.

"No!" *K*ing yells out. Felix shoves him into the hallway as Shwetz looks toward the sound.

"GO!" Felix roars at *K*ing. It looks as though he's saying more but I can't hear him.

Trent's image flashes in my head. "You've got to let me go!" I say to Shwetz. If I don't make it back to the city, what will they do to my brother? To Corwin. Corwin has no idea about Becca. Will Trent and Corwin be safe if I don't make it back?

"Why would I do that, Alyx?" she says.

I need to convince Shwetz to let me go. "Because if you don't, you won't be able to get them all."

"What says I can't?" She digs her fingers into my wrist.

"This," I say as I hold up the other wrist, showing her my bracelet. "I've been promoted. You'll have someone on the inside. There's a private beach at the end of the dock where you came in. Go there, you'll find Corwin Thwaite's daughter and another *package* that you're going to need if you want to find out who is behind all of this. Now, I'm sorry, but," I quirk a smile then punch her square in the face as hard as I can.

Shwetz tumbles backwards down the stairs, and I take off running toward *K*ing and Felix. I won't let the opportunity to save my brother and more children pass me by. Not when there is something I can do about it.

I make it to the roof as the doors to the helicopter

are closing. I scream and run forward. The doors open and Felix's hand shoots out. I grab it as the helicopter lifts into the air. My legs dangle as the helicopter flies.

The doors open further, and another hand comes out and grabs me. It's *K*ing. He pulls hard and I'm in the helicopter. Felix closes the doors.

"My *Q*ueen, thank god!" *K*ing wraps his arms around me. "Fucking hell, I don't know what I would've done without you." He kisses the top of my head.

I wrap my arms around him. My eyes find Felix. I smile. I mouth the words, 'she's safe.'

Felix nods and sits down. He looks out the window. "My *K*ing!" He points out the door.

*K*ing and I both look out the window. Agent Shwetz is on the private beach, Becca hugging her. Everleigh is holding onto Becca's leg.

"Fuck!" *K*ing screams.

Felix's head rolls back, and a tear escapes him. He leans forward and puts his head in his hands as a tremor runs through his shoulders.

"What's wrong with you?" *K*ing yells.

Felix looks up. "I've failed you." He puts his head back in his hands.

Felix is good at lying, too. I know the tears he cries are happy tears. His promise to his sister has been fulfilled.

His sister's daughter is safe now.

With Becca going back, she'll help Corwin keep Trent safe, too. I know it.

I want to smile because I know that Corwin will soon have Becca back. He'll be over the moon with joy very soon. I want to be there when that reunion happens. I can't be though. I have bigger Fish to fry. I hide my smile because I need to live a while longer. I have more people to save. I will stay with King, until they are all out.

I'll go back to the city and save everyone that I can. I'll get King back for killing my parents.

Then my brother and I will disappear.

Hell, Felix can come with us, too.

We'll get Everleigh and we'll all be safe.

EPILOGUE

"The FBI recovered one-hundred-eighty people today. Four adults were apprehended and charged with human trafficking and a slew of other charges. The FBI was quoted saying 'We will not rest until we find all of those responsible.' Those rescued from the buses range in age from four to twenty years old. The FBI is working with local authorities to identify all the individuals."

"Fuck!" Fitzroy yells from beside me as he throws the remote at the television. The remote misses its mark and he huffs. He is still a *King*, but I am now allowed to call him by his name. The news reports filing in have put a damper on the business and he is quite upset by it.

I lean back against the headboard. "It's crazy!" I say,

hiding the fact that I am the one who told Shwetz where and when to find the school buses today. Well, I didn't tell her. I had Felix drive out of the city, get a burner phone, call the 5212 number, and he told her.

My place has been by Fitzroy's side since we returned from the Island. I had a few moments to tell Felix what to do when we returned to the manor. I told him to follow Jennson and find out. Felix did one better. He offered Jennson a ride and told Fitzroy it would be better if he stayed with Jennson for a little while to keep him safe. Especially since Collin was still around to protect Fitzroy.

It worked like a charm. Felix went with Jennson, and I stayed with Fitzroy. He wanted to teach me everything. He wanted his *Q*ueen to shine—despite all the shit going on. Collin was usually close by, too.

I'd figured out how to help the kids while on the helicopter ride back to the city with *K*ing and the five *U*ncles who escaped The Island. Jennson had been one of them. He and *K*ing had pushed Tuesday's sale back because of everything that happened. It's also when I found out that Jennson handled all of *K*ing's financials —even the secret ones that no one else knows about. The loss of assets due to the raid had lost them both upwards of seventy million dollars.

The loss of the people on the buses today lost additional millions. With the news report coming out now,

I'm sure that number will rise. Not everyone wants to keep paying for services when the FBI is closing in.

"In another raid last month, the FBI located one hundred and sixty people at an undisclosed location. The numbers aren't clear yet how many were victims and how many will be charged. Many believe there must be someone on the inside helping them," the reporter says as her brow goes high. "I myself hope whoever is helping, continues to do so."

"Fucking cunt!" Fitzroy grabs the glass of water on the bedside table and chucks it at the television. The television screen breaks when the glass hits its mark. This is the third television he's broken since we returned. "Who do you think it is?" he looks at me.

I huff. "Peter!" I say throwing blame. "He was one of those arrested on The Island, but I bet he's also the one who called. Who else could it have been?" Fitzroy's brow furrows as he thinks it over. I'll try to drive it home even more. "Think about it. He was pissed because of his punishment. He didn't get to have any of the *Queen* for himself. That *Fucker*. Or not as much as he wanted anyway." I shiver at the thought of him touching me. I hated what he'd done to me. It makes me sick to my stomach every time the memory pops into my head. Fitzroy rubs my leg. "When he was punished…"

"That asshole didn't get punished enough." Fitzroy

blows out an angry breath through his nose. "I should have had him shot and thrown into the ocean." His hand squeezes my thigh. "Touching my Queen." He clenches his fists.

I nod. "Maybe you should have. Who else had access to the phones? I didn't even know there were phones on The Island until you picked up the one on your bedside table."

"You're right." Fitzroy nods his head. "It had to be one of the Uncles. No one else had access to phones." He tilts his head back and blows out a breath. "I need some tension released," he says, and he places his hand on the back of my head.

He pulls my head down to his crotch. "Of course, my King," I still have to use the term whenever sex is involved. I'd rather blow him than have him try to get me pregnant again. I've been doing all sorts of things to keep him from coming inside me. I hope Felix returns soon with more plan B pills. If he doesn't, I'll have more things to worry about.

As his fingers dig into my hair pressing my head up and down, I do all that is required of me. Flicking my tongue, sucking the right amount, doing the things that Fitzroy likes. There are still more people to save, but I need to find out who the other three Kings are. There'll be no reason to turn in Fitzroy if I don't know the others, because one of them will swoop in and take over his area. How will that help anyone?

He comes in my mouth. Fitzroy's smile is smug as I make a show of swallowing his fluid. I take a drink of the hibiscus tea that I have next to the bed to wash away the tar taste.

"Go get me some food." He picks up his cell phone.

"Of course, my *K*ing," I smile, get up, and leave the room.

We've been at the manor for five weeks now. There are sixty other people in the house. This includes Estelle, Deidra, Misty, and Collin. It also still houses the few *U*ncles—apart from Jennson—who made it off The Island to safety. They're waiting until things calm down to return to wherever they hail from.

I'm not sure why the FBI only located a hundred and sixty people on the Island. There were at least three hundred there. Where had the others gone? Estelle heads toward me as I walk down the stairs. She passes me, not daring a look at me.

Since we got back, Estelle keeps her distance from me—literally leaving any room I enter. I still don't know how to feel about it. Is she doing this because I am Queen now and she isn't? She can have the title if she wants it. I'd be happy to trade places. She can get pregnant instead of me, it won't bother me at all.

As I walk through the halls, I'm glad I'm not in

denial anymore. I know who I am. I know what I am. I'm someone who has been used and sold for sex. I am a victim of human trafficking.

Though not like some of the others.

I've had it easy compared to all of the others. I don't have to think of myself as a victim either. Though sometimes it does feel like I am one.

I still have to do what I need to do to stay alive.

I still have to have sex with Fitzroy, or whomever else he orders me to have sex with.

But I can also help the others.

And I will.

I will help anyone I can. I will pretend to be Queen. I will be good at it. Though as far as I can tell right now all being Queen entails is opening my legs—or whatever other orifice my King requires—whenever he wants. Allowing him to use my body in any way he deems necessary. Even if that means opening my legs for others.

Thus far that hasn't been required of me, but the first month of him being King has come to a close. We'll see how the rest of the week goes. Fitzroy will soon tire of having only one girl.

Not a single word about Trent has come my way. Fingers crossed that no news is good news.

I hope he's still with Corwin. No information has come about Ruby, Becca, or any of the others that were on The Island either. Does Corwin have Becca back yet? I'm not sure when or if I'll get to know.

Maybe it's better not to know any of that yet. I need to stay on my toes. I need to keep my head straight. It will be difficult though. This is the longest I've ever gone without talking to my brother. Maybe Felix can check in on him somehow.

Felix has more leeway with his comings and goings. He is a bodyguard and a personal assistant. If Fitzroy, Estelle, or I need anything Collin or Felix are sent out to get it.

I enter the kitchen and prepare a plate of food for Fitzroy. I take bites of food as I do. No one else is in the kitchen so it is safe to stuff my face a little bit. The strawberry cheesecake bites are most excellent. As are the chicken livers. I take a drink of the apple juice, too. Fresh squeezed tastes better.

Fitzroy comes into the kitchen. He's on his phone so I smile and hold the plate up so he can see what I have prepared. He nods and continues his conversation. I sneak one more cheesecake bite.

"I'm aware of that, Langdon, but it doesn't matter." He pops one of the cheesecake bites into his mouth, too. "I have about fifty here at the manor that I could move if I needed to." He swats my butt as I pass him.

I give him a wink and set his plate down on the bar. I pull the stool out and encourage him to sit down. He takes the offered seat. I go back over to the buffet to prepare my own plate.

"No, due to the loss of inventory I'll have to up the prices. Yeah, there's a team going out this week. Kentucky. No, apparently there's prime inventory there. Jennson says there's a great area that's ready for plucking. Yes, we've sent teams there before. No, their local news doesn't press the issue too much. I'm not sure. Yes. Okay. Fine then we won't go there. What about Estelle's girls that are still in Florida? Yeah, they'll work. We'll call in Iris's from Houston, too. Yes, Iris has a large enough group. It should help cover the difference."

I listen and take note of the names. Jennson, Iris, Estelle. I'll need to try and remember everyone's names and locations. Houston, and something about a place in Kentucky. I'll have to speak to Shwetz soon myself. I'll need to find a way to communicate with her so that others can be saved.

"No, I'll call you when I get a new line. Yes, everyone is changing their numbers just in case. I have five here at the manor. I don't think any of the others escaped. There were about a hundred members there when the FBI arrived. Yes, we lost two hundred units that day. That number includes some of the body-guards, too. I'm not sure. The newscast said they found around a hundred sixty in total. No, it doesn't make any sense. I assume Ruby will come back when they let her out. Because she's loyal to me. If not, we'll send someone to her family's house. She'll come back then. I don't know. Maybe the bunker did work out for some. Yes, good. I'll wait for that." Fitzroy hangs up the phone.

I store the word bunker away in my vault.

"Thank you for preparing me a plate my *Queen*." Since our return Fitzroy has been treating me as an equal. I'm not sure if it's to throw me in Estelle's face or not. His hands are always on my body if she's in the room though.

"Anything for my *King*." I run my hand through his hair and sit down by him.

Collin comes into the kitchen as we eat. "Hey boss. I finished that errand. I couldn't find anyone."

Fitzroy nods then he inclines his head toward the door. Collin returns a quick nod then heads for the exit. Looking at me and raising a brow as he leaves. From what I know of Collin that look means he's happy he knows something I don't.

I'll have to figure that out, too.

I eat the small plate of food that I prepared for myself. Glad that I ate some things before Fitzroy came into the room. Having to watch every single bite that goes into your mouth is tedious work. I'm not sure if the rules on eating still pertain to me though now that I've been promoted. Will I still get slapped for eating too many bites of food in front of Fitzroy or Estelle?

I push my luck and see. I get up and choose a few more items from the table. I put some fruit on my plate, as well as two chicken tenders. I sit back down, and Fitzroy looks over at me as I pop a strawberry in my mouth.

He leans back and watches me eat. He doesn't put out a hand to smack me. His brow doesn't quirk the way it does when he is about to strike either. "Enjoying the newfound freedom my *Queen*?"

I smile. "How much freedom are we talking about?" I eat a blueberry.

"I've been waiting for you to ask." He strokes his hand down my back. "As long as you don't gain any weight, anything is fine. So, more exercise. Okay?"

I nod.

"However, if you're pregnant the staff doctor will let you know how much weight you can gain, but exercise will still be a priority. Understood?"

"Of course." I took my last plan B pill two days ago. I need Felix to come back soon.

"Also, Estelle should give you a few girls to start with. I don't want to overwhelm you."

"What?" I ask unsure what he means. "Why would I need any girls?"

"Well. I'm sending her back to Florida. I'll need

someone here to handle the schedules for a while. Jennson will also require tending to. He requested that I send you back, but I told him that wouldn't be allowed yet. I'm not quite finished with my Queen." He laughs.

"I'll be scheduling appointments?" Why haven't I thought of this? I knew that I'd learn what Estelle does but somehow, I've neglected to realize all that that would entail. I'll have to send people out. To perform sexual acts on other people. I'll *have* to do this.

"Yes," Fitzroy's head bobs up and down. He drops his hand from my back and takes another bite of food from his own plate. "Is this not something you're interested in?" He asks hopefully not guessing that I don't want to. Hopefully he thinks of me as worried I can't do the job as well as Estelle. I'll need to make sure that's what he thinks.

"Do you think I'll do as well as Estelle? I've never done anything like this before. I don't want to mess anything up," I say. Fingers fucking crossed that my tone matches that of someone nervous for new tasks.

"I'll have Estelle go over things with you before she leaves. There are a few clients right now that aren't worried about the FBI. I've tried convincing everyone to hold off for a while, but some feel untouchable. Well, some *are* untouchable." Fitzroy shrugs, sets his fork down, and takes a swig of my apple juice. He looks over at me. His lip curves up in the right corner. That means sex is on his mind. He pushes his plate and mine to the side. Turning my stool, he puts his hands on my waist and makes me stand.

I do as I'm told. Fitzroy stands next to me, then he bends down and removes my shorts. He takes my tank top off and lifts me up and puts me on the bar. He pushes against my chest until I'm lying down, then he sits back at his stool. "This is the dessert I choose," he says then he goes down on me. His hands trailing over my breasts as he does so.

As his tongue finds its pleasure, I try to decide if I can do something like this. Can I schedule others to do what I do? Will they get paid the way I had? I know some others are paid, but not all of them. I make sure to tug on his hair to show my excitement.

Can I ask him to pay the ones who don't get paid? Would I be asking to make myself feel better? I was okay with *my* job, but I thought of it as a job. Some of the others might not. Some of the others could be like Phallon—kidnapped and forced to do what they're told.

I can't be a part of that, can I?

I refocus my attention as Fitzroy grunts. He wants me to come. As I yell out a moan of satisfaction the kitchen door opens, and several people come in.

Fitzroy's head lifts from my crotch. "What is the meaning of this?" He yells.

Several men come inside, followed by, holy shit, *Ruby*. Behind her is Phallon. They are both wearing handcuffs.

Fitzroy jumps up and goes over to them. "Thank fucking Christ!" He hugs Ruby. "Why on earth is she cuffed?" He yells at the man in the front of the group. "Uncuff them both, now!" he orders.

Ruby looks at me as I get down from the counter. I pull my top on as one of the men comes closer to me. He reaches down and grabs my shorts.

"Allow me to assist my *Queen*." He holds them out for me.

I take the shorts from him and put them on. He licks his lips. He also still wears a peach bracelet. One of the *Cousins* has escaped the island a free man.

"We've got about ten kids in the van outside, too." The man in the front of the group un-cuffs Ruby and Phallon.

"Chris," Fitzroy says, "how many others got out?"

"The bunker was well prepared. There were about a hundred and twenty of us down there. Two *Uncles* were apprehended. All our *Brothers* were in the bunker. Two *Grandpas* were in there as well as three *Fathers* and twenty *Cousins*."

"How many units did we lose?" Fitzroy asks.

"One hundred and seven units were taken by the FBI. We managed to get sixty-eight into the bunker and hidden before the FBI arrived."

"How did you get out?" Fitzroy asks with intense interest. He crosses his arms over his chest as he listens.

"The bunker worked how it was supposed to. The provisions were well stocked. We stayed down there until the FBI left The Island. It took a while. We were able to take the tunnel to Island Two, and from there we all got on boats. We secured the units with Idowu. He's taken them with him. He wanted me to tell you that he will hold the units for his *K*ing until told otherwise. We brought these two back to you because we know of their importance. We brought the children, too, because we know Idowu's vice for the little ones. Since they belong to *U*ncles and *K*ings, we didn't want to risk it."

"How many did the FBI get in total?" I ask.

"My *Q*ueen," the man bows his head. "In total the FBI took one hundred and seventy-four."

"Tell Idowu to sell off the ones he took. He can keep ten percent for his trouble," Fitzroy says. "Let's discuss everything else in my office." Fitzroy leads the way out of the kitchen.

Ruby and Phallon stay behind as everyone else follows their *K*ing to his office.

Ruby runs over to me when they're all gone. "Alyx."

She hugs me. "I'm not sure what to do. Idowu dragged me to the bunker. Yuen brought Phallon."

Phallon rubs her wrists then picks up a plate and gathers food. I don't know her well enough to know for sure, but she looks as though she's nervous-eating. Her hands quake as she holds tongs placing food on her plate.

Maybe she's just hungry.

I don't know how safe the manor is or how many cameras are all around. Ruby probably knows more than I do about the manor—like she knows more about The Island. "But you're, okay? The FBI didn't get you?" I raise my brow. "I'm so glad," my brow goes even higher. Hopefully she'll understand my questions. Who was saved? How were you not saved?

Ruby's shoulders tremble. "I'm one of the lucky ones. Phallon, too." I know by lucky she means the opposite. "Is my family still safe?" she whispers to me.

I nod. "As far as I know, yes."

"I didn't get to tell you." She leans in close to my ear. "There were texts on that cell. He is safe. He loves you." She pulls away.

I know she means Trent. I also know that those texts happened weeks ago and don't mean anything about where he is now. I smile thanking her for the news anyway. "Have some food."

I pull my plate back over and eat while Phallon and

Ruby join me. I go back for seconds because I know they won't care.

"So," Phallon says. "How far along are you?"

"What do you mean?" I stuff a chicken liver in my mouth.

"Chicken livers, potato chips, and ambrosia. Girl, you're pregnant."

I look up and drop my fork.

ACKNOWLEDGMENTS

My heart goes out to all who have supported me throughout my life and those who supported me while writing and publishing this novel.

First and foremost, I want to thank the many people who helped make this book a reality. Though, many of those people wish to remain anonymous, they know who they are, so I'll just say this… Without you this book wouldn't have happened. Thank you for your time, effort, editing, and your many reads. To others, your formatting expertise was a godsend. To all of you, your support helped me through so much during the drafting process and beyond.

To my family and friends who offered feedback and cheered me on during my moments of self-doubt, thank you for your motivation. I love you all.

To my readers—whether you have followed me for years or have only just discovered my work—I appreciate each one of you. Your support is what makes books like this worth writing.

I wrote this book as a way to defeat my own experiences with sexual assault and grooming. It may not be the way some would choose to share portions of their stories, but it is the way I chose to do so. For any and all who have experienced grooming or assault, I am on your side, the monsters were wrong for what they did, and I send love to you every single day.

This novel would not be possible without each and every one of you. Thank you for being part of my writing journey. My heart is overjoyed to have each of you on this path with me.

All my best,
T.M. Lore

ABOUT THE AUTHOR

T.M. Lore is a pseudonym used by Author Carmen DaVinleam. Since Carmen writes children and young adult books as well, she thought it best to have any adult themes written under a pseudonym.

Born and raised in Kentucky, Carmen has always enjoyed animals and the simple life. She shares a home with her two children and their many animals, three dogs, three cats, a green iguana named Boomer, and their ball python who wishes to remain nameless.

Some years back, Carmen was involved in a series of car accidents that disabled her. —Carmen would like to note here that none of the accidents were her fault— Carmen suffers from chronic pain, post-concussion syndrome, as well as many other injuries that prevent her from doing many things. Luckily writing isn't one of the things she can no longer do.

Having loved the written word since she was a child fighting dyslexia, Carmen has been writing stories for as long as she can remember. Even though reading challenged her she never gave up. In early 2023, Carmen won a spot for her short horror story 3:02 a.m. in the

Louisville Literary Arts 2023 Writer's Block Anthology. The anthology was published by Hydra Publications later that year, and you can find Carmen's winning story in The 2023 Writer's Block Anthology on Amazon.

Carmen has written many novels, though this is the first one she has published.

tiktok.com/@carmendavinleam

instagram.com/carmendavinleam

threads.net/@carmendavinleam

x.com/CarmenDaVinleam

facebook.com/CarmenDaVinleamAuthor

Milton Keynes UK
Ingram Content Group UK Ltd.
UKHW031903260924
448786UK00001B/43